WRITINGS ON THE WALL

WRITINGS ON THE WALL
A Radical and Socialist Anthology 1215–1984

edited by
TONY BENN

faber and faber
LONDON · BOSTON

First published in 1984
by Faber and Faber Limited
3 Queen Square London WC1N 3AU

Printed in Great Britain by
Redwood Burn Ltd Trowbridge Wiltshire
All rights reserved

This collection © Tony Benn, 1984

British Library Cataloguing in Publication Data

Writings on the wall.
1. Radicalism—Great Britain—History
I. Benn, Tony
320.941   HN400.R3
ISBN 0−571−13334−7
ISBN 0−571−13335−5 Pbk

Dedicated,

IN THE NAME OF THE WEARY AND OPPRESSED

OF EVERY LAND, TO ALL WHO ARE WORKING TOWARDS

A NEW ORGANISATION OF SOCIETY,

OF WHICH USEFUL LABOUR SHALL BE

THE TRUEST FOUNDATION,

AND IN WHICH THE PEOPLE S SERVICE SHALL BE

THE HIGHEST REWARD.

First edition of the *Labour Annual*, 1895

CONTENTS

PREFACE

This book developed from talks with Andrew Franklin and the support of Faber and Faber. Most of the research was carried out by Andrew Franklin and Suzanne Franks, who went through all the documents that might yield suitable material. Everything that I had collected on the same themes, over the years, went into the pool too, and we sorted, arranged and discussed every passage in detail.

I would like to express my sincere thanks to Andrew and Suzanne for their commitment and effort. Our editorial seminars gave us much encouragement and hope, and we believe that the book itself will do the same for its reader.

TONY BENN
January 1984

NOTE OF THANKS

Compiling a book like this must be a collective activity. Lots of people have helped with advice, information and suggestions, but particular thanks are due to the following: Jenny Mundy for her expertise and help with the Middle Ages; John Bowers, Caroline Elton and Tom Franklin for their extensive reading and support. We also want to thank Matthew Faber, Hedy Franks, Barbara Posen, Julian Stanley and Ian Wylie for their enthusiasm and advice.

Librarians of the following libraries were also helpful: the British Library, the British Library of Political and Economic Science, Edinburgh University Library, David Doughan at the Fawcett Library, the Labour Party Library, the London Library, Nick Wetton at the Marx Memorial Library, and the Museum of Labour History Library.

ANDREW FRANKLIN
SUZANNE FRANKS
January 1984

INTRODUCTION
Tony Benn

This book explores the radical and revolutionary tradition which we have inherited from those who went before us and established, here in our country, a set of values based on the ideas of freedom, equality and democracy to set against the prevailing political culture. This culture, which rests on the worship of authority and the elevation of personal privilege above the common good, is so strongly entrenched in the mass media and the educational system that the very fact that an alternative tradition has been in existence for centuries is simply not known to many people.

We are all taught to accept, almost without question, that our freedom and welfare depend on centralized power structures, and that we have a duty to obey the orders that are passed down to us from on high. A few individuals make it to the top in every generation, but once they have got there they are expected to defend the status quo which has made it possible for them to advance personally. Meanwhile the source of much authority remains with the old élites and with some new ones. The crown, the lords, the land, the church, and the professions retain considerable political power. These have now been joined by the new financial, multinational, military and media establishments which have skilfully integrated themselves into the hierarchies of the older order. Parliament itself has lost many of the powers that it won so painfully over the centuries, and the electors have witnessed their own rights shrinking too. This oppressive political culture has now spread over the whole of our society, affecting the lives of women as well as men, black as well as white, limiting our freedom and narrowing our vision.

There is no reason why we should accept these values, which have been consistently questioned by great numbers of people throughout our history. This book records the sayings and writings of those people, as they challenged the established order, relying on a rival analysis and a rival tradition, and campaigned for its replacement by a set of values based on social justice, solidarity and democracy.

What is that rival tradition and that rival analysis? Where does it come from and on what does it depend for its authority and support? This reader sets out to provide some of the answers to those questions, and to do so through the minds, pens and voices of the people who created that tradition for themselves, and for us.

We are so used to the idea that Britain is an industrialized country and, overall, among the richest in the world, that it is easy to forget our past. For most of our history we were, like so many of the Third World countries today, a peasant society dominated by a feudal hierarchy which owned the land and lived off the people. Thus the roots of our radicalism lie in peasant resistance, and many of the demands for revolutionary change, recorded here, are the same as those that we hear and read about today in Asia, Africa and Latin America. For example, the theme of 'liberation from the Norman yoke' shows us people opposing the invaders and the oppression they brought. That resistance was based on the denial of the legitimacy of a Crown, which derives its legal claim to the throne from the Conquest, when William I, having defeated Harold at Hastings, proclaimed his personal authority.

Not only are there echoes of these sentiments in Britain's resistance to Common Market membership, but also in the deep distrust that we now feel as a result of the presence in this country of a foreign army—the American army—with its missiles and nuclear weapons, both of which have taken power away from the Parliament that we elect. Such feelings, together with a distrust of the power of the landowners, bishops and lawyers who sustained that Norman oppression, fuelled radical and revolutionary movements long before trade-unionism and socialism appeared on the scene to reinforce those emotions with a scientific analysis of the role of class.

At the very beginning it was religious belief that provided the basis of opposition to the oppressors, and there are many references to the revolutionary message of the Bible. This is why the authorities would not allow the Bible to be made available in English, so that the people could read it freely until 1535. The Establishment feared that the same liberation theology—which today brings peasants, industrial workers, trade-unionists and socialists together in Latin America as they struggle for justice—might have united resistance to its authority.

The most basic feeling of all, and the one that could never be suppressed, was the idea of inherent rights, which recurs throughout this book. It derives originally from the belief that God, as the creator of all humanity, had implanted those rights in each man and woman as His gift, and that no person, however rich or powerful, had any moral or legal right to take them away. This is why radicals and dissenters, and many in the Labour Movement today, have always put the claims of conscience above the law, and have been quite ready to pay a personal price for doing so.

As the years passed, religious belief was supplemented, or replaced, by a more secular view of history. These inherent rights were restated in terms of reason, a humanist view that in the transition lost none of its ethical force, although it had been stripped of its theological significance. The concept has come to be expressed in terms of the rights of a freeborn Englishman, or the rights of the Scots, Irish or Welsh, of Women and of Blacks, to enjoy equality of treatment under the law. Yet the political battles that have been fought over the centuries were for the most part fought under the banners of religion and religious freedom. So it is important that we should remember that many of the ideas of solidarity, democracy, tolerance, equality and socialism owe their origin to the Old Testament and the teachings of the carpenter of Nazareth, as they were interpreted by those who were looking for some justification for their own struggles. Modern socialists should never forget that fact, lest we accidentally cut ourselves off from our own history and come to believe what our enemies say of us: that we are proponents of some foreign creed which has no roots in our own national history.

Indeed this is one reason why the Establishment historians ignore our real history. They fear that if it was made intelligible to the mass of the people we would quickly connect past with present, and draw great strength from that understanding. And so indeed we would, as we come to realize that we are engaged on a campaign for justice and freedom that has gone on, in varying forms, for nearly two thousand years. It is not, as the Establishment would have people believe, only a few trouble-makers, perhaps owing their allegiance to some foreign revolutionaries, who are pressing for change.

This, then, is the moral and historical basis for that alternative political tradition, and we only have to read a few of the passages to find ourselves immediately familiar with the arguments. For those who have not read them before, it is rather like meeting distant cousins for the first time, exploring the common relationship and exchanging family legends, so that, quite soon, total strangers begin to feel at ease with each other, and can almost imagine that they have known each other all along. But this personal selection also opens up direct communication between generations that will reawaken in us some of the anger experienced by those who have gone before and help fuel the present pressure for change, accelerating the process of reform here and now.

What is written here should not just be read as a collection of historical writings. It should allow us to use the past to serve the present; by making us familiar with the old battles to harden us for what may lie ahead, and to unite us with all people everywhere who are struggling for the same objectives and are using their own history to help them—a history that may turn out to be much like ours. In short this is a book for our times to give us knowledge that we can use, to provide hope and courage and, above all, the certainty that we are not alone in what we believe.

If we are to use this book, as it is intended to be used, we have to do a lot more than read it. For we are living at a time when the clock is being deliberately put back in order to cheat us of the gains that were won in earlier years. Unless we resist there is no guarantee that this skilful campaign of regression will not succeed. The attempt to restore Victorian values is only a beginning. It may help us to learn about the struggles that took place in Victorian times so that we can mobilize the forces for progress that achieved so much during that century, and laid the foundation for the advances that followed. We can call up Robert Owen, Charles Kingsley and Anna Wheeler, William Morris and H. M. Hyndman, Marx and Engels, the Chartists and the Tolpuddle martyrs together with all their progressive contemporaries, to reinforce us as we gird our loins to fight these old battles again. If they want to go back to the eighteenth century and resurrect the blind conservatism of Edmund Burke we have Tom Paine and his *Rights of Man* still at our disposal. Now that the divine right of Prime Ministers is being wheeled out, almost as Charles I would have argued it in the seventeenth century, we have John Lilburne and William Walwyn and the Levellers and Diggers in our camp.

In 1983 the Greenham Common women were gaoled under the Justices of the Peace Act of 1361, and if that is how they want to have it they should not forget that twenty years later Wat Tyler and John Ball marched across the bridge to occupy the City of London. Whichever century they choose to fight us in we have our champions too. Nor should we ever forget Pelagius—Britain's earliest and greatest heretic, who challenged St Augustine on the central question of original sin. He asserted the essential goodness of man, an idea that undermined the authority of the Papacy and anticipated by 1,800 years the socialists who argued the same case.

Some of the passages quoted here are explicitly revol-

17

utionary and we should not forget that the right to revolt is an ancient one that must always be held in reserve as a protection against the possibility that one day democracy and self-government might be removed, leaving us no alternative but to defend these rights by force. At this very moment in our history the other side should be reminded of this so that they do not miscalculate in what they may plan to do to us. For in the counter-revolution which they are trying to carry through it is already clear that they are prepared to attack our ancient freedoms, as with the attack on the rights of the people of London and of the other metropolitan boroughs who are to lose the power to elect their own councils. The trade unions are facing—in effect—the reintroduction of the Combination Acts which made it impossible for them to function. Women are under attack, both at work and in the home where they are expected to take on their shoulders the tasks that the Welfare State was set up to discharge.

We are losing the power to govern ourselves, and a foreign president may make war from our own country. The armed forces, the security services and the police, all heavily armed and trained in counter-insurgency operations, are now virtually unaccountable and work behind barriers of almost impenetrable secrecy. There is not a single democratic gain made by our people that is not now under some sort of threat, not a single major political issue that has not been discussed over the centuries that has not now been placed once more upon the agenda. The role of the crown, of the lords, and of the church are being discussed again. So is the question of Ireland, imperialism, our relations with America and Europe, and the rights of all working men and women.

It is not clear yet how far they want to go but we would be well advised to be ready for anything, since if they go too far it may be much harder, if not actually too late, to stop them. There is no law of God or Nature that exempts this nation from the fate that befell Germany and Italy, Spain and Portugal in the 1930s, and overtook Greece and Turkey more recently. The only guarantee of our freedom lies with us, here and now, and we had better wake up to that simple truth before it is too late. An ex-imperial power, as we are, with a decaying capitalist system of the kind we have, can be very dangerous to other countries and to its own people too. But even if we are spared the horrors of a domestic struggle to retain, or regain, our freedom, other countries will not be so fortunate.

Those who live now under corrupt military dictatorships, financed and supported by Washington, or London, to protect Western investments from the danger of a popular uprising, will almost certainly be forced to take to arms to liberate themselves. Herein lies one of the major risks of a global confrontation with nuclear weapons. For it is not the risk of a major invasion by one superpower across a European frontier that we have to fear so much as the danger of war by proxy or by accident, in the absence of any effective democratic control of the fearsome military machines that we have allowed to grow within our own societies. If humanity does survive the appalling dangers that now confront us, it will be, in part, because we have listened to these voices from the past, reproduced in these pages, and have taken seriously those who are warning us now.

Indeed hope must stem from the possibility that we might also allow these voices to reach the people in other countries, where the same calls for justice and peace are to be heard. Although the religious traditions, and the historical experiences of these peoples are different from ours, these writings on the wall are to be seen all over the globe, and have appeared in every generation to enrich the understanding of those to whom they were addressed. The only power strong enough to contain and control the unimaginable destructive force released by the splitting of the atom is the greater power that could be generated by the unification of all these voices into one great clamour for justice. Therein lies our greatest hope, and, however it is defined, it must mean radical, if not revolutionary, changes in all societies to make that possible. It must also mean that the United

Nations must be reconstituted on a basis of popular consent, as the British Parliament once was, to give it the public acceptance it needs to unite the nations.

It is when we contemplate the enormity of that task and the urgency with which it has to be attempted that we can appreciate the value of the very ancient traditions of liberty and democracy that emerge from these pages. Great as the task may seem to be to us, can it really be any greater or more difficult than the ones which faced our forebears when they made their demands? Those demands must have seemed as far-fetched to many of their contemporaries as they were unacceptable to those who stood to lose their privileges. But, as history teaches us, time and time again, it is not enough to speak or write, or compose poems or songs, about freedom if there are not people who are ready to devote to their lives to make it all come true. Some of those whose writings we are able to read worked, and others died, to uphold the principles that they proclaimed. It is only a matter of merest chance who is remembered and who lies forgotten in some graveyard known only to those friends and comrades who lived in the same town or village at the same time.

This book is therefore dedicated to the nameless thousands who worked, where they lived, to advance our common cause. They can never have known that what they believed in, and worked for, would survive in legend and tradition to encourage us so many years after they were gone, nor realize that the gift they have passed on to us is the most priceless gift of all—hope. For our greatest enemy is the fear that our opponents seek to instil in our minds to force us to accept the unacceptable, and so to paralyse our will and render us incapable of thinking out the alternative or working to bring it about. If we were ever to allow that to happen, we would have conceded a final victory to the other side, but as this book shows we all have it in our power to deny them that victory; and to establish a better society by our own efforts, provided that we remember our own history and the lessons of unity and courage that it teaches us.

PART ONE
POVERTY, INJUSTICE
AND OPPRESSION

The Rich make merry,
But in tears the Commons drown.
ANON, *c.* 1400

In its presentation of poverty, injustice and oppression this first section opens up the theme of the whole volume by recording the experiences that have led so many men and women, over the centuries, to demand change. Experience is the only real teacher. The lessons it teaches can, and do, radicalize those who have never heard any but the most conventional ideas, and may not even have realized that there is another way.

Here we can read about slavery, robbery, inequality and unemployment, about the corruption that sustained it, and the kings, landlords, priests and lawyers who propped up the whole rotten system. We learn of the tyranny of the Norman kings, of the emergence of class struggle—and the way that reform is sometimes used to defuse opposition by offering just enough to fend off real change.

Some of the passages that follow are in poetry and some in prose. The language of resistance comes in many forms: by complaining or pleading or appealing to the better nature of the oppressors; or by a sterner resolution to fight the system and change it once and for all. No one reading what is written here can doubt that the roots of revolution go deep into our history and that the remedies sought were fundamental in character, as the demands themselves show. It is also clear that the experiences of our generation have many parallels in the past, and are shared by people all over the world.

TONY BENN

A SONG OF THE TIMES

The state of the world is at the present day constantly changing; it is always becoming miserably worse; for he who spares nobody, and who is bent most on gain, is most beloved and most commended. The King and his nobles are sufficiently bitter; almost all the rich men are too avaricious; the poor man, who possesses little, must be robbed and spoiled of his property to enrich the wealthy. The rich man is blinded by superfluous wealth; his whole mind is occupied with temporal matters; and, since he is too much pleased with vanities, he puts off the doing good, but avoids not the evil.

ANON, FOURTEENTH CENTURY
Translated from the Latin

A SONG OF THE TIMES

Where money speaks, there all law is silent.
ANON, REIGN OF HENRY III (1216-72)
Translated from the Latin

THE VISION OF PIERS PLOUGHMAN

The neediest are our neighbours if we care to take note,
Such as prisoners in dungeons and poor folk in hovels,
Burdened with bairns and the rent of the barons.
What with spinning they save, they spend it on house-hire,
And on milk and on meal with which to make porridge,
To give to their children who clamour for food.
And also themselves they suffer sore hunger,
And woe in the winter, and waking at night,
To rise to the bed-side to rock the child's cradle,
To card and to comb, to patch and to wash,
To scrape flax, to wind yarn and to peel rushes.

24

It is piteous to read or in rhyme to show,
The woe of the women that dwell in these hovels,
And of the many poor men that much misery suffer.
                              WILLIAM LANGLAND, 1385–6
        C Text passus X, translated by Julian Gibbs

POEM ON THE TIMES

England, awake now,
And good heed take thou.

The Rich make merry,
    But in tears the Commons drown.
The People are weary,
    They are almost trampled down.
The Church is grieved,
    Left is the spiritual call.
And so some are mischieved,
    They fear greater loss will befall.

At Westminster Hall
    They well enough know the laws,
Nevertheless for them all
    The mighty bear down the right cause.
                              ANON, c. 1400

THE WAY TO WEALTH

No customs, no law or statute can keep them [the rich] from
oppressing us [the poor] in such sort, that we know not which
way to turn us to live. Very need therefore constrains us to
stand up against them! In the country we cannot tarry, but
we must be their slaves and labourers till our hearts break,

and then they must have all. And to go to the cities we have no hope, for there we hear that these insatiable beasts have all in their hands. Some have purchased, and some have taken by leases, whole alleys, whole rents, whole rows, yea whole streets and lanes, so that the rents be raised, some double, some triple, and some fourfold to that they were within these twelve years past. Yea, there is not so much as a garden ground free from them. No remedy therefore, we must need fight it out, or else be brought to the like slavery that the French men are in! These idle bellies will devour all that we shall get by our sore labour in our youth, and when we shall be old and impotent, then shall we be driven to beg and crave of them that will not give us so much as the crumbs that fall from their tables. Such is the pity we see in them! Better it were therefore, for us to die like men, than after so great misery in youth to die more miserably in age!

ROBERT CROWLEY, 1550

THE JEWEL OF JOY

CHRISTOPHER: Rich men were never so much estranged from all pity and compassion toward the poor people, as they be at this present time: 'They devour the people as it were a morsel of bread.' If any piece of ground delight their eye, they must needs have it, either by hook or crook. If the poor man will not satisfy their covetous desire, he is sure to be molested, troubled and disquieted . . . .

PHILEMON: And the cause of all this wretchedness and beggary in the Commonweal are the greedy men, which are sheepmongers and graziers. While they study for their own private commodity, the Commonweal is like to decay.

THOMAS BECON, c. 1550

26

SONG OF HUNGER

Thousandes have famishede for food,
And thousandes mor be lek,
Change nowe therfor your crewell moode,
And them to sucoure sek.

Thousandes ar pyned to the bonys
With hongge, thrist and cold;
And thousandes in strong fettars gronnes
Yowe caus thereof behold.

The fatharles and wydowe pore,
The syk, the sor, the lame,
Ly dyeng nowe at every dore,
And non but youe in blame.

ANON, 1550s

A REMONSTRANCE OF MANY
THOUSAND CITIZENS

One of the first revolutionary Leveller tracts, this was 'occasioned through the illegall and barbarous imprisonment of that famous and worthy sufferer for his countries freedoms, Lieutenant col. John Lilburne'.

The History of our Fore-fathers since they were Conquered by the *Normans* doth manifest that this Nation hath been held in bondage all along ever since by the policies and force of the Officers of Trust in the Common-wealth, amongst whom, wee always esteemed Kings the chiefest: and what (in much of the former-time) was done by warre, and by impoverishing of the People, to make them slaves, and to hold them in bondage, our latter Princes have endeavoured

27

to effect, by giving ease and wealth unto the People, but withall, corrupting their understanding, by infusing false Principles concerning Kings, and Government, and Parliaments, and Freedoms.

RICHARD OVERTON, JULY 1647

THE TEARS OF SCOTLAND

Mourn, hapless Caledonia, mourn
Thy banished peace, thy laurels torn!
Thy sons, for valour long renowned,
Lie slaughtered on their native ground;
Thy hospitable roofs no more
Invite the stranger to the door;
In smoky ruins sunk they lie,
The monument of cruelty.

TOBIAS SMOLLETT, 1746
Written after the Battle of Culloden (1745)

THE DESERTED VILLAGE

Written in protest at the eviction of villagers and the enclosure of farmland to create parkland for the gentry.

Ye friends to truth, ye statesmen, who survey
The rich man's joys increase, the poor's decay,
'Tis yours to judge, how wide the limits stand
Between a splendid and a happy land.
Proud swells the tide with loads of freighted ore,
And shouting Folly hails them from her shore;
Hoards, e'en beyond the miser's wish abound,
And rich men flock from all the world around.

28

Yet count our gains. This wealth is but a name
That leaves our useful products still the same.
Not so the loss. The man of wealth and pride
Takes up a space that many poor supplied;
Space for his lake, his park's extended bounds,
Space for his horses, equipage, and hounds;
The robe that wraps his limbs in silken sloth
Has robb'd the neighbouring fields of half their growth,
His seat, where solitary sports are seen,
Indignant spurns the cottage from the green;
Around the world each needful product flies;
For all the luxuries the world supplies:
While thus the land adorn'd for pleasure, all
In barren splendour feebly waits the fall.

OLIVER GOLDSMITH, 1770. *Lines 265–86*

PARABLE OF THE PIGEONS

If you should see a flock of pigeons in a field; and if (instead of each picking where and what it liked, taking just as much as it wanted, and no more) you should see ninety-nine of them gathering all they got into one heap, reserving nothing for themselves but the chaff and the refuse, keeping this heap for one, and that the weakest, perhaps worst, pigeon of the flock; sitting round and looking on all the winter, whilst this one was devouring and throwing about and wasting it; and if one pigeon more hardy or hungry than the rest touched a grain of the hoard, all the others instantly flying upon it and tearing it to pieces; if you should see this, you would see nothing more than what is every day practised and established among men.

Among men you see ninety-nine toiling and scraping together a heap of superfluities for one (and this one too oftentimes the feeblest and worst of the whole set), a child, a woman, a madman, or a fool, getting nothing for themselves all the while, but a little of the coarsest of the provision which their own industry produces, looking quietly on while they see the fruits of all their labour spent or spoiled, and if one of the number take or touch a particle of the hoard, the others joining against him and hanging him for the theft.

ARCHDEACON WILLIAM PALEY, 1785
Moral and Political Philosophy, Book III, chapter 1

MAN WAS MADE TO MOURN

If I'm designed yon lordling's slave
By nature's law designed—
Why was an independent wish
E'er planted in my mind?

ROBERT BURNS, 1786

LETTER ADDRESSED TO
THE MUNSTER PEASANTRY

O'Driscol was the self-styled 'General to the Munster Peasantry' of Southern Ireland in the 1786 rebellion.

In every age, country and religion the priesthood are allowed to have been artful, usurping and tenacious of their ill-acquired prerogatives. Often have their jarring interests and opinions deluged with Christian blood this long-devoted isle.

Some thirty years ago our unhappy fathers—galled beyond human sufferance—like a captive lion vainly struggling in the toils, strove violently to snap their bonds asunder, but instead rivetted them to more tight. Exhausted by the bloody struggle, the poor of this province submitted to their oppression, and fattened with their vitals each decimating leech.

The luxurious parson drowned in the riot of his table the bitter groans of those wretches that his proctor fleeced, and the poor remnant of the proctor's rapine was sure to be gleaned by the rapacious priest, but it was blasphemy to complain of him; Heaven, we thought, would wing its lightning to blast the wretch who grudged the Holy Father's share. Thus plundered by either clergy, we had reason to wish for our simple Druids again.

WILLIAM O'DRISCOL, JULY 1786

A WINTER NIGHT

See stern Oppression's iron grip,
  Or mad Ambition's gory hand,
Sending, like blood-hounds from the slip,
  Woe, Want, and Murder o'er a land!
Ev'n in the peaceful rural vale,
  Truth, weeping, tells the mournful tale:
How pamper'd Luxury, Flatt'ry by her side,
  The parasite empoisoning her ear,
  With all the servile wretches in the rear,
Looks o'er proud Property, extended wide;
  And eyes the simple, rustic hind,
  Whose toil upholds the glitt'ring show—
  A creature of another kind,
  Some coarser substance, unrefin'd—
Plac'd for her lordly use, thus far, thus vile, below!

ROBERT BURNS, 1787

LONDON

I wander thro' each charter'd street,
Near where the charter'd Thames does flow,
And mark in every face I meet
Marks of weakness, marks of woe.

In every cry of every Man,
In every Infant's cry of fear,
In every voice, in every ban,
The mind-forg'd manacles I hear.

How the Chimney-sweeper's cry
Every black'ning Church appalls;
And the hapless Soldier's sigh
Runs in blood down Palace walls.

But most thro' midnight streets I hear
How the youthful Harlot's curse
Blasts the new born Infant's tear,
And blights with plagues the Marriage hearse.

WILLIAM BLAKE, 1789–94
From The Songs of Experience

POLITICAL JUSTICE

And here with grief it must be confessed, that, however great and extensive are the evils that are produced by monarchies and courts, by the imposture of priests and the iniquity of criminal laws, all these are imbecil and impotent, compared with the evils that arise out of the established administration of property.

Its first effect is that which we have already mentioned, a sense of dependence. It is true that courts are mean-spirited, intriguing and servile, and that this disposition is transferred by contagion from them to all ranks of society. But accumulation brings home a servile and truckling spirit, by no circuitous method, to every house in the nation. Observe the pauper fawning with abject vileness upon his rich benefactor, speechless with sensations of gratitude for having received that which he ought to have claimed, not indeed with arrogance, or a dictatorial and overbearing temper, but with the spirit of a man discussing with a man, and resting his cause only on the justice of his claim. Observe the servants that follow in a rich man's train, watchful of his looks, anticipating his commands, not daring to reply to his insolence, all their time and their efforts under the direction of his caprice. Observe the tradesman, how he studies the passions of his customers, not to correct, but to pamper them, the vileness of his flattery and the systematical constancy with which he exaggerates the merit of his commodities.

WILLIAM GODWIN, 1793
Volume II, book viii

THE PRELUDE

And when we chanc'd
One day to meet a hunger-bitten Girl,
Who crept along, fitting her languid gait
Unto a Heifer's motion, by a cord
Tied to her arm, and picking thus from the lane
Its sustenance, while the girl with her two hands
Was busy knitting, in a heartless mood
Of solitude, and at the sight my Friend
In agitation said, ''Tis against that
Which we are fighting,' I with him believed
Devoutly that a spirit was abroad
Which could not be withstood, that poverty

33

At least like this, would in a little time
Be found no more, that we should see the earth
Unthwarted in her wish to recompense
The industrious, and the lowly Child of Toil,
All institutes for ever blotted out
That legalized exclusion, empty pomp
Abolish'd, sensual state and cruel power
Whether by edict of the one or few,
And finally, as sum and crown of all,
Should see the People having a strong hand
In making their own Laws, whence better days
To all mankind.

WILLIAM WORDSWORTH, 1805
Book IX, lines 509–32

LETTERS FROM ENGLAND

There is a shrub in some of the East Indian islands which the French call *veloutier*; it exhales an odour that is agreeable at a distance, becomes less so as you draw nearer, and, when you are quite close to it, is insupportably loathsome. Alciatus himself could not have imagined an emblem more appropriate to the commercial prosperity of England.

Mr.—— remarked that nothing could be so beneficial to a country as manufactures. 'You see these children, sir,' said he. 'In most parts of England poor children are a burthen to their parents and to the parish; here the parish, which would else have to support them, is rid of all expense; they get their bread almost as soon as they can run about, and by the time they are seven or eight years old bring in money. There is no idleness among us: they come at five in the morning; we allow them half an hour for breakfast, and an hour for dinner; they leave work at six, and another set relieves them for the night; the wheels never stand still.' I was looking,

34

while he spoke, at the unnatural dexterity with which the fingers of these little creatures were playing in the machinery, half giddy myself with the noise and the endless motion: and when he told me there was no rest in these walls, day nor night, I thought that if Dante had peopled one of his hells with children, here was a scene worthy to have supplied him with new images of torment.

Wealth flows into the country, but how does it circulate there? Not equally and healthfully through the whole system; it sprouts into wens and tumours, and collects in aneurisms which starve and palsy the extremities.

ROBERT SOUTHEY, 1807
Volume II, letter 38: Manchester

THE BANKS OF THE DEE

A Durham coal-miners' song, with a tune dating from the mid-eighteenth century.

Last Saturday night on the banks of the Dee,
I met an old man, in distress I could see.
We sat down together and to me he did say,
I've lost my employment 'cause my hair it's turned grey.
  I am an old miner, aged fifty and six,
  If I could get lots, I would raffle my picks,
  I'd raffle them, sell them, I'd throw them away,
  For I can't get employment, my hair it's turned grey.

When I was a young chap I was just like the rest,
Each day in the pit I'd do my very best.
When I had a loose place, I'd be filling all day,
Now at fifty and six, my hair it's turned grey.

Last Wednesday night to the reckoning I went.
To the colliery office, I went straight fornenst.
I'd just got my pay packet, I was walking away,
When they gave me my notice, 'cause my hair it's turned grey.

Now all you young fellows, it's you that's to blame.
If you get good places, you'll do just the same.
If you get good prices, you'll hew them away,
But you're sure to regret it when your hair it's turned grey.
  I am an old miner, aged fifty and six,
  If I could get lots I would raffle my picks,
  I'd raffle them, sell them, I'd throw them away,
  For I can't get employment, my hair it's turned grey.

TRADITIONAL (recorded 1951)

COMMERCE HAS SET THE MARK
OF SELFISHNESS

Commerce has set the mark of selfishness,
The signet of its all-enslaving power
Upon a shining ore, and called it gold:
Before whose image bow the vulgar great,
The vainly rich, the miserable proud,
The mob of peasants, nobles, priests, and kings,
And with blind feelings reverence the power
That grinds them to the dust of misery.
But in the temple of their hireling hearts
Gold is a living god, and rules in scorn
All earthly things but virtue.

Since tyrants, by the sale of human life,
Heap luxuries to their sensualism, and fame
To their wide-wasting and insatiate pride,

Success has sanctioned to a credulous world
The ruin, the disgrace, the woe of war.
His hosts of blind and unresisting dupes
The despot numbers; from his cabinet
These puppets of his schemes he moves at will,
Even as the slaves by force or famine driven,
Beneath a vulgar master, to perform
A task of cold and brutal drudgery;—
Hardened to hope, insensible to fear,
Scarce living pulleys of a dead machine,
Mere wheels of work and articles of trade,
That grace the proud and noisy pomp of wealth!

PERCY BYSSHE SHELLEY, 1813
Queen Mab, *Section V, lines 52–78*

OBSERVATIONS ON THE EFFECT OF THE MANUFACTURING SYSTEM

Shall we then make laws to imprison, transport, or condemn to death those who purloin a few shillings of our property, injure any of our domestic animals, or even a growing twig; and shall we *not* make laws to restrain those who otherwise will not be restrained in their desire for gain, from robbing, in the pursuit of it, millions of our fellow creatures of their health, their time for acquiring knowledge and future improvement, of their social comforts, and of every rational enjoyment? This system of proceeding cannot continue long; it will work its own cure by the practical evils which it creates, and that in a most dangerous way to the public welfare, if the Government shall not give it a proper direction.

ROBERT OWEN, 1815

37

THE BLACK DWARF

The Black Dwarf *was an influential satirical radical paper.*

Learn then your duty, ye hewers of wood, and drawers of water! Buckle to the wheel of necessity, and draw your lordly superiors through the dirt. They have kindly consented to provide for all your wants. They have given you laws to keep you good members of society. They have removed far from you all the benefits of the world, lest you should be puffed up with pride, and be vain glorious, and deny the LORDS. They have taken from you all temptation to sin; and to remedy the inherent and deep-rooted depravity of your nature, they have provided for you seventy thousand priests to pray for you, and to shew you the way to heaven. They have appointed lawyers to *secure* your property, lest ye should waste it without thought, and tax-gatherers to collect quarterly your savings, in that root of all evil—*money*. . . . When you meet them in the public way, you will fall down before them, and worship them, saying—'The LORD giveth, and the LORDS take away. Blessed be the ways of the *Lords*.' This sentence, which is now rendered as it ought to be, from the original, contains the whole of your business, and your duty. It speaks all the law, and the prophets which concerns you. It is plain and easy. It involves no sophistry. Read it attentively, learn it, and engrave it on the tablets of your heart. It is of the *last* consequence to you, for to its acknowledgment you must come at last.

Your well wisher,
THE BLACK DWARF
5 FEBRUARY 1817

JAIL JOTTINGS

Written while in prison for sedition and blasphemy.

CRIMES AND JURIES

The much boasted laws of England are not now the terror of the guilty, they are become a mere trap for the incautious and unwary. Our police establishments have grown into nurseries of crime; the persons employed in them are preferred in proportion to their abilities to instigate and to lay the snare for the innocent. The whole system of government is corrupt, from the monarch to its meanest instruments; and the church system too much resembles it from the primate to the grave-digger. The whole stable issues forth such a stench that is intolerable; and it will become more than the work of a day to cleanse it. Prepare your brooms, fellow countrymen, make them of the toughest birch, and you shall finally succeed.

RICHARD CARLILE, 1820

HAND-WEAVERS' LAMENT

The hand-weavers—skilled and educated artisans—were pauperized by the introduction of steam looms at the beginning of the nineteenth century.

You pull down our wages, shamefully to tell;
You go into the markets, and say you cannot sell;
And when that we do ask you when these bad times will mend,
You quickly give an answer, 'When the wars are at an end.'

When we look on our poor children, it grieves our hearts full
*   sore,*
Their clothing it is worn to rags, while we can get no more,
With little in their bellies, they to their work must go,
Whilst yours do dress as manky as monkeys in a show.

39

You go to church on Sundays, I'm sure it's nought but pride,
There can be no religion where humanity's thrown aside;
If there be a place in heaven, as there is in the Exchange,
Our poor souls must not come near there; like lost sheep they
*   must range.*

TRADITIONAL, c. 1820

Lancashire ballad, sung to the tune of 'A-hunting we will go'

CAPTAIN SWING

*'Captain Swing' was the name used on the warning notes left
by rick-burners, protesting against the loss of jobs caused by
new farming machinery.*

The next morning [I] journeyed homewards, begging for
subsistence along the road: everywhere I went I heard of
fires and notices signed 'SWING'. 'How happens this?'
thought I. 'I am not the author of those burnings! What can
have caused them?' A few minutes reflection on the history
of my own life, which without any alteration may stand for
that of thousands of others, enabled me to give myself a satisfactory answer. 'Those fires', said I, 'are caused by farmers
having been turned out of their lands to make room for
foxes—peaceable people assembled to petition Parliament,
massacred by the military—peasants confined two years in
prison for picking up a dead partridge—English labourers set
up to auction like slaves, and treated as beasts of burthen—
and pluralist parsons taking a poor man's only cow for the
tithe of his cabbage-garden. These are the things that have
caused the burnings, and not unfortunate "SWING"!'
    I continued my route, reached home, and am again har-
nessed like a horse to the gravel cart. But I bear it, with
patience, under the conviction that, in a very short time,
Reform or Revolution must release me from it.

ANON (*possibly Richard Carlile*), 1820. *Pamphlet*

A FEW DOUBTS AS TO THE CORRECTNESS OF SOME OPINIONS GENERALLY ENTERTAINED ON THE SUBJECT OF POLITICAL ECONOMY

CAPITALISM

A cold and dreary system which represents our fellow creatures as so many rivals and enemies, which makes us believe that their happiness is incompatible with our own, which builds our wealth upon their poverty, which would persuade us to look on the world in the light of a besieged town, where the death of our neighbours is hailed with secret satisfaction, since it augments the quantity of provision likely to fall to our own share.

'PIERCY RAVENSTONE' (*pseudonym?*), 1821

ENGLISHMEN READ! A LETTER TO THE KING FOR THE PEOPLE OF ENGLAND

The whole of the laws passed within the last forty years, specially within the last twenty years, present one unbroken series of endeavours to enrich and to augment the power of the aristocracy, and to empoverish and depress the middle and labouring part of the people.

ANON, 1830. *Yorkshire handbill*

CAGED RATS

Ye coop us up, and tax our bread,
And wonder why we pine;
But ye are fat, and round, and red,
And filled with tax-bought wine.
Thus twelve rats starve while three rats thrive,

41

(Like you on mine and me,)
When fifteen rats are caged alive,
With food for nine and three.

Haste! Havoc's torch begins to glow—
The ending is begun;
Make haste! Destruction thinks ye slow;
Make haste to be undone!
Why are ye called 'my Lord', and 'Squire',
While fed by mine and me,
And wringing food, and clothes, and fire,
From bread-taxed misery!

EBENEZER ELLIOTT, 1831
From The Corn Law Rhymes

THE POOR MAN'S ADVOCATE

The Poor Man's Advocate *was an underground unstamped, radical paper.*

Henry Wooley was born at a place called Bolsterstone, in Yorkshire, in the year 1804. At eight years old, he went to work in the factory of the late John and Edward Chadwick, at a place called Park Hall Clough, about half way between Ashton and Staley-bridge, Lancashire. He began as a piecer, and ultimately became a spinner. His hours of work were 14½ a day, exclusive of over time.

For the first six years he stood the system pretty well. At the age of fourteen, his limbs began to grow crooked. They continued to get worse every succeeding year, until he had reached his eighteenth year. He had then become so feeble, from the deformity of his limbs, as to be unable to stand for any length of time; and as his occupation required constant standing, he was obliged to quit it altogether. At this time he

42

was earning four and twenty shillings a week. He had then been ten years in the factory, and had thus served two moderate apprenticeships to a business which he found he was unable to follow, and had to seek a fresh employment, and to learn a new trade. He was, like too many of his class, extremely poor; and the only employment which he could procure was the unhappy one of cotton weaving. He exchanged his one pound four shillings per week for less than half that sum, in order to enable him to exist at all. . . . But for the monstrous factory system, this man would have stood more than six feet high. Even as it is, he measures five feet nine inches. His arms, when extended, measure six feet three and a half inches; and his brother stands six feet four inches. Wooley is now in his 28th year, and at that age, as far as regards agility and strength, is an old man. Here is a man who was intended by nature to be a tall, robust, and athletic figure, converted into a miserable, deformed, and almost helpless cripple, even before he had attained his eighteenth year.

23 JUNE 1832

THE ROTTEN PARLIAMENT

An address by the London Working Men's Association.

There are persons among the moneyed classes who, to deceive their fellow men, have put on a cloak of reform; many boast of freedom while they help to enslave us, preach justice while they help to oppress us. Many are for step-by-step improvement, lest we should see our political degradation too soon, and make an advance towards depriving them of their privileges. These persons, under various pretences, enlist some portion of our deluded countrymen— and, by opposing them to each other, accomplish their object of deceiving and fleecing the whole. So long as we are duped this way and we continue to seek political salvation through the instrumentality of others, so long will corrupt legislation prevail, so long must we continue to be the cringing vassals of a proud, arrogant, speech-making few.

Drafted by WILLIAM LOVETT, 1836

OF HUMAN SLAVERY

In the principal states of Europe and America, in our colonies generally, and indeed in most modern countries called 'civilized', wages-slavery is the normal condition of the labouring classes. This latter kind of slavery is *caeteris paribus*, more or less intensely severe according to the degree of perfection to which civilization is carried. Thus in our limited kingdom, which is accounted the most civilized country in the world, wages-slavery is attended with greater hardships, and subject to more privations and casualties, than anywhere else. Nowhere else do we find employment so precarious; nowhere else such multitudes of people over-worked at one time and totally destitute of employment at other times; nowhere else do we see such masses of the population subsisting upon pittances wholly inadequate to sustain human beings in health and strength; nowhere else do we find gaols and workhouses so overcrowded; nowhere else do we hear of whole districts depopulated by famine; nor of upwards of 1,500,000 out of eight millions of people being cut off by actual starvation and forced expatriation in the course of twelve months, as has happened in Ireland in our own times. All this too we find to be contemporaneous and in juxtaposition with granaries, warehouses, and shops teeming with a superabundance of the choicest produce of all climes—with cries of over-production and glutted markets ringing in our ears wherever we pass—and with the most

44

opulent and numerous aristocracy, territorial and commercial that was ever known to be congregated in any country of seven times the extent—to say nothing of a still more numerous middle class. . . .

JAMES BRONTERRE O'BRIEN, c. 1840

BROTHER CHARTISTS

Handbill from the Executive of the National Chartist Association to the People.

The great Political Truths which have been agitated during the last half century have at length aroused the degraded and insulted White Slaves of England, to a sense of their duty to themselves, their children, and their country. Tens of Thousands have flung down their implements of Labour. Your taskmasters tremble at your energy, and expecting masses eagerly watch this the great crisis of our cause. Labour must no longer be the common prey of masters and rulers. Intelligence has beamed upon the mind of the bondsman, and he has been convinced that all wealth, comfort, and produce, every thing valuable, useful, and elegant, have sprung from the palm of his hand; he feels that his cottage is empty, his back thinly clad, his children breadless, himself hopeless, his mind harrassed, and his body punished, that undue riches, luxury, and gorgeous plenty might be heaped in the palaces of the taskmasters, and flooded into the granaries of the oppressor. Nature, God, and Reason have condemned this inequality, and in the thunder of a people's voice it must perish for ever.

1842

THE SONG OF THE SHIRT

Written following a Police Report in *The Times* of a starving woman in court for being unable to redeem a pawn. She was a tailoress, with two children, earning less than seven shillings a week.

'Work—work—work!
  My labour never flags;
And what are its wages? A bed of straw,
  A crust of bread—and rags.
That shatter'd roof—and this naked floor—
  A table—a broken chair—
And a wall so blank, my shadow I thank
  For sometimes falling there!

'Work—work—work!
From weary chime to chime,
  Work—work—work—
As prisoners work for crime!
  Band, and gusset, and seam,
  Seam, and gusset, and band,
Till the heart is sick, and the brain benumb'd,
  As well as the weary hand.'

With fingers weary and worn,
  With eyelids heavy and red,
A Woman sate in unwomanly rags,
  Plying her needle and thread—
    Stitch! stitch! stitch!
  In poverty, hunger, and dirt,
And still with a voice of dolorous pitch,
Would that its tone could reach the Rich!
  She sang this 'Song of the Shirt!'

THOMAS HOOD, 1843
From Punch (*December 1843*)

THE CONDITION OF THE WORKING CLASS
IN ENGLAND IN 1844

MANCHESTER

The town itself is peculiarly built, so that a person may live in
it for years, and go in and out daily without coming into
contact with a working-people's quarter or even with
workers, that is, so long as he confines himself to his business
or to pleasure walks. This arises chiefly from the fact, that by
unconscious tacit agreement, as well as with out-spoken conscious determination, the working-people's quarters are
sharply separated from the sections of the city reserved for
the middle-class; or, if this does not succeed, they are concealed with the cloak of charity. ... The finest part of the
arrangement is this, that the members of this money aristocracy can take the shortest road through the middle of all the
labouring districts to their places of business, without ever
seeing that they are in the midst of the grimy misery that lurks
to the right and the left. For the thoroughfares leading from
the Exchange in all directions out of the city are lined, on
both sides, with an almost unbroken series of shops, and are
so kept in the hands of the middle and lower bourgeoisie,
which, out of self-interest, cares for a decent and cleanly
external appearance and *can* care for it. True, these shops
bear some relation to the districts which lie behind them, and
are more elegant in the commercial and residential quarters
than when they hide grimy working-men's dwellings; but
they suffice to conceal from the eyes of the wealthy men and
women of strong stomachs and weak nerves the misery and
grime which form the complement of their wealth. ... In
this way any one who knows Manchester can infer the
adjoining districts, from the appearance of the thoroughfare,
but one is seldom in a position to catch from the street a
glimpse of the real labouring districts. I know very well that
this hypocritical plan is more or less common to all great
cities; I know, too, that the retail dealers are forced by the
nature of their business to take possession of the great

highways: I know that there are more good buildings than bad ones upon such streets everywhere, and that the value of land is greater near them than in remoter districts; but at the same time I have never seen so systematic a shutting out of the working-class from the thoroughfares, so tender a concealment of everything which might affront the eye and the nerves of the bourgeoisie, as in Manchester. And yet, in other respects, Manchester is less built according to a plan, after official regulations, is more an outgrowth of accident, than any other city; and when I consider in this connection the eager assurances of the middle-class, that the working-class is doing famously, I cannot help feeling that the liberal manufacturers, the 'Big Wigs' of Manchester, are not so innocent after all, in the matter of this sensitive method of construction.

FREDERICK ENGELS, 1845
Not published in English until 1892

MARY BARTON:
A TALE OF MANCHESTER LIFE

'Thou never could abide the gentlefolk,' said Wilson, half amused at his friend's vehemence.

'And what good have they ever done me that I should like them?' asked Barton, the latent fire lighting up his eye: and bursting forth, he continued, 'If I am sick, do they come and nurse me? If my child lies dying (as poor Tom lay, with his white wan lips quivering, for want of better food than I could give him), does the rich man bring the wine or broth that might save his life? If I am out of work for weeks in the bad times, and winter comes, with black frost, and keen east wind, and there is no coal for the grate, and no clothes for the bed, and the thin bones are seen through the ragged clothes, does the rich man share his plenty with me, as he ought to do, if his religion was not a humbug? When I lie on my death-bed, and Mary (bless her) stands fretting, as I know she will fret,' and here his voice faltered a little, 'will a rich lady come and take her to her own home if need be, till she can look round, and see what best to do? No, I tell you, it's the poor, and the poor only as does such things for the poor. Don't think to come over me with the old tale, that the rich know nothing of the trials of the poor. I say, if they don't know, they ought to know. We are their slaves as long as we can work; we pile up their fortunes with the sweat of our brows; and yet we are to live as separate as if we were in two worlds; ay, as separate as Dives and Lazarus, with a great gulf betwixt us. . . .

ELIZABETH GASKELL, 1848

THE BAD SQUIRE

There's blood on your new foreign shrubs, squire,
  There's blood on your pointer's feet;
There's blood on the game you sell, squire,
  And there's blood on the game you eat.

You have sold the labouring-man, squire,
  Body and soul to shame,
To pay for your seat in the House, squire,
  And to pay for the feed of your game.

You made him a poacher yourself, squire,
  When you'd give neither work nor meat,
And your barley-fed hares robbed the garden
  At our starving children's feet;

49

When, packed in one reeking chamber,
  Man, maid, mother, and little ones lay;
While the rain pattered in on the rotting bride-bed,
  And the walls let in the day.

When we lay in the burning fever
  On the mud of the cold clay floor,
Till you parted us all for three months, squire,
  At the dreary workhouse door.

We quarrelled like brutes, and who wonders?
  What self-respect could we keep,
Worse housed than your hacks and your pointers,
  Worse fed than your hogs and your sheep?

CHARLES KINGSLEY, 1848–9

PROPERTY IS ROBBERY

If of any property it ever was true that it was *robbery*, it is literally true of the property of the British aristocracy. Robbery of Church property, robbery of commons, fraudulent transformation, accompanied by murder, of feudal and patriarchal property into private property—these are the titles of British aristocrats to their possessions.

KARL MARX, 1853
From the People's Paper (21 January 1853)

FELIX HOLT: THE RADICAL

The group round the speaker in the flannel shirt stood at the corner of a side-street, and the speaker himself was elevated by the head and shoulders above his hearers, not because he was tall, but because he stood on a projecting stone. At the opposite corner of the turning was the great inn of the Fox and Hounds, and this was the ultra-Liberal quarter of the High Street. Felix was at once attracted by this group; he liked the look of the speaker, whose bare arms were powerfully muscular, though he had the pallid complexion of a man who lives chiefly amidst the heat of furnaces. He was leaning against the dark stone building behind him with folded arms, the grimy paleness of his shirt and skin standing out in high relief against the dark stone building behind him. He lifted up one fore-finger, and marked his emphasis with it as he spoke. His voice was high and not strong, but Felix recognized the fluency and the method of a habitual preacher or lecturer.

'It's the fallacy of all monopolists,' he was saying. 'We know what monopolists are: men who want to keep a trade all to themselves, under the pretence that they'll furnish the public with a better article. We know what that comes to: in some countries a poor man can't afford to buy a spoonful of salt, and yet there's salt enough in the world to pickle every living thing in it. That's the sort of benefit monopolists do to mankind. And these are the men who tell us we're to let politics alone; they'll govern us better without our knowing anything about it. We must mind our business; we are ignorant; we've no time to study great questions. But I tell them this: the greatest question in the world is, how to give every man a man's share in what goes on in life—'

GEORGE ELIOT, 1866

THE JUSTICE OF THE PEACE

My name is Squire Puddinghead,
   A Justice of the Peace, sir;
And if you don't know what that means,
   Just ask the rural police, sir!
When culprits nabbed for petty crimes
   Within my court assemble,
If I am sitting on the bench,
   Oh! don't the wretches tremble
      At the Great Unpaid!
      Ask anything but justice
      Of the Great Unpaid.

If Polly Brown but takes a stick
   From Farmer Giles' fences,
I fine her twopence as its worth,
   And fourteen bob expenses;
And if a tramp sleep in a field,
   Such is my lordly bounty,
I give him lodgings for a week,
   Provided by the county.

The Union leaders I would hang,
   'Twould be a task delightful:
But since I can't I am content
   To do the mean and spiteful;
And if my colleague, Captain Fair,
   Would be the poor's protector,
The vilest things I dare to do
   Are backed up by the Rector.

So Policeman Hobbs, and Gnobs my clerk,
   Their paltry charges trump up,
To vex and harass Union men,
   And don't I make 'em stump up!
What good to me to be J.P.

Over my wretched drudges,
If I can't strain and twist the law
To pay off all my grudges?

ANON, 1870S
A country song

IN THE WORKHOUSE: CHRISTMAS DAY

It is Christmas Day in the Workhouse,
    And the cold bare walls are bright
With garlands of green and holly,
    And the place is a pleasant sight:
For with clean-washed hands and faces
    In a long and hungry line
The paupers sit at the tables,
    For this is the hour they dine.

And the guardians and their ladies,
    Although the wind is east,
Have come in their furs and wrappers,
    To watch their charges feast:
To smile and be condescending,
    Put pudding on pauper plates,
To be hosts at the workhouse banquet
    They've paid for—with the rates.

Oh, the paupers are meek and lowly
    With their 'Thank'ee kindly, mum's'
So long as they fill their stomachs,
    What matter it whence it comes?
But one of the old men mutters,
    And pushes his plate aside:
'Great God!' he cries; 'but it chokes me!
    For this is the day she died.'

53

The guardians gazed in horror,
　　The master's face went white;
Did a pauper refuse their pudding?
　　Could their ears believe aright?
Then the ladies clutched their husbands,
　　Thinking the man would die,
Struck by a bolt, or something,
　　By the outraged One on high.

But the pauper sat for a moment,
　　Then rose 'mid a silence grim,
For the others had ceased to chatter
　　And trembled in every limb.
He looked at the guardians' ladies,
　　Then, eyeing their lords, he said,
'I eat not the food of villains
　　Whose hands are foul and red:

'Whose victims cry for vengeance
　　From their dank, unhallowed graves.'
'He's drunk!' said the workhouse master.
　　'Or else he's mad, and raves.'
'Not drunk or mad,' cried the pauper,
　　'But only a hunted beast,
Who, torn by the hounds and mangled,
　　Declines the vulture's feast.

'Do you think I will take your bounty,
　　And let you smile and think
You're doing a noble action
　　With the parish's meat and drink?
Where is my wife, you traitors—
　　The poor old wife you slew?
Yes, by the God above us,
　　My Nance was killed by you!
54

'Last winter my wife lay dying,
  Starved in a filthy den;
I had never been to the parish,—
  I came to the parish then.
I swallowed my pride in coming,
  For, ere the ruin came,
I held up my head as a trader,
  And I bore a spotless name.

'I came to the parish, craving
  Bread for a starving wife,
Bread for the woman who'd loved me
  Through fifty years of life;
And what do you think they told me,
  Mocking my awful grief?
That "the House" was open to us,
  But they wouldn't give "out relief".'
                                      GEORGE SIMS, 1881

USEFUL WORK v. USELESS TOIL

The misery and squalor which we people of civilization bear
with so much complacency as a necessary part of the manufacturing system, is just as necessary to the community at
large as a proportionate amount of filth would be in the
house of a private rich man. If such a man were to allow the
cinders to be raked all over his drawing-room, and a privy to
be established in each corner of his dining room, if he habitu-
ally made a dust and refuse heap of his once beautiful
garden, never washed his sheets or changed his table-cloth,
and made his family sleep five in a bed, he would surely find
himself in the claws of a commission *de lunatico*. But such
acts of miserly folly are just what our present society is doing
daily under the compulsion of a supposed necessity, which is
nothing short of madness.

                                    WILLIAM MORRIS, 1885
                              A Socialist League pamphlet

In every shipbuilding port there are to be seen thousands of idle men vainly seeking for an honest day's work. The privation that has been endured by them, their wives and children, is terrible to contemplate. Sickness has been very prevalent, whilst the hundreds of pinched and hungry faces have told a tale of suffering and privation which no optimism could minimise or conceal. Hide it—cover it up as we may, there is a depth of grief and trouble the full revelations of which, we believe, cannot be indefinitely postponed.

The workman may be ignorant of science and the arts and the sum of his exact knowledge may be only that which he has gained in his closely circumscribed daily toil; but he is not blind, and his thoughts do not take the shape of daily and hourly thanksgiving that his condition is not worse than it is; he does not imitate the example of the pious shepherd of Salisbury Plain, who derived supreme contentment from the fact that a kind Providence had vouchsafed him salt to eat his potatoes. He sees the lavish display of wealth in which he has no part. He sees a large and growing class enjoying inherited abundance. He sees miles of costly residences, each occupied by fewer people than are crowded into single rooms of the tenement in which he lives. He cannot fail to reason that there must be something wrong in a system which effects such unequal distribution of the wealth created by labour.

WHAT A COMPULSORY 8-HOUR DAY MEANS TO THE WORKERS

The effect of our so-called labour-saving machinery (used really by its owners to save *wages* and not *labour*) is to cause continual distress amongst the workers by mercilessly throwing them out of employment without any compensation. It may then take a man often months, sometimes years, to find an occupation of any kind and when found it is at a price much below that he was in receipt of before the machine disturbed him. Yet the machine has increased the ease and rapidity of wealth-production. This increase of wealth is of course enriching *someone*—a class of which many perform but little really useful work while the bulk of them serve no function useful in any way to the community.

TOM MANN, 1886
Pamphlet

FOURPENCE A DAY

The ore is waiting in the tubs, the snow's upon the fell;
Canny folk are sleeping yet, but lead is reet to sell.
Come, my little washer lad, come let's away,
We're bound down to slavery for fourpence a day.

It's early in the morning we rise at five o'clock,
And the little slaves come to the door to knock, knock, knock.
Come, my little washer lad, come let's away,
It's very hard to work for fourpence a day.

My father was a miner and lived down in the town,
'Twas hard work and poverty that always kept him down.
He aimed for me to go to school, but brass he couldn't pay,
So I had to go to the washing rake for fourpence a day.

My mother rises out of bed with tears on her cheeks,
Puts my wallet on my shoulders which has to serve a week.
It often fills her great big heart when she unto me does say:
'I never thought thou would have worked for fourpence a
*   day.'*

Fourpence a day, my lad, and very hard to work,
And never a pleasant look from a gruffy-looking Turk.
His conscience may it fail and his heart may it give way,
Then he'll raise us our wages to ninepence a day.

TRADITIONAL

A song collected from a retired lead miner in Teesdale

DIARY OF BEATRICE WEBB

Every day my social views take a more decidedly socialist
turn, every hour reveals fresh instances of the curse of gain
without labour; the endless perplexities of the rich, the
never-failing miseries of the poor. In this household [there
are] ten persons living on the fat of the land in order to
minister to the supposed comfort of one poor old man. All
this faculty expended to satisfy the assumed desires of a
being wellnigh bereft of desire. The whole thing is a vicious
circle as irrational as it is sorrowful. We feed our servants
well, keep them in luxurious slavery, because we hate to see
discomfort around us. But they and we are consuming the
labour of others and giving nothing in return, except useless
service to a dying life past serving. Here are thirteen depen-
dants consuming riches and making none, and no one the
better for it.

BEATRICE WEBB, APRIL 1890
From My Apprenticeship

THE FABIAN ELECTION MANIFESTO 1892

WHAT THE CONSERVATIVES HAVE DONE

The Conservative Party is avowedly the party of privilege and monopoly. It has been in power for the last six years; and during that period it has suppressed popular rights in Ireland, and attacked them in England, using the armed forces at its disposal against the rights of Free Speech and Public Meeting. In the numerous disputes between Capital and Labour during its period of office, it has sanctioned State interference only when the blackleg needed protection against the Trade Unionist. Although the administration of the criminal law has been biased against the poor to a scandalous degree, the Government has only interfered to show extra favour to the rich. The infamous Game Laws have been mercilessly enforced; Labour leaders of unimpeachable personal character have been charged with intimidation and imprisoned; several working men and two working women have been arrested for exercising the right of Free Speech in London; no redress has been given in cases where the Government, in spite of the most vindictive efforts to blacken the characters of its victims, has been compelled by public indignation to beat a retreat; and ferocious sentences of penal servitude have been dealt out to poor offenders for trifling thefts, whilst rich criminals, convicted of robbery and manslaughter committed under circumstances which placed them beyond all excuse, have been treated with conspicuous humanity. All attempts to deal with the Land Question have had for their object the strengthening of the land monopoly by the creation of a host of petty landlords. ... The County Council of London, the capital city of England and the world, was denied an ordinary municipal borough's powers of local self-government.... Clearly a party of which this can be said, is no friend to the Working Classes.

A CHRISTMAS MESSAGE

I am afraid my heart is bitter tonight, and so the thoughts and feelings that pertain to Christmas are far from me. But when I think of the thousands of white-livered poltroons who will take the Christ's name in vain, and yet not see His image being crucified in every hungry child, I cannot think of peace. I have known as a child what hunger means, and the scars of those days are with me still and rankle in my heart, and unfit me in many ways for the work to be done.

JAMES KEIR HARDIE, 1897
From the Labour Leader

FREE SCHOOL MEALS

Speech to Bradford Council in the debate over the provision of free school meals. As a result of Jowett's efforts Bradford became the first local authority in Britain to assume responsibility for feeding poor schoolchildren.

The section of the community which is the despair of the reformer is the section which does not know where the bread is to come from tomorrow. It is not until the hunger pangs are removed that people are able to think of something higher and to respond to the best impulses and appeals. Education on an empty stomach is a waste of money.

FRED JOWETT, 1904

WORK FOR IDLE HANDS TO DO

Charity is an ugly trick. It is a virtue grown by the rich on the graves of the poor. Unless it is accompanied by sincere revolt against the present social system, it is cheap moral swagger.

In former times it was used as fire insurance by the rich, but now that the fear of Hell has gone along with the rest of revealed religion, it is used either to gild mean lives with nobility or as a political instrument. A man who has spent his life in selling adulterated food to the poor gives a hundred thousand to a hospital and buys a title, which brings him a puzzled respect from a people perplexed by the tradition of an honourable peerage, artificially perpetuated by the *Daily Mail*. Peers ride forth to war against Land Inquiries, flapping the blankets which, should heavier taxes be imposed, will not be given to the tenantry next Christmas. And nothing could be meaner than the way the charitable have of capturing the moral value of the situation by quoting, 'It is more blessed to give than to receive.'

Women know the true damnation of charity because the habit of civilization has always been to throw them cheap alms rather than give them good wages. On the way to business men give women their seats in the tube, and underpay them as soon as they get there.

REBECCA WEST, 1912
From the Clarion (*December 1912*)

THE RAGGED-TROUSERED
PHILANTHROPISTS

'I don't see how we're goin' to alter things,' answered Easton. 'At the present time, from what I hear, work is scarce everywhere. *We* can't *make* work, can we?'

'Do you think, then, that the affairs of the world are something like the wind or the weather—altogether beyond our control? And that if they're bad we can do nothing but just sit down and wait for them to get better?'

'Well, I don't see 'ow we can odds it. If the people wot's got the money won't spend it, the likes of me and you can't make 'em, can we?'

Owen looked curiously at Easton.

'I suppose you're about twenty-six now,' he said. 'That means that you have about another thirty years to live. Of course, if you had proper food and clothes and hadn't to work more than a reasonable number of hours every day, there is no natural reason why you should not live for another fifty or sixty years: but we'll say thirty. Do you mean to say that you are able to contemplate with indifference the prospect of living for another thirty years under such conditions as those we endure at present?'

Easton made no reply.

'If you were to commit some serious breach of the law, and were sentenced next week to ten years' penal servitude, you'd probably think your fate a very pitiable one: yet you appear to submit quite cheerfully to this other sentence, which is—that you shall die a premature death after you have done another thirty years' hard labour.'

Easton continued painting the skirting.

'When there's no work,' Owen went on, taking another dip of paint as he spoke and starting on one of the lower panels of the door, 'when there's no work, you will either starve or get into debt. When—as at present—there is a little work, you will live in a state of semi-starvation. When times are what you call "good", you will work for twelve or fourteen hours a day and—if you're *very* lucky—occasionally all night. The extra money you then earn will go to pay your debts so that you may be able to get credit again when there's no work.'

Easton put some putty in a crack in the skirting.

'In consequence of living in this manner, you will die at least twenty years sooner than is natural, or, should you have an unusually strong constitution and live after you cease to be able to work, you will be put into a kind of gaol and treated like a criminal for the remainder of your life.'

Having faced up the cracks, Easton resumed the painting of the skirting.

'If it were proposed to make a law that all working men

and women were to be put to death—smothered, or hung, or poisoned, or put into a lethal chamber—as soon as they reached the age of fifty years, there is not the slightest doubt that you would join in the uproar of protest that would ensue. Yet you submit tamely to have your life shortened by slow starvation, overwork, lack of proper boots and clothing, and through having often to turn out and go to work when you are so ill that you ought to be in bed receiving medical care.'

Easton made no reply: he knew that all this was true, but he was not without a large share of the false pride which prompts us to hide our poverty and to pretend that we are much better off than we really are. He was at that moment wearing the pair of second-hand boots that Ruth had bought for him, but he had told Harlow—who had passed some remark about them—that he had had them for years, wearing them only for best. He felt very resentful as he listened to the other's talk, and Owen perceived it, but nevertheless he continued:

'Unless the present system is altered, that is all we have to look forward to; and yet you're one of the upholders of the present system—you help to perpetuate it!'

''Ow do I help to perpetuate it?' demanded Easton.

'By not trying to find out how to end it—by not helping those who are trying to bring a better state of things into existence. Even if you are indifferent to your own fate—as you seem to be—you have no right to be indifferent to that of the child for whose existence in this world you are responsible. Every man who is not helping to bring about a better state of affairs for the future is helping to perpetuate the present misery, and is therefore the enemy of his own children. There is no such thing as being neutral: we must either help or hinder.'

ROBERT TRESSEL, 1914

SELF-GOVERNMENT IN INDUSTRY

What, I want to ask, is the fundamental evil in our modern Society which we should set out to abolish?

There are two possible answers to that question, and I am sure that very many well-meaning people would make the wrong one. They would answer POVERTY, when they ought to answer SLAVERY. Face to face every day with the shameful contrasts of riches and destitution, high dividends and low wages, and painfully conscious of the futility of trying to adjust the balance by means of charity, private or public, they would answer unhesitatingly that they stand for the ABOLITION OF POVERTY.

Well and good! On that issue every Socialist is with them. But their answer to my question is none the less wrong.

Poverty is the symptom: slavery the disease. The extremes of riches and destitution follow inevitably upon the extremes of licence and bondage. The many are not enslaved because they are poor, they are poor because they are enslaved. Yet Socialists have all too often fixed their eyes upon the material misery of the poor without realizing that it rests upon the spiritual degradation of the slave.

G.D.H. COLE, 1917

PARABLE OF THE WATER TANK

But when the people no more received the pennies of the capitalists for the water they brought, they could buy no more water from the capitalists, having naught wherewith to buy. And when the capitalists saw that they had no more profit because no man bought water of them, they were troubled. And they sent forth men into the highways, the byways, and hedges, crying, 'If any thirst let him come to the tank and buy water of us, for it doth overflow.' For they said among themselves, 'Behold, the times are dull; we must advertise.'

But the people answered, saying, 'How can we buy unless ye hire us, for how else shall we have wherewithal to buy? Hire ye us, therefore, as before, and we will gladly buy water, for we thirst, and ye will have no need to advertise.' But the capitalists said to the people: 'Shall we hire you to bring water when the tank, which is the Market, doth already overflow? Buy ye, therefore, first water, and when the tank is empty, through your buying, will we hire you again.' And so it was because the capitalists hired them no more to bring water that the people could not buy the water they had brought already, and because the people could not buy the water they had brought already, the capitalists no more hired them to bring water. And the saying went abroad, 'It is a crisis.'

And the thirst of the people was great, for it was not now as it had been in the days of their fathers, when the land was open before them for everyone to seek water for himself, seeing that the capitalists had taken all the springs, and the wells, and the water-wheels, and the vessels, and the buckets, so that no man might come by water save from the tank, which was the Market. And the people murmured against the capitalists and said: 'Behold, the tank runneth over, and we die of thirst. Give us, therefore, of the water, that we perish not.'

But the capitalists answered, 'Not so. The water is ours. Ye shall not drink thereof unless ye buy it of us with pennies.' And they confirmed it with an oath, saying, after their manner, 'Business is business.'

And after many days the water was low in the tank, for the capitalists did make fountains and fish-ponds of the water thereof, and did bathe therein, they and their wives and their children, and did waste the water for their pleasure.

And when the capitalists saw that the tank was empty, they said, 'The crisis is ended'; and they sent forth and hired the people that they should bring water to fill it again. And for the water that the people brought to the tank they received for every bucket a penny, but for the water which the capitalists drew forth from the tank to give again to the people they received two pennies, that they might have their profit. And after a time did the tank again overflow, even as before.

c. 1925. *Independent Labour Party Youth Pamphlet*

THE GENERAL STRIKE OF 1926

All the way through to November it was a jug of soup a day; twice we got half a crown from the money which the Russians sent, and once or twice we got eight shillings a shift for shovelling coal gum which the hospitals were allowed to have for fuel. And that was all. I was in lodgings at £2 a week and had to pay every penny back afterwards. If you were married it was worse; you had to sell your furniture; if they gave you parish relief, it was, 'You don't need that carpet; why do you want those fancy curtains?'

When I got my job back my place was a bad one, in an 18- to 22-inch seam, howking lying on my side, with a patch on my arm from wrist to shoulder like emery paper where the skin rubbed. We were digging coal for the Canadian market and every year when the St Lawrence froze up we were laid off. By 1930 the pit was worked out and I was 13 months out of work (we were married and living in rooms) cycling miles every day looking for work, until the supervisor in the Labour Exchange, who was in the same mob as I was in the 1914–18 war, sent me to the Clyde Navigation Trust as a labourer. We were shovelling road metal, building up a quay wall for loading iron ore; there were all sorts working there, out-of-work engineers, clerks. I felt sorry for some of them, for they were not used to this kind of work, and their hands were in a mess; I would give them a hand every now and then. But they had to put up with it, for in those days and for years afterwards, you had to take what work you could get.

JOHN CAMPBELL [1973]
From Strike: A Live History, 1887–1971 (*Leeson*)

LOVE ON THE DOLE

Helen! He saw her face in the murky water below; felt tight in the throat, turned away to slink homewards. Home! His spirits retched with nausea. How much longer? Daren't go to see Helen. Couldn't bear to look at that question eternally in her eyes: 'Have you got a job, yet?'

No money. She'd be like you, fed up. 'Ah'm goin' barmy. Ah'll jump in cut one o' these days.'

There was a dull vacuity in his eyes nowadays; he became listless, hard of hearing, saying, 'Eh?' when anybody asked him a question.

Nothing to do with time; nothing to spend; nothing to do tomorrow nor the day after; nothing to wear; can't get married. A living corpse; a unit of the spectral army of three million lost men.

Hands in pockets, shoulders hunched, he would slink round the by-streets to the billiard hall, glad to be somewhere out of the way of the public gaze, any place where there were no girls to see him in his threadbare jacket and patched overalls. Stealing into the place like a shadow to seat himself in a corner of one of the wall seats to watch the prosperous young men who had jobs and who could afford billiards, cigarettes and good clothes.

Watch that bloke there, Harry. . . . He'll be chucking his tab-end away in a minute. There it goes! Stoop, surreptitiously, pretend you are fastening your bootlace. Grab the cigarette end now ... there's no one looking. Aaaah! A long puff; tastes good. But it wasn't always so easy as that. Sometimes his vigilant eyes would see the butt end disappear into the spittoon, or its careless owner might crush it beneath his heel.

WALTER GREENWOOD, 1933

YOUTH'S OPPORTUNITY

*An appeal leaflet on behalf of the
Labour Party League of Youth*

Dear Comrades,

VICTIMS OF CAPITALISM

All around you there are masses of people, including perhaps friends, neighbours and even your own families, who are plunged in poverty, forced to dwell in slums, driven down by unemployment—vainly struggling under the pressure of economic and social insecurity to make life worth while, for however much they sacrifice and however carefully they contrive, they are unable to escape from these terrible conditions.

They must endure or go under.

There is something wrong—radically wrong. Men are not rich or poor, employed or unemployed, hungry or satisfied, at peace or at war, happy or miserable, by God's decree.

These are inequalities and evils that are inherent in the system under which we live—a system which puts profit and private property before the economic security and social well-being of the people.

Nature is bounteous in her gifts to mankind. Modern science and constantly improving machinery and methods enable wealth to be produced in far greater abundance than was ever dreamed of in days that are gone.

There would be enough for all and to spare if wealth were properly distributed and used.

CAPITALISM'S CRIMINAL WASTE

But the world as we know it is at once a vast storehouse abounding with plenty and a vast poor-house overcrowded with distressed humanity.

Crops are burnt and fish is thrown back into the sea because it does not pay to sell them. And millions go hungry because they cannot buy.

These things are wrong; they are stupid and criminal. No one but a fool would try to defend or justify them. But they go on only because the people like you and others allow them to go on.

The Labour Party wants to put them right. The Labour Party will put them right once the nation gives it power. It is going to build a sane Society within which there will be work, security and opportunity for all in an efficiently organized and well-directed State.

GEORGE LANSBURY, 1933

TIME TO SPARE

The whole system's wrong, and I don't think you'll ever change the hearts of these industrialists unless something very drastic is done. All they want is to get everything out of you, to the last possible ounce. One employer said to me, 'From a business point of view you're less valuable to me than a drum of oil. We must have the oil, but we can do without you.' This is the type of man responsible for the system—people working ten and twelve hours a day, sweated half to death on these point-to-point and other speeding-up-production methods. All the time the development of machinery is simplifying skill and doing away with us older fellows. It affects men over twenty—yes, it's come down to twenty now. Many employers today favour women and juveniles, who when they become entitled to a higher scale of wages find themselves on the scrapheap with the others. I'm only thirty-three, but I've been told time after time that I'm too old, and some of my friends who are over forty know for a fact that they'll never get another job whilst we live under this present system. There's plenty of gold, plenty of material, and God knows there's plenty of labour, so what's wrong? I'm not a revolutionary in the sense of violence, but we do want a revolutionary change in our conditions, and unless this change comes quick, thousands like myself are condemned to live in despair and slow starvation, watching our wives and children rot before our eyes. Neither Fascism nor Communism nor any other 'ism' holds any terror for us. *Nothing* can be worse than what we've got at present.

JOHN EVANS, 1934
From a series of BBC Radio talks given by the unemployed, later published in book form as So I'll Remember

MAIDEN SPEECH IN THE HOUSE OF COMMONS

I have heard of hundreds of cases, but one of the most outstanding in my mind at the moment is that of one of the heroes who came back from the war paralysed. He has lain in bed since the end of the war and has never moved. Do you remember the promise we made as to the treatment that these heroes were to receive? Do you remember how the duke and the worker were to walk along the road hand-in-hand, with roses on every side and happiness lying close at hand? Here is a paralysed man lying in bed. His boy grows to manhood—he is twenty-one years of age—and gets a job. The means test is operated in that home. He is persuaded to leave home and live with relatives so that the family income shall not be interfered with. He leaves his bed-ridden father and weeping mother and goes to his new home. He cannot eat; he cannot sleep. Despair settles upon him, and in a week comes the end—suicide. He is driven to death by the means test, as thousands of others have been done to death. Were you anxious for them? Are you going to change it because you have seen the ghastly work which you have done? I have seen it, and I cannot forget it. You have not defended the unemployed and the mothers and the children. It is all very well for the Prime Minister, in his introductory speech, to say that on the question of maternity and midwifery there will not be any need for political opposition. It is a very serious problem and one which is dear to his heart. The Chief Medical Officer in his report last year drew attention to the fact that we were making no headway against maternal mortality. Where does the trouble come from? It comes from low wages and low unemployment relief. The mothers and children have to suffer. You may pay tribute to, or worship, the Madonna and Child, but day after day you are doing the Madonna and Child to death.

WILLIE GALLACHER, DECEMBER 1935
Willie Gallacher was the first Communist Member of Parliament

MAIDEN SPEECH IN THE HOUSE OF COMMONS

The question before this House, in view of the apathy, neglect and lack of understanding which this House has shown to these people in Ulster which it claims to represent, is how in the shortest space it can make up for fifty years of neglect, apathy and lack of understanding. Short of producing miracles such as factories overnight in Derry and homes overnight in practically every area in the North of Ireland, what can we do? If British troops are sent in I should not like to be either the mother or sister of an unfortunate soldier stationed there.

BERNADETTE DEVLIN, 22 APRIL 1969
Bernadette Devlin was the Member of Parliament for Mid-Ulster

THE MAN THAT WATERS THE WORKERS' BEER

Chorus:
I am the man, the very fat man, that waters the workers' beer,
And I'm the man, the very fat man, that waters the workers' beer.
And what do I care if it makes them ill, if it makes them terribly queer?
I've a car and a yacht and an aeroplane and I waters the workers' beer!

Now when I makes the workers' beer, I puts in strychnine,
Some methylated spirits and a drop of parafin;
But since a brew so terribly strong might make them terribly queer
I reaches my hand for the water tap and I waters the workers' beer!

Now a drop of good beer is good for a man who's thirsty and tired and hot
And I sometimes has a drop for myself from a very special lot
But a fat and healthy working class is the thing that I most fear,

So I reaches my hand for the water tap and I waters the
    workers' beer!

Now ladies fair, beyond compare, and be ye maid or wife,
O, sometimes lend a thought for one who leads a wand'ring
    life.
The water rates are shockingly high, and 'meth' is shockingly
    dear,
And there isn't the profit there used to be in wat'ring the
    workers' beer!

PADDY RYAN, 1955
From the Labour Party Song Book

OLD AGE REPORT

When a man's too ill or old to work
We punish him.
Half his income is taken away
Or all of it vanishes and he gets pocket-money.

We should reward these tough old humans for surviving,
Not with a manager's soggy handshake
Or a medal shaped like an alarm clock—
No, make them a bit rich,
Give the freedom they always heard about
When the bloody chips were down
And the blitz or the desert
Swallowed their friends.

Retire, retire into a fungus basement
Where nothing moves except the draught
And the light and dark grey figures
Doubling their money on the screen;
Where the cabbages taste like the mummy's hand
And the meat tastes of feet;

Where there is nothing to say except:
'Remember?' or 'Your turn to dust the cat.'

To hell with retiring. Let them advance.
Give them the money they've always earned
Or more—and let them choose.
If Mr Burley wants to be a miser,
Great, let the moneybags sway and clink for him,
Pay him a pillowful of best doubloons.
So Mrs Wells has always longed to travel?
Print her a season ticket to the universe,
Let her slum-white skin
Be tanned by a dozen different planets.
We could wipe away some of their worry,
Some of their pain—what I mean
Is so bloody simple:
The old people are being robbed
And punished and we ought
To be letting them out of their cages
Into green spaces of enchanting light.

ADRIAN MITCHELL, 1971

RECTORIAL ADDRESS, GLASGOW UNIVERSITY

A rat race is for rats. We're not rats. We're human beings. Reject the insidious pressures in society that would blunt your critical faculties to all that is happening around you, that would caution silence in the face of injustice lest you jeopardize your chances of promotion and self-advancement. This is how it starts and, before you know where you are, you're a fully paid-up member of the rat pack. The price is too high. It entails the loss of your dignity and human spirit. Or as Christ puts it, 'What doth it profit a man if he gain the whole world and suffer the loss of his soul?'

Profit is the sole criterion used by the Establishment to evaluate economic activity. From the rat race to lame ducks. The vocabulary in vogue is a give-away. It is more reminiscent of a human menagerie than human society. The power structures that have inevitably emerged from this approach threaten and undermine our hard-won democratic rights. The whole process is towards the centralization and concentration of power in fewer and fewer hands. The facts are there for all who want to see. Giant monopoly companies and consortia dominate almost every branch of our economy. The men who wield effective control within these giants exercise a power over their fellow men which is frightening and is a negation of democracy. . . .

From the Olympian heights of an executive suite, in an atmosphere where your success is judged by the extent to which you can maximize profits, the overwhelming tendency must be to see people as units for production, as indices in your accountants' books. To appreciate fully the inhumanity of this situation, you have to see the hurt and despair in the eyes of a man suddenly told he is redundant without provision made for suitable alternative employment—with the prospect in the West of Scotland, if he is in his late forties or fifties, of spending the rest of his life in the Labour Exchange. Someone, somewhere, has decided he is unwanted, un-needed, and is to be thrown on the industrial scrap heap. From the very depth of my being, I challenge the right of any man or any group of men, in business or in government, to tell a fellow human being that he or she is expendable.

JIMMY REID, APRIL 1972

THE RAILWAYMAN

Now my father was a big strong man,
Who worked hard all his life,
He was always in a whisky glass,
And never out of strife.

For he called no man his master,
And a very few his friend,
A proud and stiff-necked man he was,
Who would never bow and bend,
But they broke him in the end,
When they'd no use for him.

And they took away his job,
When they'd no use for him any more,
After nearly thirty years,
They kicked him out the door,
But they let him keep his railway jacket,
Over coat and cap,
And the pension of nine bob a week,
He was lucky to get that,
And they nearly broke his heart,
When they'd no use for him.

When you're fifty-five years old,
And you're looking for some work,
Nobody wants to know your face,
No one gives you the start,
So I watched him growing older,
And more bitter every day,
As his pride and self-respect,
Well, they slowly drained away,
There was nothing I could say,
They had no use for him.

ERIC BOGLE, 1978

UNEMPLOYMENT

It is the context that gives poverty its definition. To see a child doing his homework by the light of a street lamp on a freezing December evening because the electricity in his home has been cut off; to hear the half-sad, half-proud voice of a mother saying of a handicapped 3-year-old child 'He's just had his first clothing grant', as though it were a rite of passage from infancy to childhood; to listen to the woman whose husband has been out of work for five years, and who allows herself one pot of tea that has to last all day—all this would not be shocking if you felt it served some other purpose than the humiliation of those who suffer it. But it doesn't. As one poorly paid railway worker said, 'Poverty has become a crime.'

In these towns, with their ruined industries, exhausted collieries and depleted shipyards, there is a sense of broken purpose, a draining away of meaning. What has been lost is that which sustained an older generation of the poor: their function and its importance. The poverty of living memory is allied to people's indispensable labour. An old miner said, 'Even at the worst of the depression, you knew you were waiting for trade to pick up. You never lost that feeling that you belonged to the working class. Those who had work helped the poor and the unemployed. Nobody in the community called the unemployed scroungers. Even those who were a bit feckless, they were helped just the same as canny folk, those who could cope. They were still your neighbours.'

It seems that the purpose of the poor now is more nakedly ideological: their purpose is to be poor. Not to produce, but simply to serve as a contrast, a defining edge for wealth and success, and a warning and example to the rest.

JEREMY SEABROOK, 1982

WIGAN PIER REVISITED

In the 1930s the words 'means test' was a curse, fuelling the resistance against it both among the unemployed and some of its administrators. Its renaissance with the new wave of unemployment has been echoed by a new contest of concepts. And this time the poor are losing—the notion of 'scrounger' has been mobilized as a new scourge against them, not only successfully legitimating the dole as the lowest of low benefits, but also its actual *reduction* (through the abolition of earnings-related benefit in 1981) and the enforced dependence on the means-tested supplementary benefit. And now the Thatcher Government threatens *further* reductions. Just as the Government of the 1930s defended cuts in relief and the expulsion of categories of claimants on grounds of costs to the country, so the Thatcher regime has conquered popular concern with poverty by a populist counterattack. The scourge of scroungerism has converted the unemployed into the poor, the poor into the undeserving poor and sympathy into suspicion.

BEATRIX CAMPBELL, 1984

PART TWO
RIGHTS AND DEMANDS

We will deny or defer to no one, right and justice.
MAGNA CARTA

Here we are introduced to some of the basic ideas that stem from the experience of struggle. The demands for freedom as an inherent human right and the insistence that everyone, however poor, is entitled to such rights, reflect the religious roots of revolt.

Despite the fact that many of the passages predate the emergence of socialism, it is possible to detect themes that have recurred throughout our history and are still keenly argued today. We hear demands that all government be based on the consent of the governed, about the importance of a genuinely free press, and of tolerance in a continuing public debate—an example of this is given with the armed forces of the English Revolution. There is an explicit demand for the common ownership of the land, and for co-operation and greater equality. Later, as we move beyond the Industrial Revolution, we hear the voices of the Chartists, with their call for annual Parliaments, and a much clearer definition of what freedom means, and its relationship to education.

Some of the passages take the form of humble petitions and others appear as bitter satire. Throughout we are reminded of the strength of conscience and the need for confidence in the democratic process. This brings forward arguments for workers' control as a way to extend democracy into the economic and industrial field so that people can develop their full capabilities which were then, as now, so severely cramped by an oppressive social system.

TONY BENN

MAGNA CARTA 1215

No freeman shall be taken, imprisoned, disseized, outlawed, banished, or in any way destroyed; nor will We proceed against him or prosecute him except by the lawful judgment of his peers or by the law of the land.

We will sell to no one, we will deny or defer to no one, right and justice.

We will not, by ourselves or others procure anything whereby any of these concessions and liberties be revoked or lessened; and if any such thing be obtained, let it be null and void, neither shall we ever make use of it, either by ourselves or any other.

THE BRUCE

Inspired by the successful Scottish resistance
to the English invasion.

Ah, freedom is a noble thing.
Freedom makes a man to have liking.
Freedom all solace to man gives:
He lives at ease, that freely lives:
A noble heart may have no ease,
Nor naught else that may him please,
If freedom fail; for free liking
Is yearned-for o'er all other thing.
Nay, he that aye has lived free,
May not know well the property,
The anger, nor the wretched doom
That is coupled with foul thraldom.
But if he had assayed it,
Then all perfectly he should it wit:
And should think freedom more to prize
Than all the gold in world that is.

JOHN BARBOUR, 1395

JOHN BALL'S SERMONS

An account of John Ball's sermons given 'oftentimes on the Sundays after mass'.

My good friends, matters cannot go on well in England until all things shall be in common; when there shall be neither vassals nor lords; when the lords shall be no more masters than ourselves. How ill they behave to us! for what reason do they hold us thus in bondage? Are we not all descended from the same parents, Adam and Eve? And what can they show, or what reason can they give, why they should be more masters than ourselves? They are clothed in velvet and rich stuffs, ornamented with ermine and other furs, while we are forced to wear poor clothing. They have wines, spices and fine breads, while we have only rye and the refuse of the straw; and when we drink it must be water. They have handsome seats and manors, while we must brave the wind and rain in our labours in the field; and it is by our labour they have wherewith to support their pomp. We are called slaves, and if we do not perform our service we are beaten, and we have no sovereign to whom we can complain or who would be willing to hear us. Let us go to the king and remonstrate with him; he is young, and from him we may obtain a favourable answer, and if not we must ourselves seek to amend our condition.

FROISSART, *c.* 1381
The Chronicles

THE COMPLAINT OF RODERYCK MORS

ON ENCLOSURE

God grant the King grace, to pull up a great part of his own parks, and to compel his lords, knights, and gentlemen to pull up all theirs by the roots, and to let out the ground to the people at such a reasonable price as they may live at their hands. And if they will needs have some deer for their vain pleasure, then let them take such heathy, woody, and moory ground, as is unfruitful for corn or pasture, so that the common wealth be not robbed; and let them make good defence, that their poor neighbours, joining unto them, be not devoured of their corn and grass. Thus should ye do, for the earth is the poor man's as well as the rich. And ye lords, see that ye abuse not the blessing of the riches and power which God hath lent you, and remember that the earth is the Lord's and not yours.

HENRY BRINKELOWE, c. 1545

THE CASE OF SHIP MONEY
BRIEFLY DISCOURSED

In nature there is no reason why the meanest wretches should not enjoy freedom, and demand justice in as ample measure, as those whom law hath provided for: and why lords which are above law should be more cruel than those which are more conditionate: yet we see it is a fatal kind of necessity only incident to immoderate power, that it must be immoderately used: and certainly this was well known to our ancestors, or else they would not have purchased their charters of freedom with so great an expense of blood as they did, and have endured so much so many years, rather than be betrayed to immoderate power and prerogative: let us therefore not be too careless of that, which they were so jealous of, but let us look narrowly into the true consequence of this ship-scot, whatsoever the face of it appear to be.

HENRY PARKER, 1640

AREOPAGITICA

Where there is much desire to learn, there of necessity will be much arguing, much writing, many opinions: for opinion in good men is but knowledge in the making. Under these fantastic terrors of sect and schism, we wrong the earnest and zealous thirst after knowledge and understanding which God hath stirred up in this city. What some lament of, we rather should rejoice at, should rather praise this pious forwardness among men, to reassume the ill-reputed care of their Religion into their own hands again.

JOHN MILTON, 1644

THE LIBERTY OF PROPHESYING

It is unnatural and unreasonable to persecute disagreeing opinions. Unnatural: for understanding, being a thing wholly spiritual, cannot be restrained, and therefore neither punished by corporal afflictions. It is *in aliena republica*, a matter of another world. You may as well cure the colic by brushing a man's clothes, or fill a man's belly with a syllogism.... For is an opinion ever the more true or false for being persecuted? Some men have believed it the more, as being provoked into a confidence, and vexed into a resolution; but the thing itself is not the truer: and though the hangman may confute a man with an inexplicable dilemma, yet not convince his understanding; for such premises can infer no conclusion but that of a man's life: and a wolf may as well give laws to the understanding, as he whose dictates are only propounded in violence and writ in blood: and a dog is as capable of a law as a man, if there be no choice in his obedience, nor discourse in his choice, nor reason to satisfy his discourse.

JEREMY TAYLOR, 1646

A COPIE OF A LETTER . . .
TO ALL THE HONEST SEA-MEN OF
ENGLAND

*The Levellers in the army succeeded in setting up a democratic
General Council of Agitators who had equal rights with the
officers. Here the soldier-legislators, freed from deference to
officers, are appealing to the much more conservative navy for
support.*

And we assure you upon the faith of honest Men and
Soldiers, that (whatever may be suggested to you by any) we
have no other aims, but that Justice might act in all its parts
and to all its ends, as relating to all states and persons in the
Kingdom, that the yokes of Oppression might be taken off
the necks of all and Justice equally distributed to all, and the
rights of any (though now detained from them) restored, and
settled upon them, that so they might not be taken from
them, unless they disabled themselves of the enjoyment of
them and so doing we trust we shall have the concurrent assistance of (at leastwise not any opposition from any rational
Men who love Justice and hate Tyranny, especially from you
(dear friends) who together with us, have been embarked in
the same ship, and have passed through many a desperate
encounter by Sea as we have by Land, all to free this poor
Kingdom from Tyrannical Oppression, (which notwithstanding, you and we feel too much of at this day) who we trust
with us, do hate and scorn to be kept any longer under
bondage, having purchased our freedom at so dear a rate,
(though free born).

JUNE 1647

AN APPEALE

Concerning Schools

That all ancient Donations for the maintenance and continuance of Free Schools which are impropriate or converted to any private use, and all such Free Schools which are destroyed or purloined of any freedom for propriety may be restored and erected again, and that in all parts or counties of the Realm of England, and the Dominion of Wales destitute of Free Schools (for the nurture and education of children) may have a competent number of such schools, founded, erected, and endowed at the public charges of those respective counties and places so destitute, that few or none of the free men of England may for the future be ignorant of reading and writing.

RICHARD OVERTON, JULY 1647

THE PUTNEY DEBATES

The army debates at Putney between the democratically elected Agents or Agitators and the Officers were a forum for discussion of fundamental principles of democracy, freedom and equality.

COWLING: Since the Conquest the greatest part of the kingdom was in vassalage.
PETTY: We judge that all inhabitants that have not lost their birthright should have an equal voice in elections.
RAINBOROUGH: I desired that those that had engaged in it might be included. For really I think that the poorest he that is in England hath a life to live, as the greatest he;

and therefore truly, sir, I think it's clear, that every man that is to live under a government ought first by his own consent to put himself under that government; and I do think that the poorest man in England is not at all bound in a strict sense to that government that he hath not had a voice to put himself under; and I am confident that, when I have heard the reasons against it, something will be said to answer those reasons, insomuch that I should doubt whether he was an Englishman or no, that should doubt of these things.

IRETON: Give me leave to tell you, that if you make this the rule I think you must fly for refuge to an absolute natural right, and you must deny all civil right; and I am sure it will come to that in the consequence. For my part I think it is no right at all. I think that no person hath a right to an interest or share in the disposing of the affairs of the kingdom, and in determining or choosing those that shall determine what laws we shall be ruled by here—no person hath a right to this, that hath not a permanent fixed interest in this kingdom. . . .

OCTOBER 1647

ENGLANDS FREEDOME, SOULDIERS RIGHTS

This pamphlet was addressed to the leaders of the New Model Army and argued that the army was a body of free citizens and that decisions therefore had to be agreed democratically.

I draw up this protestation against you, that by the Laws and constitutions of this Kingdome, you have not the least Indicative power in the world over me; therefore, I cannot in the least give you any Honour, Reverence or Respect, either in word, action, or gesture: and if you by force and compulsion compell me again to come before you, I must and will by Gods assistance keep on my Hat, and look upon you as a company of murderers, Robbers and Thieves, and doe the best I can to raise the Hue and Crie of the Kingdome against you, as a company of such lawlesse persons, and therefore if there be any Honor, Honesty and Conscience in you, I require you as a free-born English man, to doe me Justice and right, by a formall dismissing of me, and give me just reparation for my monthes unjust imprisonment by you, and for that lose of credit I have sustained thereby, that so things may goe no further; or els you will compell and necessitate me to study all waies and meanes in the world to procure satisfaction from you, and if you have any thing to lay to my charge, I am as an Englishman ready to answer you at the common Law of England, and in the mean time I shall subscribe my selfe.

From my arbitrary and most illegall imprisonment in Windsore, this 14. Decemb. 1647.
Your servant in your faithfull discharge of your dutie to your Masters (the Commons of England) that pay you your wages,

WILLIAM THOMPSON
(?) JOHN LILBURNE *and others*, DECEMBER 1647

TO THE COMMONS OF ENGLAND

Censorship, enforced by statute, was introduced in January 1649 by the Rump Parliament. It threatened to undermine the Levellers' main way of reaching their followers—the pamphlet; they responded with typical vigour.

We beseech you to consider how unreasonable it is for every man or woman to be liable to punishment, penal or corporal, upon one witness in matters of this Nature, for compiling, printing, selling or dispersing of Books and Pamphlets, nay to deserve even whipping (as the last years Ordinance, an Engine fitted to a Personal Treaty) doth provide a punishment, as we humbly conceive, fit only for slaves or bondmen.

JANUARY 1649
Leveller pamphlet

THE AGREEMENT OF THE PEOPLE

We, the free People of England, to whom God hath given hearts, means and opportunity to effect the same, do with submission to his wisdom, in his name, and desiring the equity thereof may be to his praise and glory; Agree to ascertain our Government to abolish all arbitrary Power, and to set bounds and limits both to our Supreme, and all Subordinate Authority, and remove all known Grievances. And accordingly do declare and publish to all the world, that we are agreed as followeth,

That the Supreme Authority of England and the Territories therewith incorporate, shall be and reside henceforth in a Representative of the people consisting of four hundred persons, but no more; in the choice of whom (according to natural right) all men of the age of one and twenty years and upwards (not being servants, or receiving alms, or having

served the late King in Arms or voluntary Contributions),
shall have their voices.

JOHN LILBURNE, RICHARD OVERTON *and* WILLIAM WALWYN
I MAY 1649. *Preamble to the Third Draft*

WALWINS WILES OR THE MANIFESTORS MANIFESTED

What an inequitable thing it is for one man to have thousands, and another want bread, and that the pleasure of God
is, that all men should have enough, and not that one man
should abound in this worlds good, spending it upon his
lusts, and another man of far better deserts, not be worth two
pence, and that it is no such difficulty as men make it to be, to
alter the course of the world in this thing, and that a few
diligent and valiant spirits may turn the world upside down,
if they observe their seasons, and shall with life and courage
ingage accordingly.

JOHN PRICE, APRIL 1649

DISCOURSES CONCERNING GOVERNMENT

*Sidney, a Republican Member of Parliament, was executed
for treason in 1683.*

A man may perhaps say, the public peace may be hereby
disturbed: but he ought to know, there can be no peace,
where there is no justice; nor any justice, if the government
instituted for the good of a nation be turned to its ruin.

ALGERNON SIDNEY, 1680

But when we would once form an arbitrary definition of freedom, who shall say what it ought to be? Ought freedom rather to be annexed to forty pence, or forty shillings, or forty pounds per annum? Or why not to four hundred or four thousand? But indeed, so long as money is to be the measure of it, it will be impossible to know who ought or who ought not to be free. According to my apprehension, we might as well make the possession of forty shillings per annum, the proof of a man's being rational, as of his being free. There is just as much sense in one as the other.

MAJOR JOHN CARTWRIGHT, 1776

ESSAY ON THE RIGHT OF PROPERTY IN LAND

Ogilvie advocated dividing England into smallholdings, each of equal size, for every able-bodied citizen who wanted one.

All right of property is founded either in occupancy or labour. The earth having been given to mankind in common occupancy, each individual seems to have by nature a right to possess and cultivate an equal share. This right is little different from that which he has to the free use of the open air and running water. . . .

No individual can derive from this general right of occupancy a title to any more than an equal share of the soil of his country. His actual possession of more cannot of right preclude the claim of any other person who is not already possessed of such equal share.

WILLIAM OGILVIE, 1781

THE RIGHTS OF MAN

If any generation of men ever possessed the right of dictating the mode by which the world should be governed for ever, it was the first generation that existed; and if that generation did it not, no succeeding generation can show any authority for doing it, nor can set any up. The illuminating and divine principle of the equal rights of man, (for it has its origin from the Maker of man) relates, not only to the living individuals, but to generations of men succeeding each other. Every generation is equal in rights to the generations which preceded it, by the same rule that every individual is born equal in rights with his contemporary. . . .

The Mosaic account of the creation, whether taken as divine authority, or merely historical, is full to this point, *the unity or equality of man*. The expressions admit of no controversy. . . .

But, after all, what is this metaphor called a crown, or rather what is monarchy? Is it a thing, or is it a name, or is it a fraud? Is it 'a contrivance of human wisdom', or of human craft to obtain money from a nation under specious pretences? It is a thing necessary to a nation? If it is, in what does that necessity consist, what services does it perform, what is its business, and what are its merits? Doth the virtue consist in the metaphor, or in the man? Doth the goldsmith that makes the crown, make the virtue also? Doth it operate like Fortunatus's wishing-cap, or Harlequin's wooden sword? Doth it make a man a conjuror? In fine, what is it? It appears to be a something going much out of fashion, falling into ridicule, and rejected in some countries both as unnecessary and expensive.

TOM PAINE, 1791
Part I

THE RIGHTS OF MAN

What is government more than the management of the affairs of a Nation? It is not, and from its nature cannot be, the property of any particular man or family, but of the whole community, at whose expense it is supported; and though by force or contrivance it has been usurped into an inheritance, the usurpation cannot alter the right of things. Sovereignty, as a matter of right, appertains to the Nation only, and not to any individual; and a Nation has at all times an inherent indefeasible right to abolish any form of Government it finds inconvenient, and establish such as accords with its interest, disposition, and happiness. The romantic and barbarous distinction of men into Kings and subjects, though it may suit the condition of courtiers, cannot that of citizens; and is exploded by the principle upon which Governments are now founded. Every citizen is a member of the Sovereignty, and, as such, can acknowledge no personal subjection; and his obedience can be only to the laws.

TOM PAINE, 1792
Part II

AGRARIAN JUSTICE

It is wrong to say that God made *Rich* and *Poor*; he made only *Male* and *Female*; and he gave them the earth for their inheritance.

TOM PAINE, 1795
Preface

THE RIGHTS OF BRITONS

Let us not deceive ourselves! Property is nothing but human labour. The most inestimable of all property is the sweat of the poor man's brow—the property from which all other is derived, and without which grandeur must starve in the midst of supposed abundance. And shall they who possess this inestimable property be told that they have no rights, because they have nothing to defend? Shall those who toil for our subsistence, and bleed for our protection, be excluded from all importance in the scale of humanity, because they have so toiled and bled? No; man and not moveables is the object of just legislation. All, therefore, ought to be consulted where all are concerned; for what less than the whole ought to decide the fate of the whole?

JOHN THELWALL, 1795

SETTING THE RECORD STRAIGHT

You have been represented by the *Times* newspaper, by the *Courier*, by the *Morning Post*, by the *Morning Herald*, and others, as the *scum* of society. They say that you have *no business at public meetings*; that you are *rabble*, and that you *pay no taxes*. These insolent hirelings, who wallow in wealth, would not be able to put their abuse of you in print were it not for *your labour*.

WILLIAM COBBETT, NOVEMBER 1816
From an article in the Political Register

REPORT TO THE COUNTY OF LANARK

From this principle of individual interest have arisen all the divisions of mankind, the endless errors and mischiefs of class, sect, party, and of national antipathies, creating the

95

angry and malevolent passions, and all the crimes and misery with which the human race have hitherto been afflicted.

In short, if there be one closer doctrine more contrary to truth than another, it is the notion that individual interest, as that term is now understood, is a more advantageous principle on which to found the social system, for the benefit of all, or of any, than the principle of union and mutual co-operation.

ROBERT OWEN, 1820

ON THE STATE OF OUR PRESS

I perceive that you want very much to be enlightened ON THE STATE OF OUR PRESS, which you appear to regard as being FREE, and which, as I am going to prove to you, is the most *enslaved* and the *vilest* thing that has ever been heard of in the world under the name of press. I say, that I am going to PROVE this; and proof consists of *undeniable facts*, and not of vague assertions.

Advertising is the great source of *revenue* with our journals, except in very few cases, such as mine, for instance, who have no advertisements. Hence, these journals are an affair of *trade* and not of *literature*; the proprietors think of *the money* that is to be got by them; they hire men to write in them; and these men are *ordered* to write in a way to please the classes who can give most advertisements. The Government itself pays large sums in advertisements, many hundreds a year, to some journals. The aristocracy, the clergy, the magistrates (who are generally *clergy* too) in the several counties; the merchants, the manufacturers, the great shopkeepers; all these *command* the press, because without their advertisements it cannot be carried on *with profit*.

WILLIAM COBBETT, AUGUST 1830
From an article in the Political Register

THE POOR MAN'S GUARDIAN

The people's press must be the chief weapon of our warfare. When the labourer knows his wrongs, the death-knell of the capitalist has been sounded.

AUGUST 1834
An anonymous letter

SPEECH AT THE GREAT MEETING ON KENSAL MOOR

Behind universal suffrage I want to see that knowledge in the mind, that principle in the heart, that power in the conscience, that strength in the right arm that would enable the working man to meet his master boldly, upright on his feet, without the brand mark of the bondman upon his brow, and without the blush of shame and slavery upon his cheek. I want to see the working man as free in the mill as when he goes into the wilderness—as free spoken when he goes for his wages as he is when he spends a part of it with his companion. I want to see every man so free as to speak his mind, act according to his conscience, and do no one any injury.

J. R. STEPHENS, 1838
Reported in the Northern Star, *the Chartist newspaper (29 September 1838)*

SPEECH AT A NEWCASTLE PUBLIC MEETING

The speech was on the motion 'that this meeting regards with deep indignation the baseness and treachery of the hireling portion of the press in labouring to perpetuate the slavery of the people, and that their resentment is especially directed

97

against the Sun *London evening paper, and the* London Weekly Chronicle, *and* Weekly Dispatch'.

Mr Lowery then came forward, and was received with loud and oft repeated cheers. He said that when in London he had denounced the baseness of the hireling press, and in return he had *The Times* driving furiously at him the next morning. In all the meetings he had subsequently attended, he had re-iterated the assertion of its baseness, and as a proof of the truth of that assertion, he pointed to *The Times* itself. But he would not point to *The Times* alone; there were Southey, Coleridge, Scott, aye, and Harry Brougham, all evidences of the prostitution of literary talent. But it was honesty the people wanted; he denied that it was so much a question of intelligence as of integrity. *(Hear, hear.)* The press was in the hands of the wealthy, and whether the wealthy were Whigs or Tories, they were, unfortunately for themselves, opposed to the rights of industry, and wanted to grasp to themselves the harvest of the labour of the country. *(Loud cheers.)*

The Chairman then put the resolution, which was carried unanimously.

ROBERT LOWERY, OCTOBER 1838
Reported in the Northern Liberator

LABOUR'S WRONGS AND LABOUR'S REMEDY

From the very nature of the thing, and the position in which man stands with regard to his fellows, he never did, and never can, individually, possess any exclusive right to one single inch of land. Wherever such an assumed right is set up and acted upon, there will always exist injustice, tyranny, poverty, and inequality of rights, whether the people be under the monarchical or the republican form of government; for all the wrongs and woes which man has ever committed or endured, may be traced to the assumption of right in the soil by certain individuals and classes to the exclusion of other individuals and classes. Equality of right can never be enjoyed until all individual claims to landed property are subverted, and merged in those of the nation at large.

JOHN FRANCIS BRAY, 1838–9
Nothing is known of Bray except that he was an Owenite and a printer by trade

PROGRAMME OF THE SOCIAL DEMOCRATIC FEDERATION, FOUNDED 1884

OBJECT

The socialization of the means of production, distribution, and exchange to be controlled by a Democratic State in the interest of the entire community, and the complete emancipation of labour from the domination of capitalism and landlordism, with the establishment of social and economic equality between the sexes.

PROGRAMME

1 All officers or administrators to be elected by equal direct adult suffrage and to be paid by the community.
2 Legislation by the people in such wise that no project of law shall become legally binding till accepted by the majority of the people.
3 The abolition of a standing army, and the establishment of a national citizen force; the people to decide on peace or war.

4 All education, higher no less than elementary, to be compulsory, secular, industrial, and gratuitous for all alike.

5 The administration of justice to be gratuitous for all members of society.

6 The land, with all the mines, railways and other means of transit, to be declared and treated as collective or common property.

7 The means of production, distribution and exchange to be declared and treated as collective or common property.

8 The production and distribution of wealth to be regulated by society in the common interests of all its members.

THE SONG OF THE SWEATER

Written for the Leeds Tailoresses' strike.

Every worker in every trade
In Britain and everywhere
Whether he labour by needle or spade
Shall gather in his rightful share.

TOM MAGUIRE, 1889

THE SOUL OF MAN UNDER SOCIALISM

But what is there behind the leading article but prejudice, stupidity, cant, and twaddle? And when these four are joined together they make a terrible force, and constitute the new authority.

In old days men had the rack. Now they have the press. That is an improvement certainly. But still it is very bad, and wrong, and demoralizing. Somebody—was it Burke?

—called journalism the fourth estate. That was true at the time, no doubt. But at the present moment it really is the only estate. It has eaten up the other three. The Lords Temporal say nothing, the Lords Spiritual have nothing to say, and the House of Commons has nothing to say and says it. We are dominated by Journalism.

OSCAR WILDE, 1891

DECLARATION OF PRINCIPLES
OF THE FABIAN SOCIETY, 1896

The Fabian Society consists of socialists.

It therefore aims at the re-organization of Society by the emancipation of land and industrial capital from individual and class ownership, and the vesting of them in the community for the general benefit. In this way only can the natural and acquired advantages of the country be equitably shared by the whole people.

The Society accordingly works for the extinction of private property in land and of the consequent individual appropriation, in the form of rent, of the price paid for permission to use the earth, as well as for the advantages of superior soils and sites.

The Society, further, works for the transfer to the community of the administration of such industrial capital as can conveniently be managed socially. For, owing to the monopoly of the means of production in the past, industrial inventions and the transformation of surplus income into capital have mainly enriched the proprietary class, the worker being now dependent on that class for leave to earn a living.

If these measures be carried out, without compensation (though not without such relief to expropriated individuals as may seem fit to the community), rent and interest will be added to the reward of labour, the idle class now living on the labour of others will necessarily disappear, and practical equality of opportunity will be maintained by the spontaneous action of economic forces with much less interference with personal liberty than the present system entails.

For the attainment of these ends the Fabian Society looks to the spread of socialist opinions, and the social and political changes consequent thereon, including the establishment of equal citizenship for men and women. It seeks to achieve these ends by the general dissemination of knowledge as to the relation between the individual and Society in its economic, ethical, and political aspects.

MANIFESTO OF THE LABOUR REPRESENTATION COMMITTEE FOR THE GENERAL ELECTION, 1900

Adequate Maintenance from National Funds for the Aged Poor.

Public Provision of Better Houses for the People.

Useful Work for the Unemployed.

Adequate Maintenance for Children.

No Compulsory Vaccination.

Public Control of the Liquor Traffic.

Nationalization of Land and Railways.

Relief of Local Rates by Grants from the National Exchequer.

Legislative Independence for all parts of the Empire.

Abolition of the Standing Army, and the Establishment of a Citizen Force. The People to decide on Peace or War.

Graduated Income Tax.

Shorter Parliaments. Adult Suffrage. Registration Reform. Payment of Members.

NEW WORLDS FOR OLD

The Socialist [asks] what freedom is there today for the vast majority of mankind? They are free to do nothing but work for a bare subsistence all their lives, they may not go freely about the earth even, but are prosecuted for trespassing upon the health-giving breast of our universal mother. Consider the clerks and girls who hurry to their work of a morning across Brooklyn Bridge in New York, or Hungerford Bridge in London; go and see them, study their faces. They are free, with a freedom Socialism would destroy. Consider the poor painted girls who pursue bread with nameless indignities through our streets at night. They are free by the current standard. And the poor half-starved wretches struggling with the impossible stint of oakum in a casual ward, they too are free! The nimble footman is free, the crushed porter between the trucks is free, the woman in the mill, the child in the mine. Ask them! They will tell you how free they are.

H. G. WELLS, 1908

THE MINERS' NEXT STEP

Today the shareholders own and rule the coalfields. They own and rule them mainly through paid officials. The men who work in the mine are surely as competent to elect these as shareholders who may never have seen a colliery. To have a vote in determining who shall be your foreman, manager, inspector, etc., is to have a vote in determining the conditions which shall rule your working life. On that vote will depend in a large measure your safety of life and limb, of your freedom from oppression by petty bosses, and would give you an intelligent interest in, and control over, your conditions of work. To vote for a man to represent you in

Parliament, to make rules for, and assist in appointing officials to rule you, is a different proposition altogether.

Our objective begins to take shape before your eyes. Every industry thoroughly organized, in the first place, to fight, to gain control of, and then to administer, that industry. The co-ordination of all industries on a Central Production Board, who, with a statistical department to ascertain the needs of the people, will issue its demands on the different departments of industry, leaving to the men themselves to determine under what conditions and how, the work should be done. This would mean real democracy in real life, making for real manhood and womanhood. Any other form of democracy is a delusion and a snare.

UNOFFICIAL REFORM COMMITTEE OF THE
SOUTH WALES MINERS' FEDERATION 1912

LABOUR PARTY CONSTITUTION
CLAUSE IV: PARTY OBJECTS

National

1 To organize and maintain in Parliament and in the country a Political Labour Party.
2 To co-operate with the General Council of the Trades Union Congress, or other Kindred Organizations, in joint political or other action in harmony with the Party Constitution and Standing Orders.
3 To give effect as far as may be practicable to the principles from time to time approved by the Party Conference.

4 To secure for the workers by hand or by brain the full fruits of their industry and the most equitable distribution thereof that may be possible upon the basis of the common ownership of the means of production, distribution, and exchange, and the best obtainable system of popular administration and control of each industry or service.

5 Generally to promote the Political, Social and Economic Emancipation of the People, and more particularly of those who depend directly upon their own exertions by hand or by brain for the means of life.

Inter-Commonwealth

6 To co-operate with the Labour and Socialist organizations in the Commonwealth Overseas with a view to promoting the purposes of the Party, and to take common action for the promotion of a higher standard of social and economic life for the working population of the respective countries.

International

7 To co-operate with the Labour and Socialist organization in other countries and to support the United Nations Organization and its various agencies and other international organizations for the promotion of peace, the adjustment and settlement of international disputes by conciliation or judicial arbitration, the establishment and defence of human rights, and the improvement of the social and economic standards and conditions of work of the people of the world.

Clause IV, parts 1–5, was drafted by SIDNEY WEBB
in 1918; parts 6 and 7 were added later

LABOUR AND THE NEW SOCIAL ORDER

Labour Party policy statement. The statement was based on four principles, referred to as the 'four pillars of the house we propose to erect':
the Universal Enforcement of the National Minimum;
the Democratic Control of Industry;
the Revolution in National Finance;
the Surplus Wealth for the Common Good.

The Party stands for complete Adult Suffrage with not more than a three months' residential qualification, for effective provision for absent electors to vote, for absolutely equal rights for both sexes, for the same freedom to exercise civic rights for the 'common soldier' as for the officer, for Shorter Parliaments, for the complete Abolition of the House of Lords, and for a most strenuous opposition to any new Second Chamber, whether elected or not, having in it any element of Heredity or Privilege, or of the control of the House of Commons by any Party or Class. But unlike the Conservative and Liberal Parties, the Labour Party insists on Democracy in industry as well as in government. It demands the progressive elimination from the control of industry of the private capitalist, individual or joint-stock; and the setting free of all who work, whether by hand or by brain, for the service of the community, and of the community only. And the Labour Party refuses absolutely to believe that the British people will permanently tolerate any reconstruction or perpetuation of the disorganization, waste and inefficiency involved in the abandonment of British industry to a jostling crowd of separate private employers, with their minds bent, not on the service of the community, but—by the very law of their being—only on the utmost possible profiteering. What the nation needs is undoubtedly a great bound onward in its aggregate productivity. But this cannot be secured merely by pressing the manual workers to more strenuous toil, or even by encouraging the 'Captains of Industry' to a less wasteful organization of their several enterprises on a profit-making basis. What the Labour Party looks to is a genuinely scientific reorganization of the nation's industry, no longer deflected by individual profiteering, on the basis of the Common Ownership of the Means of Production; the equitable sharing of the proceeds among all who participate in any capacity and only among these, and the adoption, in particular services and occupations, of those systems and methods of administration and control that may be found, in practice, best to promote, not profiteering, but the public interest.

Drafted by SIDNEY WEBB, 1918

EVIDENCE TO THE SANKEY COMMISSION ON THE COAL INDUSTRY

The root of the matter is the straining of the spirit of man to be free. Once he secures the freedom of the spirit he will, as a natural sequence, secure a material welfare equal to what the united brains and hands can wring from mother earth and her surrounding atmosphere. Any administration of the mines under nationalization must not leave the mine worker in the position of a mere wage-earner, whose sole energies are directed by the will of another. He must have a share in the management of the industry in which he is engaged, and understand all about the purpose and destination of the product he is producing; he must know both the productive and the commercial side of the industry. He must feel that the industry is being run by him in order to produce coal for the use of the community, instead of profit for a few people. He would thus feel the responsibility which would rest on him as a citizen, and direct his energies for the common good .... As that knowledge which has been denied him

107

grows, as it will do under nationalization, he will take his rightful place as a man. Only then will labour unrest, which is the present hope of the world, disappear. The mere granting of the 30 per cent and the shorter hours demanded will not prevent unrest, neither will nationalization with bureaucratic administration. Just as we are making political democracy world-wide, so must we have industrial democracy in order that men may be free.

WILLIAM STRAKER, 1919
Straker was Secretary of the Northumberland Miners'
Association

A CONSTITUTION FOR THE SOCIALIST COMMONWEALTH OF GREAT BRITAIN

It is inconceivable that any intelligent Democracy should continue to permit the capitalist manufacturer, merely in order to increase his profits, wantonly to defile what is not his but our atmosphere with unnecessary and really wasteful smoke from his factory chimneys; to pollute the crystal streams that are the property of all of us by the waste products of his mills and dye-works; to annihilate the irreplaceable beauty of valleys and mountain slopes by his quarries and scrap-heaps; to leave a whole countryside scarred and ruined by the wreckage which he fails to remove when one of his profit-seeking enterprises has exhausted its profitableness, or becomes bankrupt. In so far as any industry is left to capitalist profit-making, the community must at least see to it that the greed for private gain is not allowed to rob the citizens of their common heritage in a land of health and beauty.

SIDNEY *and* BEATRICE WEBB, 1920

THE ACQUISITIVE SOCIETY

At the very moment when everybody is talking about the importance of increasing the output of wealth, the last question, apparently, which it occurs to any statesman to ask is why wealth should be squandered on futile activities, and in expenditure which is either disproportionate to service or made for no service at all. So inveterate, indeed, has become the practice of payment in virtue of property rights, without even the pretence of any service being rendered, that when, in a national emergency, it is proposed to extract oil from the ground, the Government actually proposes that every gallon shall pay a tax to landowners who never even suspected its existence, and the ingenuous proprietors are full of pained astonishment at anyone questioning whether the nation is under a moral obligation to endow them further. Such rights are, strictly speaking, privileges. For the definition of a privilege is a right to which no corresponding function is attached.

The enjoyment of property and the direction of industry are considered, in short, to require no social justification, because they are regarded as rights which stand by their own virtue, not functions to be judged by the success with which they contribute to a social purpose. Today, that doctrine, if intellectually discredited, is still the practical foundation of social organization.

R. H. TAWNEY, 1921

SOCIALISM IN OUR TIME

The I L P believes that the Socialist policy should be concentrated upon a direct attack on poverty. It asserts that the workers have the first claim upon the wealth of the nation, and denies the claim of those who live by owning instead of working. The semi-starvation wages now paid are not only an intolerable evil in themselves; they are the immediate cause of the extensive unemployment. The machines stand idle because the masses lack the means to buy. The I L P urges that the whole Labour movement should therefore bend all its energies to the achievement of a national Living Wage, which would ensure for the workers adequate food, clothing, and housing, and the essentials of civilization.

The I L P sees the Living Wage as the first demand for justice, which has the power, if we follow its logic with courage, to carry us rapidly towards the realization of a Socialist State.

INDEPENDENT LABOUR PARTY, 1926
A resolution based on the party's Report on the Living Wage

THE MEANING OF EQUALITY

We must get on to the positive reasons for the Socialist plan of an equal division. I am specially interested in it because it is my favorite plan. . . .

First, equal division is not only a possible plan, but one which has been tested by long experience. The great bulk of the daily work of the civilized world is done, and always has been done, and always must be done, by bodies of persons receiving equal pay whether they are tall or short, fair or dark, quick or slow, young or getting on in years, teetotallers or beer drinkers, Protestants or Catholics, married or single, short tempered or sweet tempered, pious or worldly: in short, without the slightest regard to the differences that make one person unlike another. In every trade there is a standard wage; in every public service there is a standard pay; and in every profession the fees are fixed with a view to enable the man who follows the profession to live according to a certain standard of respectability which is the same for the whole profession. The pay of the policeman and soldier and postman, the wages of the labourer and carpenter and mason, the salary of the judge and the member of Parliament, may differ, some of them getting less than a hundred a year and others five thousand; but all the soldiers get the same, all the judges get the same, all the members of Parliament get the same. . . .

Therefore when some inconsiderate person repeats like a parrot that if you gave everybody the same money, before a year was out you would have rich and poor again just as before, all you have to do is to tell him to look round him and see millions of people who get the same money and remain in the same position all their lives without any such change taking place. The cases in which poor men become rich are most exceptional; and though the cases in which rich men become poor are commoner, they also are accidents and not ordinary everyday circumstances. . . . The only novelty proposed is that the postmen should get as much as the postmasters, and the postmasters no less than anybody else. If we find, as we do, that it answers to give all judges the same income, and all navy captains the same income, why should we go on giving judges five times as much as navy captains? That is what the navy captain would like to know; and if you tell him that if he were given as much as the judge he would be just as poor as before at the end of a year he will use language unfit for the ears of anyone but a pirate. So be careful how you say such things.

Equal distribution is then quite possible and practicable, not only momentarily but permanently. It is also simple and intelligible. It gets rid of all squabbling as to how much each person should have. It is already in operation and familiar over great masses of human beings. And it has the tremendous advantage of securing promotion by merit for the more capable.

GEORGE BERNARD SHAW, 1928
From The Intelligent Woman's Guide
to Socialism and Capitalism

THE LABOUR PARTY IN PERSPECTIVE

Those who attack Socialism on the ground that it will mean the enslavement of the individual belong invariably to the class of people whose possession of property has given them liberty at the expense of the enslavement of others. The possession of property in a Capitalist society has given liberty to a fortunate minority who hardly realize how much its absence means enslavement. The majority of the people of this country are under orders and discipline for the whole of their working day. Freedom is left behind when they 'clock in' and only resumed when they go out. Such liberty as they have got as workers has been the fruit of long and bitter struggles by the Trade Unions. But a far greater restriction on liberty than this is imposed on the vast majority of the people of this country by poverty. There is the narrowing of choice in everything. The poor man cannot choose his domicile. He must be prepared at the shortest notice to abandon all his social activities, to leave the niche which he has made for himself in the structure of society, and to remove himself elsewhere, if economic circumstances demand it. This is called 'transference'. How little would those who so easily recommend this to the workers appreciate being transferred from their pleasant homes in Surrey or Buckinghamshire to Whitechapel or the Black Country. Yet this is an ordinary incident of working-class life. The poor man is restricted in his food, his clothing, his amusements, and his occupation. The liberty which it is feared Socialism may restrict is the liberty of the few. Moreover, in modern Capitalist society, the power of wealth is such as to affect the lives of the people in thousands of ways. The whole organization of the country is based on the superior rights of the wealthy. Nothing is sacred to the profit-maker.

CLEMENT ATTLEE, 1937

NATIONAL SERVICE FOR HEALTH

The Labour Party's post-war policy

No agency less universal in its authority than Government can secure for the whole people the conditions necessary for health; and no ill-health in any part of the population can be a matter of indifference to the people's Government.

The service must be *national,* i.e., supplied and paid for out of taxes and rates. We cannot have a Medical Service which covers all the medical needs of all the people unless all the people contribute to the cost, and unless the doctoring can be distributed in accordance with the needs of all the people.

The service should be *full time.* Suppose that it were not full time, but that the doctor was partly employed in private practice. Either his service for the State would be just as thorough and conscientious as his service when treating fee-paying patients as a private doctor, or else his standard would differ. If patients could get his full attention, however, without paying a fee during half the day, they would hardly go to him during those hours when a fee would be charged. It would be intolerable that his service as a State doctor should be less adequate than the service rendered for private fees.

National Service for Health is a service honourable enough for any recruit; it should be a service well enough paid and protected to meet the needs of every doctor in a democratic Britain.

APRIL 1943

LET US FACE THE FUTURE

Labour Party Manifesto for the General Election

The great inter-war slumps were not acts of God or of blind forces. They were the sure and certain result of the concentration of too much economic power in the hands of too few men. These men had only learned how to act in the interest of their own bureaucratically-run private monopolies which may be likened to totalitarian oligarchies within our democratic State. They had and they felt no responsibility to the nation. The nation wants food, work and homes. It wants more than that. It wants good food in plenty, useful work for all and comfortable labour-saving homes that take full advantage of the resources of modern science and productive industry. It wants a high and rising standard of living; security for all against a rainy day; an educational system that will give every boy and girl a chance to develop the best that is in him. These are our aims. In themselves they are no more than words. All parties may declare that in principle they agree with them. But the test of a political programme is whether it is sufficiently in earnest about the objectives to adopt the means needed to realize them. It is very easy to set out a list of aims. ... What matters is whether it is backed up by a genuine workmanlike plan, conceived without regard for sectional vested interests and carried through in a spirit of resolute concentration.

1945

IN PLACE OF FEAR

The student of politics must seek neither universality nor immortality for his ideas and for the institutions through which he hopes to express them. What he must seek is integrity and vitality. His Holy Grail is the living truth, knowing that being alive the truth must change. If he does not cherish integrity then he will see in the change an excuse for opportunism, and so will exchange the inspiration of the pioneer for the reward of the lackey.

He must also be on his guard against the old words, for the words persist when the reality that lay behind them has changed. It is inherent in our intellectual activity that we seek to imprison reality in our description of it. Soon, long before we realize it, it is we who become the prisoners of the description. From that point on, our ideas degenerate into a kind of folklore which we pass to each other, fondly thinking we are still talking of the reality around us.

Thus we talk of free enterprise, of capitalist society, of the rights of free association, of parliamentary government, as though all these words stand for the same things they formerly did. Social institutions are what they do, not necessarily what we say they do. It is the verb that matters, not the noun.

ANEURIN BEVAN, 1953

CULTURE IS ORDINARY

Our specialisms will be finer if they have grown from a common culture, rather than being a distinction from it. And we must at all costs avoid the polarization of our culture, of which there are growing signs. High literacy is expanding, in direct relation to exceptional educational opportunities, and the gap between this and common literacy may widen, to the great damage of both, and with great consequent tension. We must emphasize, not the ladder but the common highway for every man's ignorance diminishes me, and every man's skill is a common gain of breath.

RAYMOND WILLIAMS, 1958

SPEECH IN THE HOUSE OF COMMONS

Opposing a Bill to restrict the immigration of Commonwealth citizens.

The whole future of the world will probably depend on whether people of different colours can live in harmony with each other. Therefore, this Measure as now put forward strikes at the very root of this principle.

It is no part of our case to pretend that any amount of immigration of people of different colour and social customs and language does not present problems, though I urge that we should beware of exaggerations here. Do the government deal with it by seeking to combat social evils, by building more houses and enforcing laws against over-crowding, by using every educational means at their disposal to create tolerance and mutual understanding, and by emphasizing to our own people the value of these immigrants and setting their face firmly against all forms of racial intolerance and discrimination? That is what we believe.

HUGH GAITSKELL, NOVEMBER 1961

MAY DAY MANIFESTO

The need to gain control over the productive process and over real wealth is the same need as that for the extended care of people, in work, education and housing, or in old age, sickness and disability. It is the assertion of different priorities, against the internal and limited priorities of capitalism. Only when there is democratic control, over the whole process of production and investment, can a human distribution be steadily achieved.

This is then the first policy we have learned: that actual human needs, in our real social conditions, cannot be set against the needs of production, as a marginal or residual claim. The continual frustration of these needs, by what are called the realities of debt or modernization, is in fact, as we have shown, the political acceptance of the internal priorities of profit in modern productive conditions.

RAYMOND WILLIAMS *et al.*, 1968

THIS NEW SEASON

The 'Problem of Education' cannot be isolated merely as a problem of schools, or of teachers. It is a problem of politics, and the economic domination of one class over another. It has to be solved politically, in the schools as in all of society. We cannot afford to divert ourselves with notions of de-schooling when we need more schools, more teachers, more books, more facilities for our working-class children, more concentration to develop their frustrated and insulted potential. The more economic and educational demands we make for our class, the working class, the more we threaten the prevailing standards peddled in the schools which divide us from ourselves and each other and weaken our strength with their mystification. We have to confront the enormity of the problem as an organized and interrelated body: teachers, parents, and school students. We can educate for stoicism and acceptance, only passing on to our children the identity of the exploited and underdeveloped, or we can educate for struggle and solidarity showing our children that we are fighting and learning with them, affirming ourselves, our class, and our right and determination to control our own social and educational future.

CHRIS SEARLE, 1973

117

THE LUCAS PLAN

Institute of Workers' Control pamphlet

The prosperity of Britain as a manufacturing nation depends to a very large extent upon the skill and ability of its people and the opportunity to use that skill and ability to produce commodities.

During the past five years the Lucas Aerospace work force has been reduced by approximately 25 per cent. This has come about either by direct sackings or by a deliberate policy of so-called natural wastage, i.e., not replacing those who leave, or encouraging early retirement. The net result has been that highly skilled teams of manual workers and design staff have been seriously diminished and disrupted; we cannot accept that such a development is in the long-term national interest.

Coupled with this development has been one inside the Company in which attempts have been made to replace human intelligence by machine intelligence, in particular the introduction of numerically controlled machine tools. This has, in a number of cases, proved to have been quite disastrous and the quality of the products has suffered in consequence.

In many instances the Company has fallen victim of the high-pressure salesmanship of those who would have us believe that all our problems can be solved by high capital equipment. We have allowed our regard for human talents to be bludgeoned into silence by the mystique of advanced equipment and technology, and so forget that our most precious asset is the creative and productive power of our people.

LUCAS AEROSPACE COMBINE COMMITTEE, 1976

The democratic programme of the Chartists has still to be fully realized. Their demand for annual parliaments was never taken seriously. But it remains, none the less, an important democratic objective. If achieved it could considerably aid in breaking the mass apathy which exists between elections. It would also bring home to millions of working people the advantages of being able to influence political change at short and regular intervals. It would challenge the growing encroachment on democratic rights which today characterizes a number of states in the West. . . .

An annual general election would destabilize bourgeois rule and induce a much greater interest in political participation of the mass of voters. It would be the closest one could probably get to the right of electors to recall their representatives from any elective assembly, which is the basic principle of a soviet-type body. Aligned to it must be the demand for proportional representation, which is the most democratic way of assessing real voting strength.

TARIQ ALI, 1978

PART THREE

STRUGGLE AND SOLIDARITY

The workers of Britain are getting off their knees....
JIMMY REID, 1971

What are the methods that can bring about change? These passages look at the need for solidarity, organization and collective action. We learn how this can be achieved, hear open calls for revolt to throw off the yoke of the oppressors, and see the establishment of a tradition extending from the Peasants' Revolt in 1381 to the Invergordon Naval Mutiny of 1931, which occurred within living memory.

We read of the protests against the land clearances—a contemporary version of privatization—under which the common land was stolen and transferred to the control and ownership of the rich landowners; a policy that Parliament officially authorized to increase agricultural productivity, but which also created an army of landless people who would be needed by the new capitalist class to work in the factories that were springing up in the towns and taking advantage of the new technologies.

Early trade union rules, probably drafted in some upstairs room, are recorded here and it is easy to imagine the circumstances that led to their adoption. The cause of Irish freedom can be heard, together with the words of John McLean from the Red Clyde, with his 'seditious' literature that might have subverted the soldiers then being deployed against the working class. As we listen to these voices we are reminded that only a decade ago the workers at Upper Clyde occupied their yard to maintain their jobs, and the Shrewsbury pickets were gaoled for seeking to defend their rights.

To be able to read all this in the words that were used at the time is to understand the continuing nature of the argument, and to realize that we are not the first generation who have had to face difficulty, nor indeed shall we be the last.

TONY BENN

THE PEOPLE OF KENT, ESSEX AND BEDFORDSHIRE AT THE TIME OF THE PEASANTS' REVOLT

The unhappy people began to murmur, saying that in the beginning of the world there were no slaves, and that no one ought to be treated as such, unless he had committed treason against his lord, as Lucifer had done against God; but they had done no such thing, for they were neither angels nor spirits, but men formed after the same likeness as these lords who treated them as beasts. This they would bear no longer; they were determined to be free, and if they laboured or did any work, they would be paid for it.

FROISSART, *c.* 1381
The Chronicles

PROCLAMATION TO THE REBELS IN KENT

The demands of the rebels in Jack Cade's Revolt

These be the points, causes and mischiefs of gathering and assembling of us the king's liege men of Kent, the 4th day of June, the year of our Lord 1450, the reign of our sovereign lord the king XXIX, the which we trust to Almighty God to remedy, with the help and grace of God and of our sovereign lord the king, and the poor commons of England, and else we shall die therefore.

We, considering that the king our sovereign lord, by the insatiable, covetous, malicious pomps, and false and of nought brought-up certain persons, and daily and nightly is about his highness, and daily inform him that good is evil and evil is good. . . .

Item, they say that our sovereign lord is above his laws to his pleasure, and he may make it and break it as him list, without any distinction. The contrary is true, and else he should not have sworn to keep it, the which we conceived for the highest point of treason that any subject may do, to make his prince run in perjury. . . .

Item, they say that the king should live upon his commons, and that their bodies and goods be the king's; the contrary is true, for then needeth he never Parliament to sit to ask good of his commons. . . .

Item, the law serveth of nought else in these days but for to do wrong, for nothing is sped almost but false matters for colour of the law for mede, drede and favour, and so no remedy is had in the court of conscience in any wise. . . .

Item, we will that it be known that we will not rob, nor reve, nor steal, but that these faults be amended, and then we will go home; wherefore we exhort all the king's true liegemen to help us, to support us. . . .

JACK CADE, 1450

THE TREE OF COMMON WEALTH

'Written by him while a prisoner in the Tower in the years 1509 and 1510 and now under sentence of death for High Treason.'

The name of the second messenger is Arrogancy, nigh cousin to Pride. His nature and property is to entice you to enable yourself to such things as nothing beseemeth, or to do such things as you can nothing skill on. He will show you that you be made of the same mould and metal that the gentles be made of. Why then should they sport and play, and you labour and till? He will tell you also that at your births and deaths your riches is indifferent. Why should they have so much of the prosperity and treasure of this world, and ye so little? Besides that, he will tell you that ye be the children and right inheritors of Adam, as well as they. Why should they have this great honour, royal castles and manors, with so much lands and possessions, and you but poor tenements and cottages? He will show you also why that Christ bought as dearly you as them, and with one manner of price, which was his precious blood. Why then should you be of so poor estate, and they of so high degree? . . .

But, you good commoners, in any wise utterly refused this messenger; for though he show the truth to you, he meaneth full falsely as afterwards you shall well know. . . . He will bid you leave to employ yourselves to labour and to till like beasts, nor suffer yourselves to be subdued of your fellows. He will promise to set you on high and to be lords and governors, and no longer to be churls as you were before. . . . He will also display unto you his banner of insurrection and say to you, 'Now set forward; your time is right good.'

EDMUND DUDLEY, 1509–10

THE YIELDING UP OF THE CITY
OF DAVENTRY

Allen was a Catholic Cardinal living in exile. This pamphlet was a plea for revolt against the 'Haeretical Quene' Elizabeth.

For that to revolt, is of its selfe, lawful or unlawful, honorable or otherwise, according to the justice, or injustice of the cause, or difference of the person, from or to whom, the revolt is made.

WILLIAM ALLEN, 1587

AN APPEALE

Overton was a 'Prisoner in the Infamous Gaole of Newgate for the Liberties and Freedomes of England'.

Now as no man by nature may abuse, beat, torment or afflict himself, so by nature no man may give that power to another.... So that if the betrusted act not for the weal and safety of the betrusters, they depart from their just power, and act by another, which cannot be termed either human or divine, but unnaturall and divellish, rendering such usurpers as Monsters amongst men. Now these premises considered, I doe confidently conclude (if confidence may be derived from the just principles of nature) that the transgression of our weal by our trustees, is an utter forfeiture of their trust, and cessation of their power: Therefore, if I prove a forfeiture of the *peoples trust* in the prevalent party at *Westminster* in Parliament assembled then an *Appeal* from them to the people is not *Anti-parliamentary, Anti-magesteriall*, not *from* that *Sovereign power*, but *to* that *Sovereign power*. For the evidence whereof I shall first present a discovery of their dealings with me....

Upon the 11 of *August* 1646 the House of Lords sent (without any summons or other due processe for appearance) their Emisaries with a file of Musqueteers who beset mine house and entered the same, one with his drawn sword, and another with a Pistoll ready cock'd in his hand, and surprised me in my bed without any appearance or shew of any warrant either legall or illegall....

I was almost incivilly and inhumanely dragged to *Newgate* headlong through the streets upon the stones through all the dirt and the mire, and being reviled, otherwise abused and beat, I was thrown into the common Gaole amongst Rogues and Fellons, and laid in double Irons. And since this time which was the 3 of *November* 1646 to this present 8 of *July* 1647 I could not prevaile with the Chairman to make my report unto the House thereby to obtaine any reliefe. But as I am informed, that worthy Gentleman hath neither to been necessitated and inforced to forbearance through an absolute indisposition to justice in the house, by the prevalency of a powerfull faction therein, though for my part I have been ever utterly averse to that lingering prudence, and have earnestly solicited the contrary, let the issue fall with me or against me.

Further, the tyranny of these Lords not ceasing here against me, they send their Catch poules to my house againe, where finding my wife in with her three small Children about her, tooke her and my brother away and brought them before the Lords prerogative Barre, rifled, plundered, and ransacked mine house exposing my 3 helplesse small children to the streets, and all this before any indictment, presentment, or other due processe of law preceeding.

RICHARD OVERTON, JULY 1647

A WATCHWORD FOR THE CITY OF LONDON

Action is the life of all, and if thou dost not act, thou dost nothing.

GERARD WINSTANLEY, 1649

SPEECH FROM THE SCAFFOLD AT EDINBURGH

Rumbold, an active Puritan and republican, was found guilty of taking part in the Monmouth Rebellion. After this speech he was hanged, drawn and quartered.

Gentlemen and Brethren, I die this day in the defence of the ancient laws and liberties of these nations; and though God, for reasons best known to himself, hath not seen it fit to honour us, as to make us the instruments for the deliverance of his people, yet as I have lived, so I die in the faith that he will speedily arise for the deliverance of his Church and people. And I desire of all you to prepare for this with speed. I may say this is a deluded generation, veiled with ignorance, that though popery and slavery be riding in upon them, do not perceive it; though I am sure there was no man born marked of God above another; for none comes into the world with a saddle on his back, neither any booted and spurred to ride him. . . .

RICHARD RUMBOLD, 1685

ARTICLES OF THE FRIENDLY AND UNITED SOCIETY OF CORDWAINERS

The Society was 'instituted at Westminster on 4 June 1792 and associated for the laudable purpose of serving the trade in general'.

We are convinced that nothing short of a general Fund can lay the foundation of a lasting union among journeymen of any trade; but when that is once effected, every man will feel an interest in being connected; he will see that a master cannot then easily take advantage of him; and should it be attempted, the Society will be able, in some shape, to do him justice which he could not do for himself. In short, such a Society holds out a community of interests where the members are encouraged to promote each other's welfare. . . .

Some of the Articles make mention of scabs. And what is a scab? He is to his *trade* what a traitor is to his *country*; though both may be useful to one party in troublesome times, when peace returns they are detested alike by all. When help is wanted, he is the last to contribute assistance, and the first to grasp a benefit he never laboured to procure. He cares but for himself, but he sees not beyond the extent of a day, and for a momentary and worthless approbation would betray friends, family and country. In short, he is a traitor on a small scale. He first sells the journeymen, and is himself afterwards sold in his turn by the masters, till at last he is despised by both and deserted by all. He is an enemy to himself, to the present age and to posterity.

1792. *Pamphlet*

AGRARIAN JUSTICE

The state of civilization that has prevailed throughout Europe is as unjust in its principle as it is horrid in its effects; and it is the consciousness of this, and the apprehension that such a state cannot continue when once investigation begins in any country, that makes the possessors dread every idea of a revolution. It is the *hazard*, and not the principles of a revolution, that retards their progress.

THOMAS PAINE, 1795–6

THE DELEGATES OF THE DIFFERENT SHIPS AT THE NORE ASSEMBLED IN COUNCIL, TO THEIR FELLOW SUBJECTS

This is the Manifesto of the Mutineers of the Nore Fleet which blockaded the Thames after the revolt of the fleet at Spithead (Portsmouth) two weeks earlier.

Countrymen, it is to you particularly that we owe an explanation of our conduct. His Majesty's Ministers too well know our intentions, which are founded on the laws of humanity, honour and national safety—long since trampled underfoot by those who ought to have been friends to us—the sole protectors of your laws and property. The public prints teem with falsehoods and misrepresentations to induce you to credit things as far from our design as the conduct of those at the helm of national affairs is from honesty or common decorum.

Shall we who have endured the toils of a tedious, disgraceful war, be the victims of tyranny and oppression which vile, gilded, pampered knaves, wallowing in the lap of luxury, choose to load us with? Shall we, who amid the rage of the tempest and the war of jarring elements, undaunted climb the unsteady cordage and totter on the topmast's dreadful height, suffer ourselves to be treated worse than the dogs of London Streets? Shall we, who in the battle's sanguinary rage, confound, terrify and subdue your proudest foe, guard your coasts from invasion, your children from slaughter, and your lands from pillage—be the footballs and shuttlecocks of a set of tyrants who derive from us alone their honours, their titles and their fortunes? No, the Age of Reason has at length revolved. Long have we been endeavouring to find ourselves men. We now find ourselves so. We will be treated as such. . . .

You cannot, countrymen, form the most distant idea of the slavery under which we have for many years laboured.

Rome had her Neros and Caligulas, but how many characters of their description might we not mention in the British Fleet—men without the least tincture of humanity, without the faintest spark of virtue, education or abilities, exercising the most wanton acts of cruelty over those whom dire misfortune or patriotic zeal may have placed in their power—basking in the sunshine of prosperity, whilst we (need we repeat who we are?) labour under every distress which the breast of inhumanity can suggest. The British seaman has often with justice been compared to the lion—gentle, generous and humane—no one would certainly wish to hurt such an animal. Hitherto we have laboured for our sovereign and you. We are now obliged to think for ourselves, for there are many (nay, most of us) in the Fleet who have been prisoners since the commencement of the War, without receiving a single farthing. Have we not a right to complain? Let His Majesty but order us to be paid and the little grievances we have made known redressed, we shall enter with alacrity upon any employment for the defence of our country; but until that is complied with we are determined to stop all commerce and intercept all provisions, for our own subsistence.

JUNE 1797

SPEECH AT KILMARNOCK

Alexander M'Laren was a Scottish weaver. For this speech he was sent to prison for six months.

We are ruled by men only solicitous for their own aggrandizement; and they care no further for the great body of the people than as they are subservient to their accursed purposes.... Shall we, I say, whose forefathers defied the efforts of foreign tyranny to enslave our beloved country, meanly permit in our day without a murmur a base oligarchy to feed their filthy vermin on our vitals, and rule us as they will? No, my countrymen! Let us lay our petitions at the foot of the throne, where sits our august Prince, whose gracious nature will incline his ear to listen to the cries of the people, which he is bound to do by the laws of the country. But should he be so infatuated as to turn a deaf ear to their just petition, he has forfeited their allegiance. Yes, my fellow townsmen, in such a case, to hell with our allegiance.

ALEXANDER M'LAREN, 1817

SONG TO THE MEN OF ENGLAND

Men of England, wherefore plough
For the lords who lay ye low?
Wherefore weave with toil and care
The rich robes your tyrants wear?

Wherefore feed, and clothe, and save,
From the cradle to the grave,
Those ungrateful drones who would
Drain your sweat—nay, drink your blood?

Wherefore, Bees of England, forge
Many a weapon, chain, and scourge,
That these stingless drones may spoil
The forced produce of your toil?

Have ye leisure, comfort, calm,
Shelter, food, love's gentle balm?
Or what is it ye buy so dear
With your pain and with your fear?

The seed ye sow, another reaps;
The wealth ye find, another keeps;
The robes ye weave, another wears;
The arms ye forge, another bears.

Sow seed,—but let no tyrant reap;
Find wealth,—let no impostor heap;
Weave robes,—let not the idle wear;
Forge arms,—in your defence to bear.
PERCY BYSSHE SHELLEY, 1819

TO THE PUBLIC

Carlile, one of the great campaigners for a free press, was imprisoned for publishing Tom Paine and William Hone. His wife carried on his publishing and bookselling business until she too was sent to gaol. Carlile's sister and many other followers were also sent to prison.

FROM DORCHESTER GAOL

For my own part, I am resolved never to cease, in consequence of any laws that come short of putting to death, in the open avowal and promulgation of such opinions as I conceive to be founded in truth, and the practice of which appear to me to be conducive to the interest of society. It matters nothing to me what another man thinks. I claim the same right to think and speak, and to write what I think, and to publish what I write as he does. I will never truckle to opinions propagated by force and violence, because it is *prima facie* acknowledgement that they are founded on falsehood and cannot bear the scrutiny of a rational criticism. I contend that there is no necessity for laws to regulate opinions in society; a diversity of opinion with mutual toleration will form the most stable base of its well being. But when we see men crushing the propagation of certain opinions, because the opposite are productive of profit to them, it is no longer society, but a nest of robbers who prey upon the weaker part.

RICHARD CARLILE, 18 OCTOBER 1820
An article in the Republican

THE POOR MAN'S GUARDIAN

People who live by plunder will always tell you to be submissive to thieves. To talk of *representation*, in any shape, being of any use to the people is sheer nonsense; unless the people have a House of working men, and represent themselves. Those who make the laws now and who are intended, by the new reform bill, to make them in future, all live by profits of some sort or other. They will, therefore, no matter who elect them, nor how often they are elected, always make the laws to raise profits and keep down the price of labour. Representation, therefore, by a different body of people to those who are represented, or whose interests are opposed to theirs, is a mockery, and those who persuade the people to the contrary are either idiots or cheats.

APRIL 1831
From an anonymous correspondent

PROPOSAL FOR FORMING A
BUILDERS' GUILD

To the United Working Builders of Great Britain
and Ireland,

Proposals for the establishment of a National Association for Building, to be called 'The Grand National Guild of

Builders', to be composed of Architects and Surveyors, Masons, Carpenters and Joiners, Bricklayers, Plasterers, Slaters, Plumbers, Glaziers and Painters, Whitesmiths, Quarrymen and Brickmakers.

Objects of the Union

1 The general improvement of all the individuals forming the building class; insuring regular employment for all.
2 To insure fair remuneration for their services.
3 To fix a reasonable time for labour.
4 To educate both adults and children.
5 To have regular superior medical advice and assistance, and to make provision for the comfortable and independent retirement of the aged and infirm.
6 To regulate the operations of the whole in harmony, and to produce a general fund sufficient to secure all these objects.
7 To ensure a superiority of building for the public at fair and equitable prices.
8 To obtain good and comfortable dwellings for every member of the Union; extensive and well-arranged workshops; places of depot for building materials; provisions and clothing; halls for the meeting of the Lodges and Central Committees; schools and academies for the instruction of adults and children in morals and the useful sciences.
9 And also the establishment of Builders' Banks in the various districts in which the grand District Lodges shall be established.

SEPTEMBER 1833
Published in the Pioneer

VICTIMS OF WHIGGERY:
THE TOLPUDDLE MARTYRS

George Loveless was the leader of the Tolpuddle Martyrs and was sentenced to seven years' transportation in 1834 for forming a Friendly Society of Agricultural Labourers.

A Mr Young, an attorney employed on our behalf, called me into the conversation room, and, among other things, inquired if I would promise the magistrates to have no more to do with the Union if they would let me go home to my wife and family? I said, 'I do not understand you.'

'Why,' said he, 'give them information concerning the Union, who else belongs to it, and promise you will have no more to do with it.'

'Do you mean to say I am to betray my companions?'

'That is just it,' said he.

'No; I would rather undergo any punishment.'

The same day we were sent to the high jail, where we continued until the assizes. . . .

On the 15th of March, we were taken to the County-hall to await our trial. As soon as we arrived we were ushered down some steps into a miserable dungeon, opened but twice a year, with only a glimmering light; and to make it more disagreeable, some wet and green brushwood was served for firing. . . . In this most dreadful situation we passed three whole days. As to the trial, I need mention but little; the whole proceedings were characterized by a shameful disregard of justice and decency. . . . I shall not soon forget [the judge's] address to the jury, in summing up the evidence: among other things, he told them, that if such Societies were allowed to exist, it would ruin matters, cause a stagnation in trade, destroy property—and if *they should not find us guilty, he was certain they would forfeit the opinion of the grand jury.* I thought to myself, there is no danger but we shall be found guilty, as we have a special jury for the purpose selected from among those who are most unfriendly towards us—the grand jury, land-owners, the petty jury, land-renters. Under such a charge, from such a quarter, self-interest alone would induce them to say, 'Guilty.' The judge then inquired if we had anything to say. I instantly forwarded the following short defence, in writing, to him: 'My Lord, if we have violated any law, it was not done intentionally: we have injured no man's reputation, character, person, or property: we were uniting together to preserve ourselves, our wives, and our children, from utter degradation and starvation. We challenge any man, or number of men, to prove that we have acted, or intend to act, different from the above statement.' The judge asked if I wished it to be read in Court. I answered, 'Yes.' It was then mumbled over to a part of the jury, in such an inaudible manner, that although I knew what was there, I could not comprehend it. . . .

Two days after this we were again placed at the bar to receive sentence, when the judge (John Williams) told us, 'that not for anything that we had done, or, as he could prove, we intended to do, but for an example to others, he considered it his duty to pass the sentence of seven years' transportation across his Majesty's high seas upon each and every one of us'.

GEORGE LOVELESS, 1837

THE CHARTIST MEETING
AT KENSAL MOOR

The meeting was to take place on Kensal Moor, outside the town. Local and district processions soon began to fill the streets and we joined them. Although I had often seen 100,000 at a meeting in Newcastle I never had a clear conception of a multitude until that day. The day was exceedingly fine, and there were processions from Rochdale and Oldham and the chief places for fourteen miles or upwards round about Manchester; I should think there were hundreds of bands of music. I could not conceive where the people came from, for at every open space or corner there would be thousands standing, besides the crowd passing. When we got out of the streets it was an exciting sight to see the processions arriving on the Moor from different places, with their flags flying and the music of the bands swelling in the air, ever and anon over-topped by a loud cheer which ran along the different lines. On ascending the hustings a still more exciting sight awaited us. *The Times* estimated the meeting at about 300,000. One dense mass of faces beaming with earnestness—as far as you could distinguish faces—then beyond still an immense crowd, but with indistinct countenances. There is something in the appearance of such multitudes—permeated with one thought or feeling,—whom no building made with human hands could hold, met beneath the mighty dome of God's sublime and beautiful creation, and appealing to Him for a cause which they believe to be right and just—something which, for the moment, seems to realize the truths of the ancient saying—'The voice of the people is as the voice of God.'

ROBERT LOWERY, SEPTEMBER 1838
From Robert Lowery's autobiography

THE CHARTIST WATCHWORD

Before the separation of the 'physical force' and 'moral force' wings.

Peacefully if we may; forcibly if we must.

c. 1838

SECOND NATIONAL CHARTIST PETITION

*The petition was signed by 3,315,572 workers,
from all parts of Britain.*

The six demands of the Charter were:

*Universal Suffrage
Annual Parliaments
Equal Representation
Payment of Members
Vote by Secret Ballot
No Property Qualifications.*

To the Honourable the Commons of Great Britain and Ireland in Parliament assembled.

Government originated from and was designed to protect the freedom and promote the happiness of, and ought to be responsible to the whole people. The only authority on which any body of men can make laws and govern society is delegation from the people. As government was designed for the benefit and protection of, and must be obeyed and supported by all, therefore all should be equally represented. Any form of government which fails to effect the purposes for which it was designed, and does not fully and completely represent the whole people, who are compelled to pay taxes for its support and obey the laws resolved upon by it, is unconstitutional, tyrannical, and ought to be amended or resisted. Your honourable House, as at present constituted, has not been elected by, and acts irresponsibly of the people; and hitherto has only represented parties, and benefited the few, regardless of miseries, grievances, and petitions of the many. Your honourable House has enacted laws contrary to the expressed wishes of the people, and by unconstitutional means enforced obedience to them, thereby creating an unbearable despotism on the one hand and degrading slavery on the other. . . .

In England, Ireland, Scotland, and Wales thousands of people are dying from actual want; and your petitioners, whilst sensible that poverty is the great exciting cause of crime, view with mingled astonishment and alarm the ill provision made for the poor, the aged, and the infirm. . . .

Your petitioners would direct the attention of your honourable House to the great disparity existing between the wages of the producing millions and the salaries of those whose comparative usefulness ought to be questioned, where riches and luxury prevail amongst the rulers and poverty and starvation amongst the ruled. . . .

Your petitioners know that it is the undoubted constitutional right of the people to meet freely, when, how, and where they choose, in public places, peaceably, in the day, to discuss their grievances, and political and other subjects, or for the purpose of framing, discussing, or passing any vote, petition, or remonstrance upon any subject whatsoever. Your petitioners complain that the right has unconstitutionally been infringed . . . . An unconstitutional police is distributed all over the country, at enormous cost, to prevent the due exercise of the people's rights. And your petitioners are of opinion that the Poor Law bastilles and the police stations, being co-existent, have originated from the same cause, viz., the increased desire on the part of the irresponsible few to oppress and starve the many. A vast and unconstitutional army is upheld at the public expense for the purpose of repressing public opinion in the three kingdoms and likewise to intimidate the millions in the due exercise of those rights and privileges which ought to belong to them.

Your petitioners complain that the hours of labour, particularly of the factory workers, are protracted beyond the limits of human endurance, and that the wages earned, after unnatural application to toil in heated and unhealthy workshops, are inadequate to sustain the bodily strength and to supply those comforts which are so imperative after an excessive waste of physical energy. Your petitioners also direct the attention of your honourable House to the starvation wages of the agricultural labourer, and view with horror and indignation the paltry income of those whose toil gives being to the staple food of the people. Your petitioners deeply deplore the existence of any kind of monopoly in this nation. . . .

From the numerous petitions presented to your honourable House we conclude that you are fully acquainted with the grievances of the working men; and your petitioners pray that the rights and wrongs of labour may be considered with a view to the protection of the one and the removal of the other; because your petitioners are of opinion that it is the worst species of legislation which leaves the grievances of society to be removed only by violence or revolution, both of which may be apprehended if complaints are unattended to and petitions despised.

MAY 1842

FATHER, WHO ARE THE CHARTISTS?

MILLIONS who labour with skill, my child,
On the land—at the loom—in the mill, my child.
 Whom bigots and knaves
 Would keep as their slaves;
Whom Tyrants would punish and kill, my child.

MILLIONS whom suffering draws, my child,
To unite in a glorious cause, my child:
 Their object, their end,
 Is mankind to befriend,
By gaining for all equal laws, my child.

MILLIONS who ever hath sought, my child,
For freedom of speech and of thought, my child,
Though stripp'd of each right
By the strong hand of might,
They ne'er can be vanquished or bought, my child.

MILLIONS who earnestly call, my child,
For freedom to each and to all, my child;
They have truth for their shield,
And never will yield
Till they triumph in tyranny's fall, my child.

ANON, 1844
From the Northern Star, *a Chartist newspaper*
(10 February 1844)

THE MANIFESTO OF THE
COMMUNIST PARTY

The history of all hitherto existing society is the history of class struggles.

Freeman and slave, patrician and plebian, lord and serf, guildmaster and journeyman, in a word, oppressor and oppressed, stood in constant opposition to one another, carried on an uninterrupted, now hidden, now open fight, a fight that each time ended, either in a revolutionary reconstitution of society at large, or in the common ruin of the contending classes.

The modern bourgeois society that has sprouted from the ruins of feudal society has not done away with class antagonisms. It has but established new classes, new conditions of oppression, new forms of struggle in place of the old ones.

Let the ruling classes tremble at a Communistic revolution. The proletarians have nothing to lose but their chains. They have a world to win.

Working Men of All Countries, Unite!

KARL MARX *and* FREDERICK ENGELS, 1848
English Translation of 1888

THE MASSACRE OF THE ROSSES IN STRATHCARRON, ROSS-SHIRE

A pamphlet account of the Women's resistance to the 'Highland Clearance' of their village.

Many of the women were subsequently attacked and seriously injured in a police baton charge when they were evicted.

When the tenants heard rumours that Mr Munro had gone *secretly* to Tain to order summonses of removal to be served upon them, they called upon him, and inquired if there was any truth in the rumours that reached them; when Mr Munro, most solemnly declared that he never authorized any one of them to be removed—that he never ordered summonses of removal to be served upon them; and, calling his Maker to witness, he declared that he never authorized any one to apply for warrants in his name, and that he would have nothing to do with their removal. The tenants were induced by these strong declarations made by Munro, to believe that he had not authorized their removal; yet, they were astonished on hearing that the Sheriff had actually granted warrants against them at Munro's instance, and in his name; and that a sheriff-officer was on his way to Green-

yard to serve them with the usual 'warnings' to quit. . . .
Macpherson said he acted under the authority of the sheriff;
but, the women replied, that Munro having disclaimed all
connexion with the removings, and having solemnly denied
that he applied for warrants, or authorized any application
for them, or for service of warnings, they refused to let him
pass on, unless he produced a mandate from Mr Munro,
authorising the service of the summonses. This, Macpherson
could not exhibit, consequently the females laid hold on him,
searched his pockets, and took the summonses from him and
burnt them. They made no attack whatever on Macpherson,
but treated him very gently; and one or two of the men who
came up after the summonses were burnt, went with him and
with his assistant 'Peter' in the Inn at Ardgay, and treated
them to refreshments and some spirits. Macpherson left the
district without any molestation, or abuse whatever. Not a
hair of his head was touched, and he returned to Tain in as
good health and with far more *spirits* than he had when he
left it. . . .

The burning of the summonses by the women of Greenyard caused considerable excitement in the surrounding
districts. It was the topic of conversation in every company:
some applauding, and some questioning the legality of their
conduct. . . . The news spread like wildfire—the swiftest
boys ran up by the banks of the Carron like roes, intimating
at every house that three sheriff-officers were on their way
up the glen to warn out the tenants of Greenyard. The
women again sallied out and met the *sham* sheriff-officers at
the march of Greenyard. They asked what was their mission
to that district? and being told by the gaugers that they were
sheriff-officers going to serve summonses on all the tenants,
it caused great excitement among them; and they demanded
their authority from Mr Munro. The gaugers said they had
sufficient authority already; and they ordered the women to
'move on'. The women would not budge one inch, but
demanded that the gaugers should leave the ground or else
show a mandate or some written authority from Munro. This

the gaugers could not produce, and the clamour got so fast and furious that the gaugers found themselves most awkwardly situated. . . .

DONALD ROSS, 1854

SPEECH ON THE ANNIVERSARY OF THE PEOPLE'S PAPER

The English working men are the first-born sons of modern industry. They will certainly not be the last in aiding the social revolution produced by that industry, a revolution which means the emancipation of their own class all over the world, which is as universal as capitalism and wage-slavery. I know the heroic struggles the English working class have gone through since the middle of the last century—struggles not less glorious because they are shrouded in obscurity and burked by the middle-class historian.

KARL MARX, APRIL 1856

A LONDON COSTERMONGER

People fancy that when all's quiet that all's stagnating. Propagandism is going on for all that. It's when all's quiet that the seed's a-growing. Republicans and Socialists are pressing their doctrines.

Quoted by HENRY MAYHEW, 1861,
in London Labour and London Poor

TO THE TRADE UNIONISTS OF
THE UNITED KINGDOM

Fellow Workmen, how often have we found some of our greatest and most combined efforts rendered nugatory by some antique piece of legislation in the shape of an unrepealed Act of Parliament, or by some action taken by the *Home Office*? Is it not fresh in your recollection that the Government lent soldiers to a private contractor at Chelsea to enable him to resist his workmen's demand? Have they not done so at Plymouth? Did they not do so at Aldershot? And in how many cases have they given assistance where the men could not bring positive proof although they have felt morally certain? Scotland Yard provided 'pickets' in blue coats for a large number of buildings in London during the Builders' Strike and Lock-out. Yet we were condemned if we sent a private citizen (without citizen's rights) simply to inform workmen in the most friendly and civil manner that a trade dispute existed.

JUNE 1865
An Address issued by the Reform League

FARMWORKERS' SONG

Sung by the farmworkers as they paraded through Warwickshire on the day the Warwickshire Agricultural Labourers' Union was founded.

The National Union of Agricultural Workers grew from the Warwickshire union.

> *We won't be idle, we won't stand still,*
> *We're willing to work, to plough and till:*
> *But if we don't get a rise we'll strike we will,*
> *For all have joined the union.*

MARCH 1872

MANIFESTO OF THE
AGUDAH HASOZIALISTIM CHAVERIM

The Agudah Hasozialistim Chaverim was the first Hebrew Socialist Union. The statutes of the union were drawn up in Hebrew and Yiddish, and it drew its support from Jewish sweated labour in the East End of London.

The emancipation of all mankind from oppression and slavery can only be brought about by the workers themselves, in their united efforts to wage war against their exploiters; first to destroy the existing order and then to replace it by workers' control, justice, freedom and the brotherhood of man.

And as the workers of Europe and America have already joined together in various organizations to rouse the dispossessed and dedicate themselves to revolution for the victory of workers' Socialism, so we Jewish sons bind ourselves to this noble alliance and to this end we have created a Jewish Socialist Union.

This our comrades understand to be true and correct, the supreme arbiter of their relationship with each other and other people, notwithstanding colour, race or creed, and undertake to accept the following:

The Union's aim to spread Socialism among the Jews as well as non-Jews; to support organizations recognized by it and to unite all workers in the fight against their oppressors.

The Union's undertaking, in brotherly fashion, to unite workers' organizations from other nations.

MAY 1876

THE DOCKERS' TANNER

At the docks there is a strike that the company don't like
A tanner on the hour they'll have to pay:
Like slaves they'd have us work far more than any Turk
And make us sweat our lives out every day.

> *Chorus:*
> *Strike, boys, strike for better wages!*
> *Strike, boys, strike for better pay!*
> *Go on fighting at the docks,*
> *Stick it out like fighting cocks*
> *Go on fighting till the bosses they give way!*

If it's slavery that you seek, for about a quid a week,
They'll take you on as soon as you come near,
Sweat your guts out with a will, or they'll try your job to fill,
But that won't wash with working men, that's clear.

We'll stand up for our rights and the company we will fight,
Supported by our brothers everywhere,
For we have friends galore—the good old stevedores,
And the seamen and the firemen they are there.

> *1889. A popular song of the Great Dockers' Strike*

THE RED FLAG

Chorus:
Then raise the scarlet standard high!
Within its shade we'll live or die,
Though cowards flinch and traitors jeer,
We'll keep the red flag flying here.

The people's flag is deepest red,
It shrouded oft our martyred dead,
And ere their limbs grew stiff and cold,
Their hearts' blood dyed its ev'ry fold.

It waved about our infant might,
When all ahead seemed dark as night;
It witnessed many a deed and vow:—
We must not change its colour now.

It well recalls the triumphs past,
It gives the hope of peace at last;
The banner bright, the symbol plain,
Of human right and human gain.

It suits today the weak and base,
Whose minds are fixed on pelf and place;
To cringe before the rich man's frown,
And haul the sacred emblem down.

With heads uncovered swear we all,
To bear it onward till we fall;
Come dungeon dark or gallows grim,
This song shall be our parting hymn.

JIM CONNELL, 1889
Written for the Great Dock Strike

THE DOCKERS' STORY

An article in the Nineteenth Century *describing the Great Dock Strike of 1889.*

On Wednesday, August 14th, a general strike was agreed upon, and after a meeting of the South Dock workers a procession was formed and a visit paid to the gates of the other docks. The enthusiastic shouts of the men soon acted as a call to arms to those working within. From the woodyard of the West India Dock the workers came out in hundreds, accompanied by a large body of stevedores. We then marched to the East India Dock, and, with added recruits, proceeded to the Milwall Dock, returning with our forces to the West India Dock, where arrangements for the next day were made. On that day I addressed twelve meetings. At six o'clock the following morning we were astir, and found the ranks of the strikers largely increased. We marched our forces in procession to the West, East, South, Victoria and Albert Docks, and at each dock speeches were made by representatives of the men. From the docks we made a complete tour of the wharves from Limehouse to London Bridge, and finally held a large meeting on Tower Hill. On the third day of the strike we marched, with banners and brass bands, to the number of 10,000 through the City, and a deputation attended at the Dock House to discuss with the directors the points in dispute. The tone of the directors, however, was anything but conciliatory, and we could only get them to say that they would consider our demands.... Later followed the mediation of the Lord Mayor, Cardinal Manning, and others. But what happened during the month of the strike is too well known to need repetition here. The dock directors were defeated on all points. The suggestion that the strike was the work of socialists and politicians is as untrue as it is unfair to the cause of labour. Neither socialism, creed, nor politics entered into the strike. The credit of the victory is due to the men themselves, and not to any speech-making from outsiders.

The rise in wages after November 4th will range from ten to thirty-five per cent, and will be shared by all connected with the shipping and wharf work. Even the carmen will benefit by the strike, and men whose connection with the docks is very remote will share in the benefit of the rise. So far as the docks are concerned the contract system may be said to have received its death blow, and already a feeling of mutual respect between employer and workman is arising. The strike has enabled the docker to appreciate what combination can do, and taught him more thoroughly to respect himself, his fellows, and his country. It now remains to keep the position gained.

BENJAMIN TILLETT, 1890

IN THE NAME OF THE
WORKERS' COMMITTEE . . .

A handbill calling for the mobilization of Jewish garment workers in London's East End.

Brother workers, our enemies, detractors and holy satraps want to convince you that riots will result during the procession so that you should not join us—your well-known dedicated friends. In reply we say that there will be no riots and disorder. As we do not intend to protest against the police, so they will not interfere with us.

Come in your masses, workers—come with us to the Great Synagogue to show the world our plight and that we will no longer be slaves to the sweaters.

LEWIS LYONS *and* PHILIP KRANZ, MARCH 1889

THE SOUL OF MAN UNDER SOCIALISM

Disobedience, in the eyes of anyone who has read history, is man's original virtue. It is through disobedience that progress has been made, through disobedience and through rebellion. Sometimes the poor are praised for being thrifty. But to recommend thrift to the poor is both grotesque and insulting. It is like advising a man who is starving to eat less. For a town or country labourer to practise thrift would be absolutely immoral. Man should not be ready to show that he can live like a badly fed animal.... Agitators are a set of interfering, meddling people, who come down to some perfectly contented class of the community, and sow the seeds of discontent amongst them. That is the reason why agitators are so absolutely necessary. Without them, in our incomplete state, there would be no advance towards civilization.

OSCAR WILDE, 1891

MANIFESTO OF THE JOINT COMMITTEE OF SOCIALIST BODIES

The socialist bodies represented on the Joint Committee were the Socialist Democratic Federation, the Fabian Society and the Hammersmith Socialist Society.

Moreover, the question of the unemployed is more pressing today than at any recent period. The incapacity of the capitalist class to handle the machinery of production without injury to the community has been demonstrated afresh by the crisis, itself following upon a very short period of inflation; since which time every department of trade and industry has suffered from lack of initiative and want of confidence and ability among these 'organizers of labour'. As a result the numbers of the unemployed have increased rapidly; the prospect of any improvement is still remote; and the stereotyped official assurance that there is no exceptional distress only emphasizes the fact that it is prosperity, not distress, which is exceptional. Indeed, the greatest 'prosperity' possible under the present system could only lessen the mass of those without occupation, and bring them down to a number manageable by the employers.

I MAY 1893

MERRIE ENGLAND

From a series of letters written to 'John Smith of Oldham, a practical working man'.

The question of Socialism is the most important and imperative question of the age. It will divide, is now dividing, society into two camps. In which camp will you elect to stand? On the one side there are individualism and competition—leading to a 'great trade' and great miseries. On the other side is justice, without which can come no good, from which can come no evil. On the one hand, are ranged all the sages, all the saints, all the martyrs, all the noble manhood and pure womanhood of the world; on the other hand, are the tyrant, the robber, the man-slayer, the libertine, the usurer, the slave-driver, the drunkard, and the sweater. Choose your party, then, my friend, and let us get to the fighting.

ROBERT BLATCHFORD, 1894

WORKSHOP TALK

I know it because I read it in the papers. I also know it to be the case because in every country I have graced with my presence up to the present time, or have heard from, the possessing classes through their organs in the press, and their spokesmen upon the platform have been vociferous and insistent in declaring the foreign origin of Socialism.

In Ireland Socialism is an English importation, in England they are convinced it was made in Germany, in Germany it is a scheme of traitors in alliance with the French to disrupt the Empire, in France it is an accursed conspiracy to discredit the army...in Russia it is an English plot to prevent Russian extension towards Asia, in Asia it is known to have been set on foot by American enemies of Chinese and Japanese industrial progress, and in America it is one of the baneful fruits of unrestricted pauper and criminal immigration.

All nations today repudiate Socialism, yet Socialist ideas are conquering all nations. When anything has to be done in a practical direction towards ameliorating the lot of the helpless ones, or towards using the collective force of society in strengthening the hands of the individual it is sure to be in the intellectual armory of Socialists the right weapon is found for the work.

JAMES CONNOLLY, JUNE 1899
Published in the Workers' Republic

LABOUR IN IRISH HISTORY

The Irishman frees himself from...slavery when he realizes the truth that the capitalist system is the most foreign thing in Ireland. .... The Irish question is a social question.

The whole age-long fight of the Irish people against their oppressors resolves itself in the last analysis into a fight for the mastery of the means of life, the sources of production, in Ireland. Who would own and control the land? The people, or the invaders; and if the invaders, which set of them—the most recent swarm of land thieves, or the sons of the thieves of a former generation?

JAMES CONNOLLY, 1910

SOCIALISM: ITS AIM AND OBJECT

We want equality of opportunity; a fair field and no favour for those who are willing to labour—an ample and secluded space in which to starve for those who are only willing to idle.

On the road to our goal, we are willing to take 'instalments'. We will agitate for softer crusts and drier hovels for the underdogs of our system. We will accept political emollients with a meaning smile. But we aim at Socialism; at complete emancipation from wage-slavery; at social order and harmony instead of social chaos.

In furthering these aims we are inspired with an abiding faith and hope. Our present system blesses no class. It curses the rich as well as the poor. It breeds panic, insecurity, and ennui. It hinders and mocks the fulfilment of human destiny.

We Socialists can afford to wait for tomorrow. We are in true line with evolution. We are aligned with the Universe. We believe—and we grow stronger by fighting.

Socialism is inevitable.

VICTOR GRAYSON, 1910

CAMBRIAN COMBINE STRIKE COMMITTEE MANIFESTO, 1910

Through all the long dark night of years
The peoples' cry ascendeth
And earth is wet with blood and tears
But our meek suffrance endeth,
The few shall not for ever hold sway
The many toil in sorrow
The powers of Hell are strong today
Our kingdom comes tomorrow.

SPEECH MADE IN GLASGOW

The Socialist question was not a religious question. It was a question to be settled in the mines and factories, not at the altar. The Socialist movement had nothing whatever to do with the next world. It was no concern of their organization whether there was a heaven or a hell, but, if there was a heaven hereafter, it was poor preparation to live in hell here.

JAMES CONNOLLY, OCTOBER 1910
Reported in Forward *(15 October 1910)*

THE LIVERPOOL STRIKE OF 1911

The whole of Liverpool looked like an armed camp. The 80,000 strikers continued successfully in spite of all the parading of the military. The soldiers were compelled to do the disgraceful work of helping the few blacklegs present. Thus, for example, when the authorities decided to open a railway goods yard and fetch out a few hundredweight of freight, they requisitioned mounted police, foot police, cavalry, infantry with fixed bayonets—altogether some hundreds of men to escort a couple of lorries.

On the other hand, goods that were intended for the hospitals and public institutions were brought out by Union drivers unaccompanied by anyone other than a couple of Committee men. On each lorry was a large placard bearing the words, 'By Authorization of the Strike Committee', and each as it appeared was cheered by thousands.

Backed by over 7,000 military and special police, the local authorities were determined to provoke disorder. Mounted and foot police were sent out in large numbers to the centre of the city, and these made many uncalled-for attacks upon peaceful pedestrians, riding them down and clubbing any young men who happened to be near. Naturally people resented this and retaliated, and this is how riots began.

TOM MANN, [1923]
From Tom Mann's Memoirs

CLOSING SPEECH AT MACLEAN'S TRIAL FOR SEDITION

Maclean was a prominent leader of the Clyde Workers Committee.

MACLEAN: It has been said that they cannot fathom my motive. For the full period of my active life I have been a teacher of Economics to the working classes, and my contention has always been that Capitalism is rotten to the foundations, and must give place to a new society. I had a lecture, the principal heading of which was 'Thou shalt not steal, thou shalt not kill', and I pointed out that as a consequence of the robbery that goes on in all civilized countries today, our respective countries have had to keep armies, and that inevitably our armies must clash together. On that and on other grounds, I consider Capitalism the most infamous, bloody and evil system that mankind has ever witnessed. My language is regarded as extravagant language, but the events of the

158

past four years have proved my contention.... I am not here then as the accused, I am here as the accuser, of Capitalism dripping with blood from head to foot. ...

I have taken up unconstitutional action at this time because of the abnormal circumstances and because precedent has been given by the British Government. I am a Socialist, and have been fighting and will fight for an absolute reconstruction of Society for the benefit of all. I am proud of my conduct. I have squared my conduct with my intellect, and if everyone had done so this war would not have taken place. I act square and clean for my principles. I have nothing to retract. I have nothing to be ashamed of. Your class position is against my class position. There are two classes of morality. There is the working-class morality and there is the capitalist-class morality. There is this antagonism as there is the antagonism between Germany and Britain. A victory for Germany is a defeat for Britain; a victory for Britain is a defeat for Germany. And it is exactly the same so far as our classes are concerned. What is moral for the one class is absolutely immoral for the other, and vice versa. No matter what your accusations against me may be; no matter what reservations you keep at the back of your head, my appeal is to the working class. I appeal exclusively to them because they and they only can bring about the time when the whole world will be in one brotherhood, on a sound economic foundation. That, and that alone, can be the means of bringing about a reorganization of Society. That can only be obtained when the people of the world get the world, and retain the world.

THE LORD JUSTICE GENERAL: The sentence of the Court is that you be sent to penal servitude for a period of five years.

MACLEAN: (*Turning to comrades in the court*) Keep it going, boys; keep it going.

JOHN MACLEAN, MAY 1918
Published by the Workers' Propaganda Defence Department
as Condemned from the Dock

THE MAN IN PETERHEAD

A poem about the imprisonment of John MacLean, the Clyde-side leader, first published as a broadsheet by the Women's Section of Glasgow District Council.

MacLean was found guilty of sedition and sentenced to serve five years in Peterhead gaol. There were widespread protests, and he was released after seven months.

When you've passed your resolutions,
  When you feel you've 'done your bit',
And you think there's nothing more that you can do,
  Why not ACT—and in your action, try to emulate
  the grit
Of the Man in Peterhead who ACTS FOR YOU?

He is grateful for your money;
  He appreciates your cheers;
And your sympathy is ample for his needs:
  There are more effective things than resolutions, cash,
  or tears.
Why not give him just a sample, say—of DEEDS?

'Twas for you he garnered knowledge,
  Sacrificed his very youth—
For he worked for you until his head was grey.
  They are killing him by inches just because he thought
  the truth;
And having thought it, had the guts to SAY. . . .

John was for the Revolution
  That will surely come in time,
For the sacred Flag of Liberty—the Red!
  That he bravely kept in flying was the burden of his
  'crime',
But he keeps it flying yet in Peterhead.

Will you suffer his destruction
  On the tyrant's battle-ground?
Will you let the cursed Wrong defeat the Right?
  He is One against an Army!—are you going to see him
  downed?
Are you going to let him die without a FIGHT?

He will pay you back in plenty,
  It is YOU who stand to gain;
For his Lion Heart is yours if he is spared.
  Then, toilers, for your own sake UP AND LIBERATE
  MACLEAN.
You could DO IT—aye, tomorrow—IF YOU DARED!

JOHN S. CLARKE, 1918

THE UNEMPLOYED ARMY

Leading article in the Strike Bulletin—Organ of the Forty
Hours Movement, *which appeared during the Glasgow Forty
Hours Strike.*

All over the land, as we are able to show in our columns
today, there are strikes and preparations for strikes. In
countries further afield the same unrest is at work, and the
cause of it there is the same as the cause here. It is the fear of
unemployment and the spectre of hunger and misery which
looms menacingly behind it. All over the world the workers,
after toiling night and day for four years and more, are faced
with unemployment—the penalty of producing too much in
the past.

The workers dread unemployment as worse than an epidemic of fever. We know what it means—low wages, hunger, soup kitchens, doles, evictions, fireless grates, ragged clothes, weeping children, frantic women, desperate men. We have been through it before, and we don't want to go through it again. Unemployment is the Workers' Hell, and it is into that Hell those who oppose the 40 hours' week want to drive us. Unable to beat us in argument, they try to make us accept unemployment at the bayonet point. Still we fight on, for we are more afraid of unemployment than their cruel bayonets—weapons we made, little thinking they would be turned in our direction.

We are going to abolish the fear of unemployment, come what may. Everywhere the remedy put forward by the workers is the same as ours. All the workers are agreed that the reduction of hours means work and bread for all, and it is just for that reason that the Profiteers and Government oppose our claim. During the war there was work and bread for all, and we want that to continue during the peace as well.

11 FEBRUARY 1919

SPEECH TO THE DOCKERS'
UNION CONFERENCE AT PLYMOUTH

Ernest Bevin was denouncing the British Government's military support for the war against Russia, after the dockers had refused to co-operate with the loading of a munitions ship, the Jolly George.

I do not believe that the present Government has the authority of the Democracy of this country to lend a single penny or supply a single gun to carry on further war against Russia....Here are people being set at each others' throats, in order that Western financiers may regain the grain belt of Southern Russia. The time has come for the more advanced Democracy of the Western world to raise its voice in protest against any Government inspiring these people to fight their battles, and then supplying them with munitions with which to shoot one another in the financiers' interests. I was glad when the London dockers refused to load the *Jolly George*, and when a shipowner appealed to me I replied: 'Ask Bonar Law and Lloyd George.' I am not going to ask the dockers to put a gun in the ship to carry on this wicked venture. The workers have a right to say how their labour shall be used. If we are called upon to make munitions or transport munitions for purposes which outrage our sense of justice we have the right to refuse to have our labours prostituted.

ERNEST BEVIN, MAY 1920
From a report in the Daily Herald

JUSTICE FOR IRELAND

We have all along abstained from the impertinence of advising the Irish people what they should do. That is their business. The business of the English people is to insist that England shall recognize the principles of liberty and justice. . . .

Consider the alternative. . . . If Great Britain insists upon taking the attitude of a nation dominating another by physical force and insisting on certain terms for no better reason than it is strong enough to enforce them by bloodshed, *then the bloodshed will come and the whole responsibility will be upon this country*. Every single man and woman who fails to raise a voice in these critical hours against the British attitude and the implied British threat will be guilty of murder—deliberate cold-blooded murder.

SEPTEMBER 1921
Leading article in the Daily Herald

LIFT UP THE PEOPLE'S BANNER

Lift up the People's banner,
  Now trailing in the dust;
A million hands are ready
  To guard the sacred trust;
With steps that never falter,
  And hearts that grow more strong,
Till victory ends our warfare
  We sternly march along.

Through ages of oppression,
  We bore a heavy load,
While others reaped the harvest
  From seeds the people sowed;
Down in the earth we burrowed,
  Or fed the furnace heats;
We felled the mighty forests,
  We built the mighty fleets.

But after bitter ages
  Of hunger and despair,
The slave has snapped his fetters,
  And bids his foes beware;
We will be slaves no longer,
  The nations soon shall know
That all who live must labour,
  And all who reap must sow.

JOSEPH WHITTAKER, 1925
From the Socialist Sunday School Song Book

CLOSING SPEECH AT HIS TRIAL FOR SEDITIOUS LIBEL AND INCITEMENT

Pollitt was General Secretary of the Communist Party.

The hostility between the classes arises as a result of the hostility of economic interests. In the early days of the capitalist system the class struggle was mainly concerned in a fight on behalf of the workers to get little concessions, such as the eight-hour day instead of the ten-hour and the fourteen-hour day; such as the abolition of the half-time system in the factories, the better ventilation of workshops and a shilling a week more on wages; that was the keynote of the struggle at that particular time. But as the system becomes more and more powerful and more and more compact, so the class war intensifies, not because we say it will intensify, but the struggle between the working class and the capitalist becomes intensified as the capitalist system itself becomes intensified. . . .

As this struggle becomes intensified, the working class must develop their organization and the capitalist class theirs. We see the development of the policy of the capitalist organization, and we see coming into existence a huge combine representing the political and economic interests of the capitalists, which is called the Federation of British Industries. On the other hand, we see the Trades Union Congress increasing its members. The two classes line up, the one to defend what it has won and to get a better existence, and the other to keep what it has and to prevent the working class getting a better existence. This mutual war intensifies as a result of ordinary economic development. Lock-outs and strikes, any political event at all, take on a much more serious character than formerly. . . .

Members of the jury, you know, as a matter of common knowledge, that this country spent 100 million pounds trying to smash the Russian Government. The lesson of history is that whatever ruling class is in power, it will retain that power peaceably and constitutionally, if it can, and if it cannot it will resort to other methods. This is not simply the view of one or two hot-heads who are now in the dock; it is very prevalent among the people in this country. It is very prevalent in the Labour Movement all over the world. We work to get our candidates on the local councils and boards of guardians and in Parliament. No one is more delighted than the members of the Communist Party to bring this about, but we have a right to warn the working classes of what happened in the past, and what is happening now before our very eyes.

HARRY POLLITT, OCTOBER 1925

THE STRIKERS' ALPHABET

A is for ALL, ALL OUT and ALL WIN,
And down with the blacklegs and scabs who stay in.
B is for Baldwin, the Bosses' Strong Man,
But he's welcome to dig all the coal that he can.
C is for Courage the workers have shown,
Class Conscious and Confident that they'll hold their own.
D is for DOPE that the Government spread—
Dishwash for Duncos and Dubbs—'nuf sed.'
E is for Energy that will carry us through,
Everyone class-conscious, steadfast and true.
F is for fight, our fight to the end,
For we're solid together, not an inch will we bend.
G is for Grab-all, the bosses, you know,
Greedy and grasping, one day they must go.
H is Hardship, we all must endure;
However, keep smiling, for Victory is sure.
I is for Interest, Profits and Rent
Into the pockets of the Indolent.
J is for Jix, the stirrer of strife,
Just waiting the chance to have your life.
K is for knife that is wielded by Jix,

166

Keep yourselves orderly and frustrate his tricks.
L is for London, where the T.U.C. meet,
Leading the workers the bosses to beat.
M is for Miners, for whose rights we must fight,
Maintaining the cause which we know to be right.

MAY 1926
From the St Pancras strikers' Bulletin, *during the*
General Strike

INTERVIEW WITH A. J. COOK

I am as anxious as any man in this country for a satisfactory and peaceful settlement of the mining problems, but must again express clearly and definitely my view that peace cannot be secured in this great basic industry unless the men who risk their lives and invest their all are secured a decent living wage.

Reductions in wages will increase neither efficiency nor output, nor will they bring harmony in this industry. Safety depends to a great extent upon economic security.

I make an appeal to all those who have been striving for peace to make their influence felt and remember that the great mining community expects the British public to treat them fairly and squarely.

MAY 1926
From the British Worker, *17 May*

MEDITATIONS OF A TRADE UNIONIST ON READING MR BALDWIN'S LATEST GUARANTEES TO STRIKE BREAKERS

An anonymous poem attacking strike breakers in the British Worker *(10 May), the official strike news bulletin published by the Trades Union Council during the General Strike.*

So you will 'guarantee' that all I'd lose
In Union benefits should be made up,
And you MIGHT keep your promise, though the woes
Of them that gave up everything to fight
And now are starving with their wives and kids
Make one a bit suspicious;
Still, you MIGHT!

Also you've promised you'd protect my skin
And save my bones, and make it safe for me
To walk about and work and earn my keep.
I'm not afraid for that. I know my mates;
They're decent, quiet chaps, not hooligans.
They wouldn't try to murder me,
Not they!

But could you make them treat me as a pal,
Or shield me from their cold, contemptuous eyes?
Could you restore the pride of comradeship?
Could you call back my ruined self-respect,
Give me protection from my bitter shame,
From self-contempt that drives out happiness?

Such guarantees are not in mortal power.
I'm sticking to my mates:
That's my reply.

MAY 1926

168

THE WINCOTT MANIFESTO

*The Wincott Manifesto was the declaration by the Inver-
gordon Mutineers, responding to the Admiralty's attempts to
impose a 25 per cent pay cut on the Navy's lower ranks. It took
its name from Len Wincott an able seaman on board the* HMS
Norfolk.

We the loyal subjects of H. M. the King do hereby present
my Lords Commissioners of the Admiralty our represen-
tations to implore them to amend the drastic cuts in pay that
have been inflicted on the lowest paid men on the lower
deck.

It is evident to all concerned that this cut is the forerunner
of tragedy, misery and immorality amongst the families of
the lower deck and unless we can be guaranteed a written
agreement from Admiralty confirmed by Parliament stating
that our pay will be revised we are still to remain as one unit,
refusing to serve under the new rate of pay.

The men are quite willing to accept a cut which they, the
men, consider in reason.

1931

THEIR THEATRE AND OURS

ALL: (*In line*) WORKERS' THEATRE! WORKERS' THEATRE!
          WORKERS' THEATRE!
FIRST: The theatre of workers like yourselves...
SECOND: ...who play in every town and country...
THIRD: ...to workers like yourselves.
ALL: WORKERS' THEATRE! WORKERS' THEATRE! WORKERS'
          THEATRE!
FOURTH: We show the life of working men and women.

FIFTH: Their hardships and their hunger.

SIXTH: Their struggles to exist.

FIRST: We are robbed at work for the profits of the rich!

SECOND: They speed us up, and throw millions out of work!

THIRD: Three millions of us and more are out of work!

FOURTH: They cut the dole and put us on the Means Test.

FIFTH: But the landlord gets his rent, or throws us out on the ear.

SIXTH: The bondholders get their hundreds of millions in interest every year.

WOMAN PLAYER: Workers' children are robbed of their milk.

ANOTHER WOMAN: And the death rate of the workers' children rises.

THIRD: (*To audience*) Why don't we workers unite and end this misery, this starvation, this mass-murder?

FIRST: *Because* many workers are still satisfied with their rotten conditions.

SECOND: *Because* others think that the workers have always been poor and oppressed and always *will* be.

FOURTH: *Because* thousands more think that the rich class are too powerful for us to overthrow.

FIFTH: And why do they think like this?

SIXTH: Because the capitalist class make you think just exactly what they want you to think.

FIRST: The Press...

SECOND: The Schools...

THIRD: The Theatres...

FOURTH: The Cinemas...

ALL: ... are controlled by the capitalist class.

SECOND: When things get bad, they sing to you at the pictures—

(*The group gathers round like a chorus on stage or film 'plugging' a 'cheer-up' song. A satirical picture of the way this stuff is put across. Faces ghastly with forced happiness.* SECOND *leads them in the song:*)

170

Happy days are here again,
The skies above are clear again—
    (*straight on to*):
There's a good time coming,
So keep your sunny side up, up—
TOM THOMAS, 1932
From one of the plays of the Workers'
Theatre Movement

INDUSTRIAL DEMOCRACY

The Labour movement feels, and rightly feels, that Labour has for too long allowed itself to be regarded as the hewer of wood and the drawer of water for the classes above.... I am of the working-class myself and I share in the revolt of its more enlightened elements against the commodity status of the workers by hand and by brain. But that commodity status will remain in greater or lesser degree as long as society is divided into owners and proletarians; and it is self-deception to think that it is ended or materially affected because, as an act of kindness, such and such a union has been allowed to nominate Brother So-and-So as a member of such and such a Board, where he sits side by side with a majority representing capitalist or non-Labour interests. They will be nice to the representative of Labour who has been allowed in, will these hail-fellow-well-met, soft-mannered capitalists. Indeed the representative of Labour must be a man of strong character if his spirit of working-class independence is not to be smothered by that kindness of which the British bougeoisie has great resources for use in circumstances which are advantageous to it....

HERBERT MORRISON, 1933

THEY SHALL NOT PASS

We stood at Gardiner's Corner,
We stood and watched the crowds,
We stood at Gardiner's Corner,
Firm, solid, voices loud.

Came the marching of the Blackshirts,
Came the pounding of their feet,
Came the sound of ruffians marching
Where the five roads meet.

We thought of so many refugees
Fleeing from the Fascist hordes,
The maimed, the sick,
The young, the old,
Those who had fought the Fascist lords.

So we stopped there at Gardiner's,
We fought and won our way.
We fought the baton charges,
No Fascist passed that day!

MILLY HARRIS, OCTOBER 1936
From They Shall not Pass: Anthology to
Celebrate the East Enders' Victory over Fascism

HUNGER MARCHERS' PETITION

A petition presented to the House of Commons by Aneurin
Bevan on behalf of the Hunger March organized by the
National Unemployed Workers' Movement.

I beg to present a humble Petition from unemployed
marchers showing the grievous hardship which is being

endured by great numbers of unemployed men and women by reason of their loss of physical well-being, the breaking up of many of their homes, the wretched condition of the villages and towns, and the harsh incidence of the family means test. Wherefore, your Petitioners pray that they, or some of their number, be heard at the Bar of the House as the representatives of the unemployed, to set forth their grievances and to urge, on behalf of the unemployed men and women, the provision of decent maintenance or employment at trade union rates of wages.

NOVEMBER 1936

MEMORIAL SOUVENIR ON
THE INTERNATIONAL BRIGADE

More than 2,000 volunteers for liberty went from Britain to fight for all the things that the best of British men and women have held dear through the centuries of their history.

Those 2,000 men fought under a hot Spanish sun in a country strange to them for the same fundamental principles as John Ball and Wat Tyler fought more than five centuries earlier. Nearly five hundred of them have died. They died for reasons that are written imperishably in the traditions of their fathers and their grandfathers.

Fifteen hundred of the 2,000 were wounded; some were incapacitated for life. They limp about Britain today in the footsteps of John Wyclif and Jack Cade, the Chartists who followed in later years, and all those other men who have built up the story of Britain's long fight for freedom. . . .

It was Pasionaria who when the attack on the Spanish people began cried proudly: 'We would rather die on our feet than live on our knees.'

173

That defiant sentence found an echo in the hearts of men in fifty-two lands. So the greatest epic of the 20th century began with the journey of volunteers for liberty from the countries of the world.

They came from all the corners of Europe. They rode under trains across half a dozen international boundaries. From Greece and Bulgaria and Jugoslavia and Hungary where liberty had always been difficult to hold, they made their way to Spain. They smuggled themselves out of Fascist Italy and Nazi Germany. Some of them had escaped from dictatorship to a hardly won peace in democratic countries; now they threw their peace away. . . .

And they came from Britain. From the Clydeside and industrial areas of Scotland where the spirit of independence has always been proud and strong; from South Wales, whose hills and valleys are haunted by memories of freedom's fight, from the North of England, where the ground is thick with traditions of a people obstinate and stiff-necked in their defiance of tyrants; from London, which has seen so many struggles for democracy.

PHILIP BOLSOVER, 1939

THE ROAD TO WIGAN PIER

Socialism is such elementary common sense that I am sometimes amazed that it has not established itself already. The world is a raft sailing through space with, potentially, plenty of provisions for everybody; the idea that we must all co-operate and see to it that everyone does his fair share of the work and gets his fair share of the provisions seems so blatantly obvious that one would say that no one could possibly fail to accept it unless he had some corrupt motive for clinging to the present system. Yet the fact that we have got to face is that Socialism is *not* establishing itself. Instead of going forward, the cause of Socialism is visibly going back. At this moment Socialists almost everywhere are in retreat before the onslaught of Fascism, and events are moving at terrible speed. . . .

There are, I believe, countless people who, without being aware of it, are in sympathy with the essential aims of Socialism, and who could be won over almost without a struggle if only one could find the word that would move them. Everyone who knows the meaning of poverty, everyone who has a genuine hatred of tyranny and war, is on the Socialist side, potentially. . . .

It is fatal to let the ordinary enquirer get away with the idea that being a Socialist means wearing sandals and burbling about dialectical materialism. You have got to make it clear that there is room in the Socialist movement for human beings, or the game is up.

For the moment the only possible course for any decent person, however much of a Tory or an anarchist by temperament, is to work for the establishment of Socialism. Nothing else can save us from the misery of the present or the nightmare of the future.

GEORGE ORWELL, 1937

INTRODUCTION TO THE COMMUNIST MANIFESTO

The Labour Party reprinted the manifesto in its centenary year.

It is not, I think, merely patriotic emotion that makes British socialists feel that here, as nowhere else, the truth of their principles will be tested. It was in Great Britain that capitalist society first came to full maturity in the generation

175

subsequent to the Napoleonic Wars. It was largely from the observation and analysis of that maturity that Marxism became the outstanding philosophic expression of socialist principles and methods; and it was largely from British socialist writers, and the early British socialist movement, alike on its political and on its trade union side, that Marx and Engels moved to the understanding that men make their history by their power, through their grasp of the forces which make it move, to give a conscious direction to that movement.

HAROLD LASKI, 1948

CONTEMPORARY CAPITALISM

We sometimes celebrate the pioneers of trade unionism, and co-operation, with more sentiment than knowledge or understanding. But, for all that, can we ever too greatly honour these men and women? For they laid the essential basis of modern democracy. In the mire of Tolpuddle and the murk of Rochdale, in a hundred other British back streets and country lanes, the social atoms began to fuse. These for the most part anonymous men and women then and there began the long, painful process by which the hitherto helpless wage earners were to forge for themselves the organizations and institutions which could alone enable them to appear as actors instead of patients on the pages of history. Nor was that development accomplished without almost unbelievably stubborn perseverance and immense self-sacrifice. The sheer doggedness, level-headedness and good sense of the nineteenth and early twentieth century British workers in using the means that were open to them constituted a kind of heroism no less noble, and far more fruitful, than that of their continental comrades who died upon the barricades.

For they gave social and economic content to the political democracy which, by the middle of the twentieth century, had been established in Britain.

Whoever has failed to understand the extreme importance of the right of association and all that goes with it—of all that is often called 'working-class democracy'—has failed to cross the true Rubicon of modern political thought and feeling. He has remained upon the other side of that sometimes invisible, but deep, stream which divides the world of the wage earner from that of the property owner. He has remained in the realm of abstract principles, of more or less unreal and papery schemes and constitutions, and of 'economic laws' which are thought to apply equally to millionaires and paupers. Paper constitutions are indeed important: or, more precisely, they *become* important as soon as the wage earners achieve a sufficient degree of solidarity, of organization, of consciousness of their own aims and interests, to fill out those otherwise empty abstractions with the content of their social purposes.

JOHN STRACHEY, 1956

A SENSE OF OUTRAGE

I am simple-minded enough to believe that we will never get a Socialist society in Britain—that is, a society based on the Christian principle that each individual is of equal worth, and has equal claims and duties—so long as we preserve historical continuity in our institutions, or indeed, and this may seem a hard thing to say, so long as we evaluate institutions in terms of their intrinsic merit and not in terms of their social consequences. I would therefore abolish the monarchy and House of Lords, dispossess the corporate bodies which control the public schools and the Oxford and Cambridge colleges; end the regimental system in the army, and destroy Service 'traditions' by amalgamating all three; disestablish the Church; replace the Inns of Court system with a central law college directly responsible to a government department; unify the chaotic hospital administration system, so that the Ministry of Health takes direct charge of training; and, finally, abolish the Honours List. What is more, we should take the offensive on all these fronts simultaneously: for, if the apostles of social change eschew violence, they must embrace speed. Our society is a many-headed hydra: it is no use chopping the heads off singly, for while you are dealing with the second or third, the first will grow again. Transforming society is rather like bombing a factory complex: if, on each raid, you concentrate on one workshop, you allow the others to employ their resources on rebuilding it in the intervals. You must destroy the whole simultaneously, otherwise the complex will survive. The British Left—whether Liberal or Labour—has tinkered with our institutions in the past, but singly and timidly, and on the assumption that what is old should command respect. It should not; it should inspire fear. A better society can only be bought at a price; we should not be afraid of inflicting damage. After all, it is no accident that wars herald and permit social transformations.

PAUL JOHNSON, 1958

THE ROAD TO ALDERMASTON

As I think of the Aldermaston march, I am reminded of the paradox that there is nothing so contemporary as the past.

One of the first bits of human writing scratched on a stone dug out of the sands of the Middle East reads: 'What a world we live in, children no longer obey their parents and everybody wants to write a book'; and that sounds up to date enough for anybody, though it is probably twenty thousand years old.

Whatever our early forefathers did about the situation thus described, it is reasonably certain that some of them got together in the open air, marched somewhere, and ended up with a demonstration at some shrine or other appropriate and significant spot.

This kind of public witness is as old as the hills and it is still potentially the most effective means of expressing and stimulating public opinion.

It provides a real though partial answer—if only by adding legs to ideas—to those who feel the irresistible urge to do something more than register a conviction.

It breaks through the 'public meeting' barrier and communicates its message to those who seem totally impervious to the appeal to assemble together indoors. . . .

It 'confirms the feeble knees' of those who are weak in the faith by giving to them the exhilaration of a public witness to the convictions.

The marcher is a marked man. He has nailed his colours to a mast that is plainly visible. To put it exactly in Miltonic words, the virtue of those who go in processions is no longer 'unexercised and unbreathed'.

DONALD SOPER, 1958
From Tribune *(4 April 1958)*

THE UPPER CLYDE SHIPYARD CAMPAIGN

A speech to a Glasgow demonstration soon after the start of the UCS work-in.

The workers of Britain are getting off their knees, getting on their feet and asserting their dignity. Asserting their abilities in a determined and disciplined way that they will have a say in the decision-making of this country. No one has the right to destroy the aspirations of young men or the security of old men. No one has the right to demand that people leave their countries if they want work.

We started off fighting for jobs, and in a matter of days we knew we were fighting for Scotland, and for the British working-class movement. The real power of this country has been forged today in Clydeside, and will be forged now in the pits, the factories, the yards and the offices. Once that force is given proper leadership—is disciplined and determined—there is no force in Britain, or indeed the world, that can stand against it.

JIMMY REID, AUGUST 1971

SPEECH AT TOMLINSON'S TRIAL

Eric Tomlinson was one of the Shrewsbury building workers tried and found guilty of conspiracy after the building workers' strike in 1972.

Over the past months I have discovered many things about myself and about the laws of this land which I had been led to believe was the finest legal system in the world. But now I can only fear for the working-class people of this country.

If a mighty trade union can be fined a vast amount of money, then building workers arrested, tried and sentenced for picketing, will the day come when it will be a crime in itself to be a member of a trade union? Who can tell?

The sentence passed on me today by this court will not matter. My innocence has been proved time and time again by building workers of Wrexham whom I led and indeed by building workers from all over the country who have sent messages of support to myself, my family and my colleagues. . . .

I would like to ask if the fantastic police enquiries and mammoth statements taken and the thousands of pounds spent on this spectacular are the usual diligent efforts used in an ordinary criminal trial?

I look forward to the day when the real culprits—the McAlpines, Wimpeys, Laings and Bovises and all their political puppets are in the dock facing charges of conspiracy and intimidating workers from doing what is their lawful right—picketing.

Politics have been mentioned in this trial and of course politics do play a part. They play a part in our very existence . . . This trial is political and at all times has been political. It has been handled in a most biased fashion against myself and Warren, and distorted and exaggerated in the extreme.

It is hoped the trade union movement and working classes of this country will act now to ensure that another charade as this trial will never take place again and that the right to picket or strike be defended even at the cost of great personal hardship or individual freedom.

ERIC TOMLINSON, OCTOBER 1973

CRISIS AS CATALYST

A speech during the Labour Party Conference debate on the public sector.

The crisis that we inherit when we come to power will be the occasion for fundamental change and not the excuse for postponing it.

TONY BENN, OCTOBER 1973

LEADERS OF MEN

Jack Davitt, alias Ripyard Cuddling, was a shipyard welder at Swan & Hunter on Tyneside.

If managers were blades of grass
And foremen grains of sand,
One half of Swan's would be a field
The other desert land.

If tears could grant me heaven's gifts
Then I'd have some to spare;
If sweat cost thirty bob an ounce,
I'd be a millionaire.

But sweat, alas, is not the thing
To make your fortune grow;
The ones who reap the biggest crops
Are those who do not sow.

If wealth was measured out to each
According to his uses,
Then some in hats of green and white
Would need some good excuses.

Relations in the industry
Are not too good at all;
There's far too many referees
And too few on the ball.

And so I struggle through it all,
Still faithful to my Class,
But sometimes how I wish that I
Could be a blade of grass.

JACK DAVITT, 1977
From Shipyard Muddling

BEYOND THE FRAGMENTS

For socialists to win a parliamentary majority will be important, but only on the basis of, and accountable to, a strong extra-parliamentary movement able to confront the existing state apparatus and the financial interests it protects. For it is this movement which, having destroyed the coercive powers of the present state, will provide the basis of the new democratic form of political power. The exact form of the political organizations that will be capable of giving this movement a lead, fighting for its interests within the existing political system and organizing its defence against repression and violence, cannot yet be seen. It cannot be determined until the working class and other oppressed groups have developed a level of consciousness, sense of purpose and degree of self-confidence to remake society. The purpose of socialist organization now should be to develop that consciousness together with a vision of an alternative society.

HILARY WAINWRIGHT, 1979
Introduction

PART FOUR
WOMEN

The ferment among women. . . .
KEIR HARDIE, 1913

For those who may be tempted to think that the demands of women for equal rights are new, this section will be of special interest as it traces these demands back for three hundred and fifty years. If proper records were available we should certainly learn that they go back for thousands of years.

In these extracts we see the emergence and articulation of issues that are still being argued today. For women have always had to contend with the idea that they are second-class people, and not just different from men. We are told of women's qualities and how they are disregarded, of the need for self-pride especially when enslaved as a servant inside an unequal marriage relationship or outside in the world. The claim to inherent rights recurs and from this develops an urgent expression of the need for political action. From their experience women came to see the relevance of class and the need for trade union protection. There is also a clear perception of the potential role of democracy, used to promote the objectives of any women's movement. The dialogue between radical and socialist feminists can be found here, as can a reasoned argument for militant action—when all else fails, or conscience calls—as a legitimate instrument to bring about political and social change.

But what comes across most strongly is the conviction that the inequality and injustice which women endure must be seen as a distinct and pressing issue, and that it is only when their oppression is lifted that all humankind will be liberated.

TONY BENN

ESTHER HATH HANGED HAMAN!

'*An answer to a lewd Pamphlet, entitled* The Arraignment of Women, *with the arraignment of lewd, idle, forward, and unconstant men, and husbands, by Esther Sowerman, neither Maide, Wife nor Widdowe, yet really all, and therefore experienced to defend all.*'

If no one thing men do acknowledge a more excellent perfection in women than in the estimate of the offences which a women doth commit: the worthiness of the person doth make the sin more markable. What an hateful thing is it to see a woman overcome with drink, when as in men it is noted for a sign of goodfellowship. And whosoever doth observe it, for one woman which doth make a custom of drunkenness, you shall find an hundred men: it is abhorred in women, and therefore they avoid it; it is laughed at and made but as a jest amongst men, and therefore so many do practise it. Likewise if a man abuse a maid and get her with child, no matter is made of it, but as a trick of youth; but it is made so heinous an offence in the maid that she is disparaged and utterly undone by it. So in all offences those which men commit are made light and as nothing, slighted over; but those which women do commit, those are made grievous and shameful.

ESTHER SOWERMAN (*? pseudonym*), 1617

SIR PATIENT FANCY

Aphra Behn was the first British woman to earn her living as a writer.

What has poor woman done that she must be
Debarred from sense and sacred poetry?
Why in this age has Heaven allowed you more,
And woman less of wit than heretofore?
We once were famed in story, and could write
Equal to men; could govern, nay, could fight.
We still have passive valour, and can show,
Would custom give us leave, the active too,
Since we no provocations want from you.
For who but we could your dull fopperies bear,
Your saucy love, and your brisk nonsense hear;
Endure your worse than womanish affectation,
Which renders you the nuisance of the nation;
Scorned even by all the misses of the town,
A jest to vizard mask and pit-buffoon;
A glass by which the admiring country fool
May learn to dress himself en ridicule,
Both striving who shall most ingenious grow
In lewdness, foppery, nonsense, noise and show.
And yet to these fine things we must submit
Our reason, arms, our laurels and our wit.
Because we do not laugh at you when lewd,
And scorn and cudgel ye when you are rude,
That we have nobler souls than you we prove,
By how much more we're sensible of love;
Quickest in finding all the subtlest ways
To make your joys, why not to make you plays?
We best can find your foibles, know our own,
And jilts and cuckolds now best please the town;
Your way of writing's out of fashion grown.

APHRA BEHN, 1678
Epilogue

A SERIOUS PROPOSAL TO THE LADIES FOR THE ADVANCEMENT OF THEIR TRUE AND GREATEST INTEREST—BY A LOVER OF HER SEX

The proposal was a plan for an academic convent where women would be able to withdraw from the world to pursue serious study.

Let us learn to pride our selves in something more excellent than the invention of a Fashion; And not entertain such a degrading thought of our own *worth*, as to imagine that our Souls were given us only for the service of our Bodies, and that the best improvement we can make of these, is to attract the Eyes of Men. We value *them* too much, and our *selves* too little, if we place any part of our desert in their Opinion and don't think our selves capable of Nobler Things than the pitiful Conquest of some worthless heart. . . .

Instead of inquiring why all Women are not wise and good, we have reason to wonder that there are any so. Were the Men as much neglected, and as little care taken to cultivate and improve them, perhaps they would be so far from surpassing those whom they now despise, that they themselves would sink into the greatest stupidity and brutality. The preposterous returns that the most of them make, to all the care and pains that is bestow'd on them, renders this no uncharitable, nor improbable Conjecture. One would therefore almost think, that the wise disposer of all things, foreseeing how unjustly Women are denied opportunities of improvement from *without*, has therefore by way of compensation endow'd them with greater propensions to Virtue, and a natural goodness of Temper *within*, which if duly manag'd, would raise them to the most eminent pitch of heroick Virtue. Hither Ladies, I desire you would aspire, 'tis a noble and becoming Ambition, to remove such Obstacles as lie in your way.

MARY ASTELL, 1694

SOME REFLECTIONS UPON MARRIAGE

If *all Men are born Free*, how is it that all Women are born Slaves? As they must be, if the being subjected to the *inconstant, uncertain, unknown, arbitrary Will* of Men, be the *perfect Condition of Slavery*? And, if the Essence of Freedom consists, as our Masters say it does, in having a *standing Rule to live by*? And why is Slavery so much condemn'd and strove against in one Case, and so highly applauded, and held so necessary and so sacred in another?

MARY ASTELL, 1700

WOMAN NOT INFERIOR TO MAN

'*A short and modest vindication of the natural right of the fair sex to a perfect Equality of Power, dignity and esteem with men.*'

Was every individual *Man* to divulge his thoughts of our sex, they would all be found unanimous in thinking, that we are made only for their use, that we are fit only to breed and nurse children in their tender years, to mind household affairs, and to obey, serve, and please our masters, that is, themselves forsooth. ...

Men seem to conclude, that all other creatures were made for them, because they themselves were not created till all were in readiness for them. How far this reasoning will hold good I will not take upon me to say. But if it has any weight at all, I am sure it must equally prove, that the *Men* were made for our use rather than we for theirs. ...

Our right is the same with theirs to all *public employments*; we are endow'd, by nature, with geniuses at least as capable of filling them as theirs can be; and our hearts are as susceptible of *virtue* as our heads are of the *sciences*. We neither want *spirit, strength*, nor *courage*, to *defend* a country, nor *prudence* to *rule* it. Our *souls* are as *perfect* as theirs, and the *organs* they depend on are generally more *refined*. . . .

I cannot help thinking that the wise author of nature suited our frames to the souls he gave us. And surely then the acuteness of our minds, with what passes in the inside of our heads, ought to render us at least EQUALS to *Men*. . . .

SOPHIA ('A person of quality'), 1739

A VINDICATION OF THE RIGHTS OF WOMEN

Ah! why do women—I write with affectionate solicitude—condescend to receive a degree of attention and respect from strangers different from that reciprocation of civility which the dictates of humanity and the politeness of civilization authorize between man and man? And why do they not discover, when 'in the noon of beauty's power', that they are treated like queens only to be deluded by hollow respect, till they are led to resign, or not assume, their natural prerogatives? Confined, then, in cages like the feathered race, they have nothing to do but to plume themselves, and stalk with mock majesty from perch to perch. It is true they are provided with food and raiment, for which they neither toil nor spin; but health, liberty, and virtue are given in exchange. But where, amongst mankind, has been found sufficient strength of mind to enable a being to resign these adventitious prerogatives—one who, rising with the calm dignity of reason above opinion, dared to be proud of the privileges inherent in man? And it is vain to expect it whilst hereditary power chokes the affections, and nips reason in the bud. . . .

It is a melancholy truth; yet such is the blessed effect of civilization! the most respectable women are the most oppressed; and, unless they have understandings far superior to the common run of understandings, taking in both sexes, they must, from being treated like contemptible beings, become contemptible. How many women thus waste life away the prey of discontent, who might have practised as physicians, regulated a farm, managed a shop, and stood erect, supported by their own industry, instead of hanging their heads surcharged with the dew of sensibility, that consumes the beauty to which it at first gave lustre; nay, I doubt whether pity and love are so near akin as poets feign, for I have seldom seen much compassion excited by the help-lessness of females, unless they were fair; then, perhaps, pity was the soft handmaid of love, or the harbinger of lust.

MARY WOLLSTONECRAFT, 1792

THE REVOLT OF ISLAM

Can man be free if woman be a slave?
  Chain one who lives, and breathes this boundless air,
To the corruption of a closèd grave!
  Can they whose mates are beasts, condemned to bear
  Scorn, heavier far than toil or anguish, dare
To trample their oppressors? in their home
  Among their babes, thou knowest a curse would wear
The shape of woman—hoary Crime would come
Behind, and Fraud rebuild religion's tottering dome.

PERCY BYSSHE SHELLEY, 1818

APPEAL OF ONE HALF OF THE HUMAN RACE

An appeal made by 'women against the pretensions of the other half [of the human race] men, to retain them in political and thence in civil and domestic slavery'.

Whatever system of labour, that by slaves or that by freemen; whatever system of government, that by one, by a few, or by many, have hitherto prevailed in human society; under every vicissitude of MAN's condition, he has always retained woman his slave. The republican has exercised over you that hateful spirit of domination which his fellow man and citizen disdained to submit to. Of all the sins and vices of your masters, you have been made the scapegoats: they have enjoyed, and you have suffered for their enjoyments; suffered for the very enjoyments of which they compel you to be the instruments! What wonder that your sex is indifferent to what man calls the progress of society, of freedom of action, of social institutions? Where amongst them all, amongst all their past schemes of liberty or despotism, is the freedom of action *for you*?

To obtain equal rights, the basis of equal happiness with men, you must be *respected* by them; not merely desired, like rare meats,to pamper their selfish appetites. To be respected by them, you must be respectable in your own eyes; you must exert more power, you must be more useful. You must regard yourselves as having equal capabilities of contributing to the general happiness with men, and as therefore equally entitled with them to every enjoyment. You must exercise these capabilities, nor cease to remonstrate till no more than equal duties are exacted from you, till no more than equal punishments are inflicted upon you, till equal enjoyments and equal means of seeking happiness are permitted to you as to men.

WILLIAM THOMPSON *and* ANNA WHEELER, 1825

THE DEMAND FOR THE EMANCIPATION
OF WOMEN, POLITICALLY AND SOCIALLY

The equality of woman and man must be our rallying cry.
Woman's slavery under Muhammadism, and her subaltern
situation under Christianity, must be repealed, and her
equality with man be acknowledged under Communism. But
although we would equalize, we would not identify the
sexes. Such identification would be unnatural, unbeautiful,
and accordant with the miserable state of the sexes among
the lowest of the low orders. Woman and man are two in
variety and one in equality. Their physical frames are as
various as are the stems of the poplar and of the oak, but yet
should the sun of equal right be alike shining upon them.

CATHERINE BARMBY, 1843
From New Tracts for the Times

THE SUBJECTION OF WOMEN

The concessions of the privileged to the unprivileged are so
seldom brought about by any better motive than the power
of the unprivileged to extort them, that any arguments
against the prerogative of sex are likely to be little attended
to by the generality, as long as they are able to say to themselves that women do not complain of it. That fact certainly
enables men to retain the unjust privilege some time longer;
but does not render it less unjust. . . .

Women do not complain of the general lot of women; or
rather they do, for plaintive elegies on it are very common in
the writings of women, and were still more so as long as the
lamentations could not be suspected of having any practical
object. Their complaints are like the complaints which men
make of the general unsatisfactoriness of human life; they
are not meant to imply blame, or to plead for any change.

But though women do not complain of the power of husbands, each complains of her own husband, or of the husbands of her friends. It is the same in all other cases of servitude, at least in the commencement of the emancipatory movement. The serfs did not at first complain of the power of their lords, but only of their tyranny. The Commons began by claiming a few municipal privileges; they next asked an exemption for themselves from being taxed without their own consent; but they would at that time have thought it a great presumption to claim any share in the king's sovereign authority. The case of women is now the only case in which to rebel against established rules is still looked upon with the same eyes as was formerly a subject's claim to the right of rebelling against his king.

JOHN STUART MILL, 1869

THE POSITION OF WORKING WOMEN, AND HOW TO IMPROVE IT

Emma Paterson was one of the pioneers of unions for women.

It is seldom disputed that the rate of wages paid to women is, in many occupations, disgracefully low. This may not be so glaringly the case in the great mills and factories of the North, but, in addition to cases which privately come to the knowledge of everyone, disclosures are not unfrequently made in the newspapers, showing how sadly many working women need some improvement in their position.

Not long ago a case appeared in the London papers which must have horrified all who read it. A woman had been working in a white-lead factory near London; the factory was three or four miles from her lodging; she had to walk to and fro morning and night. She could not pay the smallest amount for riding, nor provide herself with proper food, for her wages were but 9s per week for work occupying twelve hours each day. She bravely battled with her difficulties for some time, and managed to keep alive herself and three children, but, at last, nature could hold out no longer; she died, and her death, leaving the children unprotected, brought to light the fearful tale. Had she supported herself only, the facts might never have been known. . . .

Employers alone are not to blame for the evils of under-payment. There are many just and right-minded employers who would gladly pay their work-women a fair rate of wages: but, however willing they may be to do this, they are almost powerless so long as the women themselves make no stir in the matter.

EMMA PATERSON, APRIL 1874
An article in Labour News

A LETTER TO THE LADIES OF THE WOMEN'S SUFFRAGE MOVEMENT

A time has come in which it is needful that we should ask ourselves—What principle holds us together? Why are we associated? What is it we are trying to do? We are of many shades of political and religious opinions, of widely separated stations in life, but we are bound together by our work, by labours towards a common end. What is that end? It is to uplift one half of the human race from political and social serfdom; to save thereby the other half from the sins of injustice, and both together from the demoralization that injustice always brings; to make women more worthy of respect, and men more capable of feeling it for them; to bring the united action of men and women working harmoniously together to bear upon the sufferings of humanity, and to open to the whole human race the healing fountains of equal justice.

JESSIE CRAIGEN, *c.* 1883
Pamphlet

THE ORIGIN OF THE FAMILY, PRIVATE PROPERTY AND THE STATE

When monogamous marriage first makes its appearance in history, it is not as the reconciliation of man and woman, still less as the highest form of such a reconciliation. Quite the contrary. Monogamous marriage comes on the scene as the subjugation of the one sex by the other; it announces a struggle between the sexes unknown throughout the whole previous prehistoric period. In an old unpublished manuscript, written by Marx and myself in 1846, I find the words: 'The first division of labour is that between man and woman for the propagation of children.' And today I can add: 'The first class opposition that appears in history coincides with the development of the antagonism between man and woman in monogamous marriage, and the first class oppression coincides with that of the female sex by the male. . . .

In the great majority of cases today, at least in the possessing classes, the husband is obliged to earn a living and support his family, and that in itself gives him a position of supremacy, without any need for special legal titles and privileges. Within the family he is the bourgeois and the wife represents the proletariat. In the industrial world, the specific character of the economic oppression burdening the proletariat is visible in all its sharpness only when all special legal privileges of the capitalist class have been abolished and complete legal equality of both classes established. The democratic republic does not do away with the opposition of the two classes; on the contrary, it provides the clear field on which the fight can be fought out. And in the same way, the peculiar character of the supremacy of the husband over the wife in the modern family, the necessity of creating real social equality between them, and the way to do it, will only be seen in the clear light of day when both possess legally complete equality of rights. Then it will be plain that the first condition for the liberation of the wife is to bring the whole female sex back into public industry, and that this in turn demands the abolition of the monogamous family as the economic unit of society.

FREDERICK ENGELS, 1884

THE WOMAN QUESTION

The truth, not fully recognized even by those anxious to do good to woman, is that she, like the labour-classes, is in an oppressed condition; that her position, like theirs, is one of merciless degradation. Women are the creatures of an organized tyranny of men, as the workers are the creatures of an organized tyranny of idlers. Even where thus much is grasped, we must never be weary of insisting on the non-understanding that for women, as for the labouring classes, no solution of the difficulties and problems that present themselves is really possible in the present condition of society. All that is done, heralded with no matter what flourish of trumpets, is palliative, not remedial. Both the oppressed classes, women and the immediate producers, must understand that their emancipation will come from themselves. Women will find allies in the better sort of men, as the labourers are finding allies among the philosophers, artists, and poets. But the one has nothing to hope from man as a whole, and the other has nothing to hope from the middle class as a whole.

EDWARD AVELING and ELEANOR MARX AVELING, 1887
Pamphlet

WOMAN IN RELATION TO
THE LABOUR MOVEMENT

In the first place you are in the movement whether you will or no. If not at the centre, then on the outskirts. If not as a conscious worker, then as an unconscious one. You may abjure politics, or declare yourself an individualist. But politics or no politics you will send your child to school, where he will be influenced vitally and permanently by the inevitable growth of Collectivism. Later you will apprentice him to a trade, or send him to college; and whether in the workshop or in the students' hall, all the winds of adverse social doctrines will fiercely beat on him. You may declare for independence, but in order to attain it you may have to take your place in a Hospital, under a truly socialistic management, or possibly as a health lecturer, where your work will be considerably more drastic and revolutionary than that of the wildest agitator. Whatever you do you *must* come into contact with the labouring people, and with the Labour movement. Therefore my appeal to you is not an appeal in the interests of the people—it is not even an appeal to you to do your highest and best work. It is a suggestion that you should become a conscious instead of an unconscious worker—that you should be a willing perceiving unit, rather than an atom borne along on the torrent. . . .

The Reveille of the proletariat then is the Reveille of woman. Their emancipation must be simultaneous. Each in freeing themselves must free the other. At the bottom of all their efforts lies the same aim: self-realization, a full and conscious life of personal and social activity.

MARGARET MCMILLAN, 1895
From the Labour Annual

WORDS OF A LEADER

Lydia Becker was one of the most important pioneers in the fight for women's suffrage. In 1867 she established the Manchester Women's Suffrage Society, the first of its kind in the United Kingdom.

Women claim the right to vote, not as a boon to be granted by Parliament, although they must receive it, as any disfranchised class of the people must receive it, through the machinery of an Act of Parliament, but as a right inherent in them as human beings, a right which men can neither give nor take away, whatever their power may be to withhold from women the exercise of their rights. Women claim the suffrage because they form an integral part of the people by whose assent and for whose benefit Parliament has the power to legislate. The people do not derive their political rights from their representatives, but the representatives derive their authority from the people. By the people is not meant the electorate merely, but the whole body of the people.

LYDIA BECKER [1897]
From Words of a Leader: Being Extracts from the Writings of the late Lydia Becker, *edited by Helen Blackburn*

WHAT THE WOMEN WANT

Distributed as a Suffrage hand bill.

'Whatever do the women want?' we hear the scornful cry.
To you, O 'Christian Commonwealth'! we women make
  reply.
We want a 'Christian Commonwealth', where just and equal
  laws
Shall make a needless mission ours, who plead the woman's
  cause.

It was a wholesome lesson we were taught as girls at school
That our vaunted Constitution has a fundamental rule,
That whosoever hath no voice in voting or debate
Is free from obligation to contribute to the State.

When we women claim the Franchise, men have one
    answering note
'By reason of your womanhood, we do refuse the vote.'
But when the tax collector calls, 'tis not enough to say,
'By reason of our womanhood we do refuse to pay.'

O wise and prudent Rulers! we are women it is true,
But we are fellow citizens and fellow subjects too,
We have hearts and brains and voices, have we no right to say,
By what laws we will be governed—whose the Sceptre we
    obey?

There are wrongs that must be righted—bitter woes that seek
    redress,
We can hear our sisters calling in their weakness and distress,
We need the power to lift them from their sad and evil plight,
'Tis for this we want the Franchise—and we claim it as our
    right.

ANON, C. 1900

THE WOMEN'S CO-OPERATIVE GUILD,
1883–1904

[A] goal which all working women's organizations are bound
to seek is that of national citizenship. As soon as women are
in earnest as regards industrial and social reform, they are inevitably led to perceive how handicapped they are, by laws
which prevent their election to town and county councils,
and debar them from the parliamentary suffrage. It is not

only because women's own particular interests suffer, that they demand that such indignities should cease. The nation cannot afford to sacrifice anything in the battle for a juster life. It must inevitably suffer if it leaves more than half the community on one side, undeveloped and unrepresented; it cannot afford to dispense with the help which women can bring.

MARGARET LLEWELYN-DAVIES, 1904

REVOLUTIONARY SOCIALISM AND THE WOMEN'S MOVEMENT

The enemy of the women workers is not the male sex, but the capitalist class. That class is made up both of men and women. Many women are direct employers of labour; many are shareholders in capitalist industries; and as employers and shareholders they have equality with men. Do we find that their influence is used in favour of their women employees? By no means. Where their class interests are concerned women capitalists in general act no more mercifully than men capitalists. Their interests are to extract the fattest possible dividends out of the life-blood of the workers, without considering, or even knowing, whether the labour that creates these dividends is that of men or women. Would it not be folly in working women to expect these luxurious capitalist ladies to recognize common interests with *them*?

But the bourgeois feminists make a special appeal to the women workers under the pretence that their interests can be served along with the interests of wealthy women—that the privileged section will fight the male tyrant for the benefit of *all women*. The different class interests, different mode of life, different outlook, and different aims of the women of the bourgeoisie are ignored.

It is true that for these women also the bonds of slavery still exist, but they are rather silken cords than the iron chains borne by working women. So soft indeed are these cords that the majority of women in the capitalist class are quite oblivious to their own degradation. The affluence in which they live acts as a narcotic. Wealthy women are surrounded by a sensuous and hypocritical 'chivalry', which for the most part they blindly accept without detecting its falsity. They are content to have as their aim in life the buying and selling of themselves into that peculiar ornamental slavery and dependence which is the capitalist ideal of marriage. . . .

It is to Socialism that women must look for their freedom; and Socialism can only be achieved by a united working class. Let the women workers of today unite with their brother wage-slaves to put an end to that suffering and subjection in which the silent generations of the women of the past have lived and died.

LILY GAIR WILKINSON, c. 1906
Socialist Labour Party pamphlet

SPEECH AT THE TRIAL
OF THE SUFFRAGETTE LEADERS

Now, we have tried every way. We have presented larger petitions than were ever presented for any other reform, we have succeeded in holding greater public meetings than men have ever had for any reform, in spite of the difficulty which women have in throwing off their natural diffidence, that desire to escape publicity which we have inherited from generations of our foremothers; we have broken through that. We have faced hostile mobs at street corners, because we were told that we could not have that representation for our taxes which men have won unless we converted the whole of the country to our side. Because we have done this, we have been misrepresented, we have been ridiculed, we have had contempt poured upon us. The ignorant mob at the street corner has been incited to offer us violence, which we have faced unarmed and unprotected by the safeguards which Cabinet Ministers have. We know that we need the protection of the vote even more than men have needed it. . . .

Although the Government admitted that we are political offenders, and, therefore, ought to be treated as political offenders are invariably treated, we shall be treated as pickpockets and drunkards; we shall be searched. I want you, if you can, as a man, to realize what it means to women like us. We are driven to do this, we are determined to go on with this agitation, because we feel in honour bound. Just as it was the duty of your forefathers, it is our duty to make this world a better place for women that it is today.

EMMELINE PANKHURST, OCTOBER 1908
defending herself against the charge of 'conduct likely to provoke a breach of the peace'

THE SOLIDARITY OF WOMEN

The struggle to gain freedom for women, not for our own sake individually, but in order to win dignity and development for our own sex has given us something that history and classic literature tells us women once possessed amongst themselves. It has given us back a sense of unity with a great race, womanhood: independent in its point of view, reliant upon its judgement, confident in its standards of value, strong in the consciousness of its ideals, and determined to reach its goal and attain its purpose. . . .

This consciousness of the solidarity of women is breaking down personal rivalries, destroying class distinctions, and doing away with numberless suspicions and jealousies that have been fostered by the lives which women have led for many past generations. . . .

In this movement especially we see women losing sight of all that divides them and remembering only the ties of common experience and common destiny which bind them together.

CHRISTABEL PANKHURST, SEPTEMBER 1908
An article in Votes for Women

THE MEANING OF
THE WOMAN'S MOVEMENT

Men and Women! Those who speak of the Woman's Movement and what it means today are speaking the words of life. We tell you of a new great hope—a new great possibility for humanity. We speak to you of a better day that is dawning for the whole human family. We bring you the light of a great truth rediscovered. Those whose deeds are evil and whose thoughts are corrupt will still love darkness rather than light, but in spite of them the sun will rise and the day will dawn, and just as certainly will come the new time, and just as surely will it bring with it victory for the Woman's Cause, which is essentially the Cause of Progress and the great Cause of Humanity.

EMMELINE PETHICK LAWRENCE, c. 1908
Pamphlet

A CHALLENGE!

This article, defending the tactic of smashing windows, was originally supposed to appear in the 8 March 1912 issue of Votes for Women. *But it was censored and the page left blank. Instead, the article was published as a pamphlet a few days later.*

Gratitude to the women in prison, reverence for their courage and selflessness—these are the feelings that stir the hearts of every one of us. A cause must triumph that is fought by such soldiers as these. Our prisoners in Holloway take rank with those heroes and liberators whose names are set like jewels in our national history.

The stupid will exclaim at this. What! The women who broke shop windows? Do you call that action glorious? Why not? we answer. The breaking of windows is infinitely less cruel and violent than the acts of destruction to property and even to life which are committed in wars for freedom, whether such wars be international or civil. Two statues, standing outside the House of Commons, hand down from generation to generation the memory of a man and a woman. They are Boadicea, who fought for national independence, and Cromwell, who, in pursuit of his ideal of freedom, plunged the country into civil war. For their deeds the State itself, which has raised these statues, asks our admiration and reverence. But were these deeds either more dignified or more virtuous than the breaking of windows? . . .

The Suffragettes are happy indeed in knowing that, not only is their object as great as that of any soldiers or militant reformers, but that their action has been infinitely less harmful to life or property.

CHRISTABEL PANKHURST, MARCH 1912

GOODWILL MESSAGE

The ferment among women is far and away the most important event in the history of the world. So far as I know this is the first time in which women have come boldly forward, claiming equal rights with men, with their corresponding duties and responsibilities. Just what they may mean cannot be foretold. The one thing certain is that things can never again be what they have been. Under the influence of the Women's Movement the existing relationships are bound in process of time to undergo great changes. Let anyone who doubts this try to picture what is likely to emerge out of a state of society in which women have fought their way to economic freedom and have ceased to be dependent upon men. That one fact of itself must change the whole basis upon which society now rests.

For men and women alike Socialism means economic freedom, but men may as well realize the fact, sooner rather than later, that freedom must come to all or it cannot come to any. So long as there is a class or a sex which is not free that fact anchors all the rest of society in a like bondage. It is a law of the universe from which there is no escape. If this be so then, the cause of women is the cause of humanity. Political equality will, as in the case of men, precede economic equality. Votes for women will not only be a recognition of the equality of the sexes, but will also enable women to stand with men in the greater fight for economic freedom.

JAMES KEIR HARDIE, MAY 1913
An article in the first edition of Labour Woman

A TRAINING IN TRUCULENCE

It is a very serious thing that working women do not take a more active part in Labour and trade-unionist organizations. In trades confined to women one understands that the workers have the militancy sweated out of them by evil conditions, but even in the prosperous mixed unions women appear to feel that so long as they support them by funds and obedience they may leave the government of the unions to men. But men should never govern women, for it makes the men purr with self-admiration and the women whine with self-contempt. One would not wish women to become the kind of bureaucrats that the men's unions have in certain cases brought upon themselves, for it is one of the chief dangers to feminism that women may learn to play the fool as successfully as men. But one would wish them to lead by the ardour of their propaganda and the pride of their policy. One would wish them to form the most aggressive quarter of the Trade Union Congress, instead of merely the distinguished handful that now represent their sex.

REBECCA WEST, FEBRUARY 1913
From the Clarion

IN MEMORIAM:
MISS EMILY WILDING DAVISON

On 4 June 1913 Emily Wilding Davison threw herself underneath the King's horse at Epsom. Four days later she died and became the first and only martyr in the cause of Women's Suffrage. She was buried on 14 June. This is part of the pamphlet printed for her funeral.

A PETITION TO THE KING

The yielding up of life is the highest and most eloquent proof of love for others that human beings have it in their power to give—only the very strongest and most urgent reasons can call for such a sacrifice. Had Miss Davison such strong and urgent reasons? Yes, for deep in her heart burned the knowledge of the intolerable wrongs from which women are suffering. She knew of the Widow's struggle to exist on the pittance paid for making Government clothing, and of the horrors of the sweating system, under which women work for less than 1/- a day, until their eyes grow dim and their hands stiff and misshapen. She knew that out of every 1,000 babies born, on an average 110 are destined to die within a year of birth, because of their mothers' pitiable condition. She knew, too, that women are exploited, bought and sold into a life of shame and suffering, so that vice may flourish unchecked. She knew that every day of the year, little children are outraged and defiled, and that these wrongs will continue undiminished so long as the womanhood of the country is held in subjection and dishonour. And so she offered up her life as a PETITION TO THE KING, praying that women might be freed to aid their sisters.

JUNE 1913

OUR COMMON HUMANITY

A speech to a demonstration at the Albert Hall, London.

When government passed to a class, and was shared by thousands of men, they could not suppose themselves all divine, but they easily believed that they alone were truly human. The poor—the working people—were not denied all human personality; they were alluded to in a quaint and interesting phrase as *'that sort of person'*. And when government passed, as it has passed, from a class to a sex, the same feeling persisted. When a man says 'human being', he is generally thinking 'man'. Women indeed are not wholly denied human personality; it is admitted that they have some sort of claim to it; they are, in fact, in a still more curious phrase, 'persons' (or 'not persons') 'within the meaning of the Act'. . . .

Women indeed are not naturally a class. They belong to all classes. But men have made of them a class; for there is no class distinction in the world—not birth, or wealth, or education, or tradition—which makes so deep a cleavage as the distinction between the governing and the governed, and women, learning this, have learnt to work together, whatever their class, realizing that in unfreedom they are *solidaire*.

MAUDE ROYDEN, FEBRUARY 1914

A MEMBER'S VIEW OF THE GUILD

I can hardly gauge what the [Women's Cooperative] Guild has done for me. I feel it has affected me in so many different ways. There were certain latent sparks which it has kindled and caused to burn brightly. It has given me a much greater understanding of life and an immense feeling of sympathy with men and women in general. How our lives are linked together and each may work for a common good, though we may never see or speak to one another. I feel more and more what an immense power united action can be, and how the humblest may attain to it in its best form. I think that is one of the best features in the Guild.

'A LONDON GUILDSWOMAN', 1919
From Life as we have known it

WHAT WE WANT AND WHY

Like every other problem menacing to the well-being of the community, that of women's labour is anything but a simple one. It cannot be solved by the legal or trade union exclusion of women from industry, if that were possible. Neither can it be completely settled by raising the banner of equal pay for equal work. The ultimate ideal must surely be the payment for work, irrespective of sex, of such a wage as no man or woman would be afraid or ashamed to accept, and that this remuneration should be the same for men and for women doing the same work and doing it equally well.

ETHEL SNOWDEN, 1922

WHAT IS FEMINISM?

A leading article in the Woman's Leader

Everyone, it is to be supposed, will agree that the foundation of feminism is belief in women as human beings. A century ago such belief was a great act of faith. It could not be deduced from the broad aspect of society. It must have been built up from disconcerting gleams and instances from almost terrifying moments of insight. It was the perception that these curious creatures hampered throughout their lives by dozens of yards of cloth and dozens of rules for respectable female behaviour—that these weak, ignorant, garrulous, fanciful, submissive creatures were almost the opposite of what they seemed. All these qualities, which seemed so inherently feminine, must suddenly be regarded as merely the results of environment and training. Women were not born delicate for the benefit of doctors. Their way of living was unhealthy. They were not irremediably stupid, only untaught. They were fanciful because a narrow life forced them back upon ill-grounded imagination; garrulous because they were helpless, submissive, not on account of some indwelling glory of man, but because they were unselfish and timid. In short they were beings especially framed for liberty and fresh air, peculiarly bound to suffer if those were denied. It is easy enough to understand all this now. We can take it for granted and proceed to scrutinize more narrowly our definition of feminism. We can go on to agree that women and men should be made equal as citizens and before the law, and differ as to what we mean by that. If we say that no rights are to be denied to a woman because she is a woman, we part company not only with all those who think that there has been enough of this progress but with heavily burdened married men, and unenterprising wives, who view with dismay the competition of unencumbered, eager, diligent, and unfairly attractive young women. These people, however, would not call themselves feminists, so our definition remains unattacked. When we pass on to the corollary, that women should not be subject to restrictions merely because they are women, we are, if we push it far enough, at variance among ourselves. To one party it seems logical that because men do not bear children, the community has no right to regulate the conduct of a pregnant or newly-delivered mother. To the other party this does not seem to be a feminist issue at all, but merely a question of cruelty to children. If a man had an infant fastened to him by a chain and on the grounds that he was a free citizen he went for his usual swim before breakfast on a December morning, he would be found guilty of murder unless the doctors succeeded in getting him off on the score of insanity. This, however, and all the less extreme cases which flow from the fact that there is a physical difference between women and men are matters of interpretation or tactics, rather than of principle.

23 MARCH 1928

213

IN DEFENCE OF CHILDREN

Children like women and the proletariat are an oppressed class.

DORA RUSSELL, 1932

INTERVIEW WITH JESSIE McCULLOUGH

Jessie McCullough, a former Lucas factory worker, remembers the 1930s.

We were filing shock absorbers, weighing three or four pounds, standing up at a bench. It's rough work even when nobody's pushing you around.

One day I turned round and saw someone standing behind me while I was working. I asked them what they were doing and they said they were timing me. Why me and not her, I said, pointing to another woman. The fact was I've always worked quickly, and we were getting so much per gross, so that if you wanted to earn anything, you had to get a move on. You were lucky if you got 25 or 30 shillings. They obviously wanted to set the time by me and the others would have to keep up with it. Well, I had a talk with the girls about it and in the end they had us all in the office, offering us cups of tea and cigarettes. But the other girls just watched what I did and we all refused.

I decided to go to the union. The AEU wouldn't take in women, so I went to the Transport and General Workers', and got forms for the girls to join. Now unions were something new for them and they wouldn't go to the branch meeting unless I was with them. And when they went they found it very dull. The union officials were very lax and they used to look at me amazed when I brought in the application forms filled up. They just didn't believe women would join the union. But every week I took down more forms, and eventually we had a big meeting outside the gates and most of the girls joined. When the strike came, all the girls walked out.

[1971]. *From* Strike: A Live History, 1887–1971 (*Leeson*)

CHANGES IN PUBLIC LIFE

Now there is indeed a task for the women's movement—in my view, incomparably the greatest task still left to it—to give back to the disinherited family that share in the world's wealth which men have continued to filch from them; to assert the claims of the children to direct provision, preferably through allowances paid in cash to the mother; perhaps to some extent by communal provision in kind, such as that already received, imperfectly, in the one matter of education. . . .

Poverty is an old story, but it gets new listeners when it begins to be told not by sociologists and Labour agitators, but by agriculturists and manufacturers clamouring for new markets. The fact that the greatest of all causes of poverty and malnutrition—greater than all other causes put together—is the burden of child maintenance, is also an old story. I have been telling it myself for the past twenty years. But it acquires a new significance now that it is beginning to be realized that the children are the greatest unsatisfied market for consumable goods of the very kinds that are being over-produced. Plainly that market cannot be exploited if the poverty-stricken parent remains the only purchaser.

ELEANOR RATHBONE, 1936

HUMILIATION WITH HONOUR

One of the reforms most successfully carried through by a small minority was woman suffrage. There has been some confusion on this issue, since the First World War broke out before the effect of the suffragist propaganda was fully apparent. The gap between the demand for female suffrage, and the first partial acceptance of it in Britain in 1918, enabled the opponents of the feminist campaign to say that the vote was conceded to women as a reward for their part in winning the war. But in some countries, such as the United States, where woman suffrage was also granted at the end of the war, the amount of war service performed by women had been very small. The vote would never have been conceded had not a hard-working and articulate minority brought their claims, before the war, to a point where these appeared not only conceivable, but rational and just.

VERA BRITTAIN, 1942

IN A MAN'S WORLD:
THE ECLIPSE OF WOMAN

But what in effect is this State, on which we tend to rely more and more to play father and mother to its citizens? It is mechanical, bureaucratic, power-loving, sadistic, war-like, repressive. By its very nature, history and principles, it cannot deal constructively with human problems. It is founded on the principle of keeping order by force within the State and by force giving battle to enemies without. In accord with this concept, for instance, it seeks to deal with crime and juvenile delinquency by a great increase in the pay of the police, while insulting and underpaying the teaching and nursing profession. The tragedy of its traditional attitude in foreign affairs needs no emphasis.

Ultimately it is with this encroaching industrial State machine that women have been engaged in battle ever since they first sought emancipation. At first confused, they made for the vote. But events have made them aware that unless they emerge from their streamlined or dingy kitchens to demand much more, not only their families but all humanity may stand in great peril.

DORA RUSSELL, 1965

WOMEN: THE LONGEST REVOLUTION

Women are essential and irreplaceable; they cannot therefore be exploited in the same way as other social groups can. They are fundamental to the human condition, yet in their economic, social and political roles they are marginal. It is precisely this combination—fundamental and marginal at one and the same time—that has been fatal to them. Within the mould of men their position is comparable to that of an oppressed minority: but they also exist outside the world of men. The one state justifies the other and precludes protest. In advanced industrial society, women's work is only marginal to the total economy. Yet it is through work that man changes natural conditions and thereby produces society. Until there is a revolution in production, the labour situation will prescribe women's situation within the world of men. But women are offered a universe of their own: the family. Like woman herself, the family appears as a natural object, but it is actually a cultural creation. There is nothing inevitable about the form or role of the family any more than there is about the character or role of women. It is the function of ideology to present these given social types as aspects of Nature itself. Both can be exalted paradoxically, as ideals. The 'true' woman and the 'true' family are images of peace and plenty: in actuality they may both be sites of violence and despair.

JULIET MITCHELL, 1966
From New Left Review (*November–December 1966*)

MANIFESTO OF THE
WOMEN'S LIBERATION WORKSHOP

[The Women's Liberation Workshop] believes that women in our society are oppressed. We are economically oppressed: in jobs we do full work for half pay, in the home we do unpaid work full time. We are commercially exploited by advertisements, television and press; legally we often have only the status of children. We are brought up to feel inadequate, educated to narrower horizons than men. This is our specific oppression as women. It is as women that we are, therefore, organizing.

The Women's Liberation Workshop questions women's role and redefines the possibilities. It seeks to bring women to a full awareness of the meaning of their inferior status and to devise methods to change it. In society women and girls relate primarily to men; any organization duplicates this pattern: the men lead and dominate, the women follow and submit.

We close our meetings to men to break through this pattern, to establish our own leaderless groups and to meet each other over our common experience as women. If we admitted men there would be a tendency for them, by virtue of their experience, vested interests, and status in society, to dominate the organization. We want eventually to be, and to help other women to be, in charge of our own lives; therefore, we must be in charge of our own movement, directly, not by remote control. This means that not only those with experience in politics, but all, must learn to take their own decisions, both political and personal.

From Shrew *(November–December 1969)*

POEM

Mis-fit	*refuses to conform.*
Mis-conception	*demands free abortions for all women.*
Mis-fortune	*demands equal pay for all women.*
Mis-judged	*demands an end to beauty contests.*
Mis-directed	*demands equal opportunity.*
Mis-laid	*demands free contraception.*
Mis-governed	*demands liberation.*
Mis-used	*demands 24-hour child-care centres.*
Mis-placed	*demands a chance to get out of the house.*
Mis-treated	*demands shared housework.*
Mis-nomer	*demands a name of her own.*
Mis-quoted	*demands an unbiased press.*

ANON, 1969
From Shrew *(November–December 1969)*

WOMAN'S CONSCIOUSNESS, MAN'S WORLD

At one side we live in capitalism. To some extent we are forced to play along with the system in order to make life tolerable at all. We have to bargain within a particular historical situation and with opponents of flesh, blood and power. Equal pay is part of our bargain, more or less the least we expect within the system. We cannot afford the misconceived purity which does not go for immediate gains. But beyond just asking for more, if we are ever to end the spiralling whirlwind of simply economic inroads into the structure of capitalist society which are recouped by the political power of the ruling class, we need to develop notions of what an alternative society would be like. Similarly, the organization of women into trade unions is a necessary first step but women must also have control over union policy and make new forms of organizing which connect work and home. Simply because women have different expectations from men, simply because women have been kept out of certain areas of capitalism, they are well equipped to reach out to another form of social organization. They are able to see through some of the 'realities' men have come to regard as 'normal'. Capitalism itself has produced the contradictory need of being dependent on women's labour power in the home but in the process of its self-expansion seeking also to exploit women's labour in industry. It is up to us who want to transform the family and end the exploitation of all human beings to study carefully what is going on and use the knowledge we accumulate like a crowbar to crank open the tender and unprotected slits in Mr Moneybags's defences.

SHEILA ROWBOTHAM, 1973

GRUNWICK WOMEN

Jayaben Desai was one of the women workers at the Grunwick film-processing factory who went on strike for nearly two years for trade union recognition.

All this time I have been watching the strikes and I realized that the workers are the people who give their blood for the management and that they should have good conditions, good pay and should be well fed. The trade unions are the best thing here—they are not so powerful in other countries. They are a nice power and we should keep it on.

We didn't think about trade unions at Grunwick—they harass you so much there that you couldn't have any idea about joining a union.

This dispute is bringing us so many good things. Before the mass picketing began in June the issue was not so clear in our community, it was misty before. But now the Asian community sees what we are fighting for.

And before, the trade unions in this country were feeling that our community was not interested—that was always a gap in our community. But this will bring the distance nearer. We can all see the result—people coming here from all over the country and seeing us as part of the workers now.

In our community ladies are always obedient. So some had problems at the start. There was some bad feeling. But men know the women are always obedient, and in his heart a man knows he must not disturb a woman.

JAYABEN DESAI, 1977
From an interview in Spare Rib (*August 1977*)

MOVING BEYOND THE FRAGMENTS

We are not holding out the organization of the women's movement as a complete model on which the Left should base itself. But the women's movement has made an absolutely vital achievement—or at least the beginnings of it—which no socialist should ignore. It has effectively challenged, on a wide scale, the *self-subordination*, the acceptance of a secondary role, which underpins most forms of oppression and exploitation. This may not be confronting the state—though the women's movement does plenty of that—but unless such a self-subordination is rejected in the minds of men, of the unemployed, of blacks, gays, and all other groups to which socialists aim to give a lead, there will never be much chance of confronting the existing state with a democratic socialist alternative.

HILARY WAINWRIGHT, 1979

EDITORIAL

We believe that men as a group benefit from the oppression and exploitation of women as a group. We do not see women's oppression as secondary in importance to class or any other oppression; nor do we see it as produced by or maintained because of class or any other oppression. Although we recognize that women experience additional oppressions, particularly through race, ethnic origin, age, disability, class, and that these additional oppressions may benefit and be contributed to by women who do not share them, *all* women are oppressed *as women*.

Men oppress women, but not because of their (or our) biology—not because men are physically stronger, nor because men have phalluses and women may bear children and breast feed, nor because men are innately more aggressive. Neither is universal heterosexuality 'natural', but rather one of the institutions which organizes women's oppression.

We consider men oppress women because they benefit from doing so. All men, even those at the very bottom of male hierarchies, have advantages which flow from belonging to the category male. Even the men most sympathetic to women's liberation derive benefits from women's subordination. The social structure has been developed in such a way as to ensure that the collective and individual actions of men support and maintain them in power. We believe change can come about only through women's collective action, and we therefore do not see convincing men of the need for feminism to be a priority in our struggle against male supremacy.

We seek a movement of *all* women to overthrow male supremacy.

1983

From the first edition of Trouble and Strife (*Winter 1983*)

PART FIVE

VISIONS

. . . another and a better Kingdom come.
LOUIS MACNEICE, 1939

While most of the quotations reproduced in this volume arose directly from the experience of struggle, there has always been a special place reserved for the dreams and visions that have inspired people to lift their eyes beyond the miserable drudgery of their daily lives and to contemplate a new society in which they would be free. Such dreams have played an essential role in keeping the flames of hope burning, and thus maintaining the impetus for change at times when the immediate prospects were bleak, and the temptation to give up completely became almost irresistible.

The sources from which these visions came were many and various, ranging from the religious through the rational to the scientific. As we trace the imagery used, we can actually observe the emergence of a humanistic socialism as it grew out of the earlier pictures of a golden age devised by the Creator and still referred to today, by Christian socialists. Indeed the rich variety of the socialist heritage, derives, in part, from the fact that each strand can trace its own ancestry directly back to its source and is thus sustained by its own particular tradition. But there is also a great deal of common ground in the shared belief in high ethical standards whether deriving from God, or from the necessity of respecting the rights of humankind as the basis of any good society. The rejection of class oppression and the urge to put first things first so that basic needs can be met, are combined with the commitment to democracy as the main instrument for advance.

If it is true, as I believe it is, that the future lies with social-ism then our arguments are going to rotate around the various interpretations of what that socialism should be like, and here we have an introduction to some of the debates that lie ahead for us all.   TONY BENN

CORPUS CHRISTI SERMON

Preached to the assembled masses of the Peasants' Revolt, by John Ball, 1381.

> *Whan Adam dalf, and Eve span,*
> *Wo was thanne a gentilman?*

From the beginning all men were created equal by nature and ... servitude had been introduced by the unjust and evil oppression of men, against the will of God, who, if it had pleased Him to create serfs, surely in the beginning of the world would have appointed who should be a serf and who a lord. Let them consider, therefore, that He had now appointed the time wherein, laying aside the yoke of long servitude, they might, if they wished, enjoy their liberty so long desired. Wherefore they must be prudent, hastening to act after the manner of a good husbandman, tilling his field, and uprooting the tares that are accustomed to destroy the grain; first killing the great lords of the realm, then slaying the lawyers, justices and jurors, and finally rooting out everyone whom they knew to be harmful to the community in future. So at last they would obtain peace and security, if, when the great ones had been removed, they maintained among themselves equality of liberty and nobility, as well as of dignity and power.

From Thomas Walsingham, Historia Anglicana II

UTOPIA

[This is] the most accurate account I can give you of the Utopian Republic. To my mind, it's not only the best country in the world, but the only one that has any right to call itself a republic. Elsewhere, people are always talking about the public interest, but all they really care about is private property. In Utopia, where there's no private property, people take their duty to the public seriously. And both attitudes are perfectly reasonable. In other 'republics' practically everyone knows that, if he doesn't look out for himself, he'll starve to death, however prosperous his country may be. He's therefore compelled to give his own interests priority over those of the public; that is, of other people. But in Utopia, where everything's under public ownership, no one has any fear of going short, as long as the public storehouses are full. Everyone gets a fair share, so there are never any poor men or beggars. Nobody owns anything, but everyone is rich—for what greater wealth can there be than cheerfulness, peace of mind, and freedom from anxiety?

THOMAS MORE, 1516
Book II

REGAL TYRANNIE DISCOVERED

Pamphlet: 'A discourse shewing that all lawfull . . . instituted power by God amongst men is by common agreement and mutual consent'.

Power is originally inherent in the People, and it is nothing else but that might and vigour, which such and such a Society of men contains in itself, and when by such and such a Law of common consent and agreement, it is derived into such and such hands, God confirms the Law. And so man is the free and voluntary author, the Law is the instrument, and God is the establisher of both.

JOHN LILBURNE, 1647

THE TRUE LEVELLERS'
STANDARD ADVANCED

'The State of the Community opened, and presented to the Sons of Men: A Declaration to the Powers of England, and to all the Powers of the world, showing the cause why the Common People of England have begun, and gives Consent to dig up, manure and sow corn upon George Hill in Surrey, by those that have subscribed and thousands more that gives consent'.

In the beginning of Time, the great Creator Reason made the Earth to be a Common Treasury, to preserve Beasts, Birds, Fishes, and Man, the lord that was to govern this Creation; for Man had Domination given to him, over the Beasts, Birds, and Fishes; but not one word was spoken in the beginning, that one branch of mankind should rule over another.

And the Reason is this, Every single man, Male and Female, is a perfect Creature of himself; and the same Spirit that made the Globe, dwells in man to govern the Globe; so that the flesh of man being subject to Reason, his Maker, hath him to be his Teacher and Ruler within himself, therefore needs not run abroad after any Teacher and Ruler without him, for he needs not that any man should teach him, for the same Anointing that ruled in the Son of man, teacheth him all things.

GERARD WINSTANLEY *(and others)*, 1649

REFLECTIONS ON THE CASE OF MR WILKES, AND ON THE RIGHT OF THE PEOPLE TO ELECT THEIR OWN REPRESENTATIVES

John Wilkes, despite being duly elected as Member of Parliament for Middlesex by the voters, was prevented from taking his seat and declared ineligible because of his attacks on the King and the Tories.

That State is truly free, where the People are governed by Laws, which they have a Share in making, and to the Validity of which their Consent is essentially necessary. And that Country is absolutely and totally enslaved where one single Law can be made or repealed without the Interposition or Consent of the People.

JOHN WILKES, 1768

POLITICAL DISQUISITIONS

All lawful authority, legislative, and executive, originates from the people. Power in the people is like light in the Sun, native, original, inherent and unlimited by any thing human. In governors, it may be compared to the reflected light of the moon; for it is only borrowed, delegated, and limited by the intention of the people.

JAMES BURGH, 1774

LETTER TO THE PRINTER OF THE PUBLIC ADVERTISER

The identity of 'Junius' has yet to be discovered.

I would have the manners of the people purely and strictly republican. I do not mean the licentious spirit of anarchy and riot. I mean a general attachment to the common-weal, distinct from any partial attachment to persons or families; an implicit submission to the laws only, and an affection to the magistrate, proportioned to the integrity and wisdom with which he distributes justice to his people, and administers their affairs.

JUNIUS, OCTOBER 1777

THE RESTORER OF SOCIETY TO ITS NATURAL STATE

Societies, Families, and Tribes being originally nothing but Banditties they esteemed War and Pillage to be honourable, and the greatest Ruffians seize on the principal shares of the spoils as well of Land as Movables, introduced into the World all the curst varieties of Lordship, Vassalage, and Slavery as we see it at this Day.

Now Citizen, if we really want to get rid of these evils from amongst Men, we must destroy not only personal and hereditary Lordship, but the cause of them, which is Private Property in Land. For this is the Pillar that supports the Temple of Aristocracy. Take away this Pillar, and the whole Fabric of their Dominion falls to the ground. Then shall no other Lords have dominion over us, but the Laws, and Laws too of our own making; for at present it is those who have robbed us of our lands, that have robbed us also of the privilege of making our own Laws: so in truth and reality we are in bondage, and vassalage to the landed interest. Wherefore let us bear this always in mind, and we shall never be at a loss to know where the root of the Evil lies.

THOMAS SPENCE, 1801

JERUSALEM

And did those feet in ancient time
Walk upon England's mountains green?
And was the holy Lamb of God
On England's pleasant pastures seen?

And did the Countenance Divine
Shine forth upon our clouded hills?
And was Jerusalem builded here
Among these dark Satanic mills?

Bring me my bow of burning gold!
Bring me my arrows of desire!
Bring me my spear! O clouds, unfold!
Bring me my chariot of fire!

I will not cease from mental fight,
Nor shall my sword sleep in my hand
Till we have built Jerusalem
In England's green and pleasant land.

WILLIAM BLAKE, 1804

THE SPIRIT OF THE AGE

The spirit of the age is an irresistible power—unions will continue; more strikes and more blunders will succeed each other. However productive they may be of temporary mischief and misery, better associations shall be formed, and from the difficulties of the time the nation will learn. A new world will gradually unfold itself; the financial delusions and blunders which clog and shackle society will become evident to every one; a new kind of knowledge and of liberty will arise and spread itself, from that single reason that no remedy can be found in the old, worn-out basis of thought and action far too narrow for the mental fecundity and for the mechanical powers of the age now begun!

1834. *Leading article in the* Pioneer (*20 September 1834*)

HARD TIMES

'I am almost ashamed,' said Sissy, with reluctance. 'But today, for instance, Mr M'Choakumchild was explaining to us about Natural Prosperity.'

'National, I think it must have been,' observed Louisa.

'Yes, it was. But isn't it the same?' she timidly asked.

'You had better say, National, as he said so,' returned Louisa, with her dry reserve.

'National Prosperity. And he said, Now, this schoolroom is a Nation. And in this nation, there are fifty millions of money. Isn't this a prosperous nation? Girl number twenty, isn't this a prosperous nation, and a'n't you in a thriving state?'

'What did you say?' asked Louisa.

'Miss Louisa, I said I didn't know. I thought I couldn't know whether it was a prosperous nation or not, and whether I was in a thriving state or not, unless I knew who had got the money, and whether any of it was mine. But that had nothing to do with it. It was not in the figures at all,' said Sissy, wiping her eyes.

'That was a great mistake of yours,' observed Louisa.

CHARLES DICKENS, 1854

THE SONG OF THE WAGE SLAVE

The land it is the landlord's,
  The trader's is the sea,
The ore the usurer's coffer fills—
  But what remains for me?
The engine whirls for master's craft;
  The steel shines to defend,
With labour's arms, what labour raised,
  For labour's foes to spend.

The camp, the pulpit, and the law
  For rich men's sons are free;
Theirs, theirs the learning, art, and arms—
  But what remains for me?
    The coming hope, the future day,
      When wrong to right shall bow,
    And hearts that have the courage, man,
      To make that future now.

ERNEST JONES, 1856

THE FUNERAL OF KARL MARX

An immeasurable loss has been sustained both by the militant proletariat of Europe and America, and by historical science, in the death of this man. The gap that has been left by the death of this mighty spirit will soon enough make itself felt.

Just as Darwin discovered the law of evolution in organic nature, so Marx discovered the law of evolution in human history; he discovered the simple fact, hitherto concealed by an overgrowth of ideology, that mankind must first of all eat and drink, have shelter and clothing, before it can pursue politics, science, religion, art, etc.; and that therefore the production of the immediate material means of life and consequently the degree of economic development attained by a given people or during a given epoch, form the foundation upon which the forms of government, the legal conceptions, the art and even the religious ideas of the people concerned have been evolved, and in the light of which these things must therefore be explained, instead of vice versa as had hitherto been the case.

But that is not all. Marx also discovered the special law of motion governing the present-day capitalist method of production and the bourgeois society that this method of production has created. The discovery of surplus value suddenly threw light on the problem in trying to solve which all previous investigators, both bourgeois economists and socialist critics, had been groping in the dark....

Marx was before all else a revolutionary. His real mission in life was to contribute in one way or another to the overthrow of capitalist society and of the forms of government which it had brought into being, to contribute to the liberation of the present-day proletariat, which he was the first to make conscious of its own position and its needs, of the conditions under which it could win its freedom. Fighting was his element. And he fought with a passion, a tenacity and a success such as few could rival....

236

And consequently Marx was the best hated and most calumniated man of his times. Governments, both absolutist and republican, deported him from their territories. The bourgeoisie, whether conservative or extreme democrat, vied with one another in heaping slanders upon him. All this he brushed aside as though it were cobweb, ignoring them, answering only when necessity compelled him. And now he has died—beloved, revered and mourned by millions of revolutionary fellow workers—from the mines of Siberia to California, in all parts of Europe and America—and I make bold to say that though he may have many opponents he has hardly one personal enemy.

His name and his work will endure through the ages!

FREDERICK ENGELS, 17 MARCH 1883
Speech at Marx's graveside in Highgate Cemetery

ART, WEALTH AND RICHES

I will, with your leave, tell the chief things which I really want to see changed ... lest I should seem to have nothing to bid you to but destruction, the destruction of a system by some thought to have been made to last for ever. I want, then, all persons to be educated according to their capacity, not according to the amount of money which their parents happen to have. I want all persons to have manners and breeding according to their innate goodness and kindness, and not according to the amount of money which their parents happen to have. As a consequence of these two things I want to be able to talk to any of my countrymen in his own tongue freely, and feeling sure that he will be able to understand my thoughts according to his innate capacity;

and I also want to be able to sit at table with a person of any occupation without a feeling of awkwardness and constraint being present between us. I want no one to have any money except as due wages for work done; and, since I feel sure that those who do the most useful work will neither ask nor get the highest wages, I believe that this change will destroy that worship of a man for the sake of his money, which everybody admits is degrading, but which very few indeed can help sharing in. I want those who do the rough work of the world—sailors, miners, ploughmen, and the like—to be treated with consideration and respect, to be paid abundant money-wages, and to have plenty of leisure. I want modern science, which I believe to be capable of overcoming all material difficulties, to turn from such preposterous follies as the invention of anthracine colours and monster cannon to the invention of machines for performing such labour as is revolting and destructive of self-respect to the men who now have to do it by hand. I want handicraftsmen proper, that is, those who make wares, to be in such a position that they may be able to refuse to make foolish and useless wares, or to make the cheap and nasty wares which are the mainstay of competitive commerce, and are indeed slave-wares, made by and for slaves. And in order that the workmen may be in this position, I want division of labour restricted within reasonable limits, and men taught to think over their work and take pleasure in it. I also want the wasteful system of middlemen restricted, so that workmen may be brought into contact with the public, who will thus learn something about their work, and so be able to give them due reward of praise for excellence.

WILLIAM MORRIS, 1883

ENGLAND, ARISE!

England arise! the long night is over,
Faint in the east behold the dawn appear;
Out of your evil dream of toil and sorrow,
Arise, O England, for the day is here;
From your fields and hills,
Hark! the answer swells
Arise, O England, for the day is here.

By your young children's eyes so red with weeping,
By their white faces aged with want and fear,
By the dark cities where your babes are creeping
Naked of joy and all that makes life dear;
From each wretched slum
Let the loud cry come;
Arise, O England, for the day is here.

EDWARD CARPENTER, 1886

WHY I AM A SOCIALIST

Take two healthy week-old babies, one the child of a plough-man and the other the child of a duke; place them side by side, and the keenest eye will not be able to separate the aristocrat and the plebeian. But give to one the best education and to the other none, and place them side by side when each is grown to manhood, and the easy polished manner and soft speech of the one will be contrasted with the clumsy roughness and stumbling articulation of the other. Education, training, culture, these make class distinctions, and nothing can efface them save common education and equally refined life-surroundings. Such education and life-surroundings cannot be shared so long as some enjoy wealth

239

they do not earn, and others are deprived of the wealth they do earn. Land and capital must be made common property, and then no man will be in a position to enslave his brother by placing before him the alternative of starvation or servitude. And because no system save that of Socialism claims that there shall be no individual monopoly of that on which the whole nation must depend, of the soil on which it is born and must subsist, of the capital accumulated by the labour of its innumerable children, living and dead; because no system save that of Socialism claims for the whole community control of its land and its capital; because no system save that of Socialism declares that wealth created by associated workers should be shared among those workers, and that no idlers should have a lien upon it; because no system save that of Socialism makes industry really free and the worker really independent, by substituting co-operation among workers for employed and employing classes; because of all this I am a Socialist. My Socialism is based on the recognition of economic facts, on the study of the results which flow inevitably from the present economic system. The pauper and the millionaire are alike its legitimate children; the evil tree brings forth its evil fruits.

ANNIE BESANT, 1886
Pamphlet

AN ADDRESS

Miss Reddish, of Bolton, had left school at the age of 11 to become a weaver. She was a leading member of the Women's Co-operative Guild.

I believe that all the physical, social, and moral evils have their source for the most part in a bad economic and industrial system, and, therefore, I would have society and the industry of the kingdom established and worked on new lines—on the lines of true and universal Co-operation, or the

principle of equal efforts in producing and equal participation in results. I would have no superior recognized but
the superior in intelligence, morals, and honour, which
should be based on commendable service to all.... The
first and highest duty I would have taught in schools is the
sacred duty of each to labour for and promote the highest
good of society, and that of society to promote the highest
good of each individual comprising it.... When we have
used our best efforts to bring about this great and desired end
of universal Co-operation we shall feel that we have done
our duty to our fellows in the endeavour to realize the hopes
and wishes of the great founders of the Co-operative
movement, that poverty and idleness should disappear from
the land; that idleness should cease to revel in luxury and
labour pine in want; that vice should no longer glitter in the
palace and virtue droop in the hovel; that man's inhumanity
to man be a thing only of the past. Let us all do our best to
bring about that possible condition of life wherein virtue and
justice and love are with and for all, and the beautiful dream
of universal brotherhood shall become a lasting and grand
reality.

MISS REDDISH, 1889

PRECEPTS OF THE SOCIALIST
SUNDAY SCHOOL MOVEMENT

1 Love your schoolfellows, who will be your fellow
workmen in life.
2 Love Learning, which is the food of the mind; be as
grateful to your teacher as to your parents.
3 Make every day holy by good and useful deeds and kindly
actions.
4 Honour the good, be courteous to all, bow down to none.

5 Do not hate or speak evil of anyone. Do not be revengeful, but stand up for your rights and resist oppression.
6 Do not be cowardly. Be a friend to the weak, and love justice.
7 Remember that all the good things of the earth are produced by labour. Whoever enjoys them without working for them is stealing the bread of the workers.
8 Observe and think in order to discover the truth. Do not believe what is contrary to reason, and never deceive yourself or others.
9 Do not think that those who love their own country must hate and despise other nations, or wish for war, which is a remnant of barbarism.
10 Look forward to the day when all men and women will be free citizens of one fatherland, and live together as brothers and sisters in peace and righteousness.

1892

MERRIE ENGLAND

Socialists do not propose by a single Act of Parliament, nor by a sudden revolution, to put all men on an equality, and compel them to remain so. Socialism is not a wild dream of a happy land, where the apples will drop off the trees into our open mouths, the fish come out ot the rivers and fry themselves for dinner, and the looms turn out ready-made suits of velvet with gold buttons, without the trouble of coaling the engine. Neither is it a dream of a nation of stained-glass angels, who always love their neighbours better than themselves, and who never need to work unless they wish.

Socialism is a scientific scheme of national organization, entirely wise, just, and practical. It is a kind of national co-operation. Its programme consists, essentially, of one demand, that the land, and all other instruments of production and exchange, shall be the common property of the nation, and shall be used and managed by the nation for the nation.

ROBERT BLATCHFORD, 1894

SOCIALISM: THE ONLY WAY OUT

It is not claimed by Socialists that Socialism will solve all human ills. They know no quack cure, no panacea, no Morrison's pills for human sorrow. Ignorance, sickness, evil, will continue to exist, they are aware, under Socialism; although, they believe, in a diminished degree. But Socialists do believe that in the *principles* of Socialism lies the one way out of *our present main industrial woes.* Nor is this a narrow position. Socialism is not a single measure like the Single Tax or Co-operation, which are sometimes preached as economic panaceas. Socialism is a collection of principles including a thousand detailed acts. It is the ism that there is no ism. It is the appeal from sectarian reforms to the essential unity of society. Even as a philosophy too, it does not claim to be universal. It recognizes truth in Individualism, in Anarchism, in Paternalism, even in Capitalism; it simply holds that Socialism is the one social principle that industry most needs today.

W. D. P. BLISS, 1895

SPEECH IN THE HOUSE OF COMMONS

We are called upon to decide the question propounded in the Sermon on the Mount as to whether we will worship God or Mammon. The last has not been heard of this movement either in the House or in the country, for as surely as Radicalism democratized the system of Government politically in the last century, so will Socialism democratize the industrialism of the country in the coming century.

JAMES KEIR HARDIE, 1901

FROM SERFDOM TO SOCIALISM

This generation has grown up ignorant of the fact that Socialism is as old as the human race and has never been without its witness. Ere civilization dawned upon the world, primitive man was living his rude Communistic life, sharing all things in common with every member of his tribe or gens and bringing forth the rudiments of the emotional, the ethical and the artistic faculties. Later when the race lived in villages and ere yet towns or cities had been built, Man, the Communist, moved about among the communal flocks and herds on communal land. The peoples who have carved their names most deeply on the tables of human story all set out on their conquering career as Communists, and their downward path begins with the day when they finally turned away from it and began to gather personal possessions. Every popular movement of the past seven hundred years has been a Socialist movement at bottom. The peasants on the Continent of Europe were, as we have already seen, first fired to enter upon their Thirty Years' War by Communists; the Peasants' Revolt in England was led by a Communist; in the struggle

244

against the divine right of kings, which ended in the establishment of the Cromwellian Commonwealth, a strong Communist sect strove mightily to make Communism the policy of the new order. Liberty, Equality, Fraternity was the slogan which roused the people of France to their mighty effort for freedom. The towns which made great the name of Italy were communal, as were also the towns of England in the days of their power. When the old civilizations were putrefying, the still small voice of Jesus the Communist stole over the earth like a soft refreshing breeze carrying healing wherever it went.

JAMES KEIR HARDIE, 1907

NEW WORLDS FOR OLD

That Anarchist world, I admit, is our dream; we do believe—well, I, at any rate, believe this present world, this planet, will some day bear a race beyond our most exalted and temerarious dreams, a race begotten of our wills and the substance of our bodies, a race, so I have said it, 'who will stand upon the earth as one stands upon a footstool, and laugh and reach out their hands amidst the stars,' but the way to that is through education and discipline and law. Socialism is the preparation for that higher Anarchism; painfully, laboriously we mean to destroy false ideas of property and self, eliminate unjust laws and poisonous and hateful suggestions and prejudices, create a system of social right-dealing and a tradition of right-feeling and action. Socialism is the schoolroom of true and noble Anarchism, wherein by training and restraint we shall make free men.

H. G. WELLS, 1908

MANIFESTO OF CHRISTIAN MINISTERS

Our Socialism is not less earnest nor less complete because it is inspired by our Christianity. The central teaching of Socialism is a matter of economics, and may therefore be advocated by all men, whether they be Christians or unbelievers; yet we feel, as ministers of the Christian faith, that this economic doctrine is in perfect harmony with our faith, and we believe that its advocacy is sanctioned and indeed required of us, by the implications of our religion.

1908

NON-GOVERNMENTAL SOCIETY

With the dying out of fear and grinding anxiety and the undoing of the frightful tension which today characterizes all our lives, Society will spring back nearer to its normal form of mutual help. People will wake up with surprise, and rub their eyes to find that they are under no necessity of being other than human.

Simultaneously (i.e., with the lessening of the power of money as an engine of interest and profit-grinding) the huge nightmare which weighs on us today, the monstrous incubus of 'business'—with its endless Sisyphus labours, its searchings for markets, its displacement and destructions of rivals, its travellers, its advertisements, its armies of clerks, its banking and broking, its accounts and checking of accounts—will fade and lessen in importance; till some day perchance it will collapse, and roll off like a great burden to the ground! Freed from the great strain and waste which all this system creates, the body politic will recover like a man from a disease, and spring to unexpected powers of health.

EDWARD CARPENTER, 1911

THE MEANING OF SOCIALISM

Socialism, in truth, consists, when finally resolved, not in getting at all, but in giving; not in being served, but in serving; not in selfishness, but in unselfishness; not in the desire to gain a place of bliss in this world for one's self and one's family (that is the individualist and capitalist aim), but in the desire to create an earthly paradise for all. Its ultimate moral, as its original biological justification, lies in the principle, human and divine, that 'as we give, so we live', and only in so far as we are willing to lose life do we gain life.

Thus, once again, we see that fundamentally Socialism is a question of right human relationship and is essentially a spiritual principle.

Socialism, therefore, is religion—not that part of religion that relates to our beliefs concerning God, immortality, and the mystery of the unseen universe, but that part, the all-essential, practical part of it, that concerns the right state of our present lives, the right state of our relation to our fellows, the right moral health of our souls.

BRUCE GLASIER, 1919

SOCIALISM: CRITICAL AND CONSTRUCTIVE

Did Socialism only mean to put Labour in power so that grouped working-class interests could pursue the same self-regarding policy as capitalist interests have pursued, gloomy indeed would be the prospect. It is true that in the imperious conflicts which divide the workman from his employer in present-day Society, Socialism has to take sides with the forces that are making for the new Society; but it is above the conflicts in spirit, and it is steadily infusing into both sides the

247

creative desire to get beyond present divisions and reach a state in which all service will be done for communal ends by men who feel the community in their hearts and know that its wealth means their own wealth.

JAMES RAMSAY MACDONALD, 1921

THE ACQUISITIVE SOCIETY

'*He hath put down the mighty from their seat, and hath exalted the humble and meek.*' A society which is fortunate enough to possess so revolutionary a basis, a society whose Founder was executed as the enemy of law and order, need not seek to soften the materialism of principalities and powers with mild doses of piety administered in an apologetic whisper. It will teach as one having authority, and will have sufficient confidence in its Faith to believe that it requires neither artificial protection nor judicious understatement in order that such truth as there is in it may prevail. It will appeal to mankind, not because its standards are identical with those of the world, but because they are profoundly different. It will win its converts, not because membership involves no change in their manner of life, but because it involves a change so complete as to be ineffaceable.

R. H. TAWNEY, 1921

MY ENGLAND

I should hope in time to obliterate for good and all the class distinction in houses. I would have no West Ends and no East Ends. All people should obtain the housing accommodation and comfort now reserved for the few. Slum towns must be improved off the face of the earth. I would ask the House of Commons for power to set up a planning commission with authority to create new industrial areas with residential districts outside. With mechanical transport at its present state of development, there is no reason at all why workers should live where they work. No rich people do this. Why should those who produce wealth submit to doing so?

I visualize England, Scotland, and Wales as a carefully planned pattern of garden land, farm land, well-defined, and sharply limited industrial areas, and, in addition, huge tracts in the Highlands and Lake districts and elsewhere set apart for pleasure.

GEORGE LANSBURY, 1934

THE LABOUR PARTY IN PERSPECTIVE

The dominant issue of the twentieth century is socialism. Socialism is not the invention of an individual. It is essentially the outcome of economic and social conditions. The evils that capitalism brings differ in intensity in different countries but, the root cause of the trouble once discerned, the remedy is seen to be the same by thoughtful men and women. The cause is the private ownership of the means of life; the remedy is public ownership.

CLEMENT ATTLEE, 1937

Most are accepters, born and bred to harness,
  And take things as they come,
But some refusing harness and more who are refused it
  Would pray that another and a better Kingdom come.
Which now is sketched in the air or travestied in slogans
  Written in chalk or tar on stucco or plaster-board
But in time may find its body in men's bodies,
  Its law and order in their heart's accord,
Where skill will no longer languish nor energy be trammelled
  To competition and graft,
Exploited in subservience but not allegiance
  To an utterly lost and daft
System that gives a few at fancy prices
  Their fancy lives
While ninety-nine in the hundred who never attend the
  banquet
  Must wash the grease of ages off the knives.

LOUIS MACNEICE, 1939

THE LION AND THE UNICORN:
SOCIALISM AND THE ENGLISH GENIUS

The difference between Socialism and capitalism is not primarily a difference of technique. One cannot simply change from one system to the other as one might install a new piece of machinery in a factory, and then carry on as before, with the same people in positions of control. Obviously there is also needed a complete shift of power. New blood, new men, new ideas—in the true sense of the word, a revolution. . . .

It is only by revolution that the native genius of the English people can be set free. Revolution does not mean red flags and street fighting, it means a fundamental shift of power. Whether it happens with or without bloodshed is largely an accident of time and place. . . . What is wanted is a conscious open revolt by ordinary people against inefficiency, class privilege and the rule of the old. It is not primarily a question of change of government. British governments do, broadly speaking, represent the will of the people, and if we alter our structure from below we shall get the government we need. Ambassadors, generals, officials and colonial administrators who are senile or pro-Fascist are more dangerous than Cabinet ministers whose follies have to be committed in public. Right through our national life we have got to fight against privilege, against the notion that a half-witted public-schoolboy is better fitted for command than an intelligent mechanic. Although there are gifted and honest *individuals* among them, we have got to break the grip of the moneyed class as a whole. England has got to assume its real shape. The England that is only just beneath the surface, in the factories and the newspaper offices, in the aeroplanes and the submarines, has got to take charge of its own destiny. . . .

An English Socialist government will transform the nation from top to bottom, but it will still bear all over it the unmistakable marks of our own civilization. . . .

It will not be doctrinaire, nor even logical. It will abolish the House of Lords, but quite probably will not abolish the Monarchy. It will leave anachronisms and loose ends everywhere, the judge in his ridiculous horsehair wig and the lion and the unicorn on the soldier's cap-buttons. It will not set up any explicit class dictatorship. It will group itself round the old Labour Party and its mass following will be in the trade unions, but it will draw into it most of the middle class and many of the younger sons of the bourgeoisie. Most of its directing brains will come from the new indeterminate class of skilled workers, technical experts, airmen, scientists, architects and journalists, the people who feel at home in the radio and ferro-concrete age. But it will never lose touch

251

with the tradition of compromise and the belief in a law that is above the State. It will shoot traitors, but it will give them a solemn trial beforehand and occasionally it will acquit them. It will crush any open revolt promptly and cruelly, but it will interfere very little with the spoken and written word. Political parties with different names will still exist, revolutionary sects will still be publishing their newspapers and making as little impression as ever. It will disestablish the Church, but will not persecute religion. It will retain a vague reverence for the Christian moral code, and from time to time will refer to England as 'a Christian country'. The Catholic Church will war against it, but the Nonconformist sects and the bulk of the Anglican Church will be able to come to terms with it. It will show a power of assimilating the past which will shock foreign observers and sometimes make them doubt whether any revolution has happened.

But all the same it will have done the essential thing. It will have nationalized industry, scaled down incomes, set up a classless educational system. Its real nature will be apparent from the hatred which the surviving rich men of the world will feel for it. It will aim not at disintegrating the Empire but at turning it into a federation of Socialist states, freed not so much from the British flag as from the money-lender, the dividend-drawer and the wooden-headed British official.

GEORGE ORWELL, 1941

INSIDE THE LEFT

The Socialist ideal expresses fraternity, service, mutual trust, truthfulness, liberty, respect for personality. The true Socialist strives to live according to this social code, and everything within the present system which prevents him doing so serves only to stimulate him to devote his energies to the cause of Socialism. One thought remains in my mind from all the thousands of forgotten words which I read during my twenty-eight months in prison. Plato wrote in his *Republic* that the man who really sees a vision of a better world becomes at that moment a citizen of that world. The inner loyalty of a man whose personality has been captured by the ideal of Socialism influences him to live honestly and fraternally towards others.

Of course, so long as we have the system of Capitalism, with its class divisions and antagonistic sectional interests, the ideal of conduct in a Socialist society is not attainable. A Socialist may be philosophic enough to understand that the members of the possessing class are as much the creatures of their environment as are workers and feel no enmity towards them as persons; nevertheless, he will devote himself to the class struggle, participate with all his energy against Capitalists in strikes and lockouts, and, if need be, defend the cause of the Socialist revolution by arms against those who attempt to destroy it. He will do this because he sees that the overthrow of the class ownership of what is necessary for all must be carried through before a classless co-operative society can be established.

As they carry on this class struggle, however, Socialists who are true to their ideal will be honest, disinterested, generous-spirited. Leaders worthy of the name will be so much citizens of the Socialist world that they will feel alien to the values of the Capitalist world. They will be indifferent to wealth, they will not be tempted by careerism. Few leaders have attained this standard, but the lives of those who have are among the inspirations of the movement. And everyone who has experience of the working-class struggle of this and other countries has met many men and women, generally simple workers, unknown outside a small circle, whose way of life is a continual inspiration. They have lived entirely for the Cause, undergoing victimization, careless of material gain or social status, devoting their 'leisure hours' to unrecognized routine tasks, striving to gain the knowledge which will help them to be more useful Socialists, and all the time breathing a spirit of comradeship and acting with an uprightness towards their fellows which commands affection and respect. These men and women are the salt of the Movement. When one meets them the conviction is renewed that the ideal is attainable.

FENNER BROCKWAY, 1942

CAN WE MAKE THE LABOUR PARTY A SOCIALIST PARTY?

Men and women have come to realize the old system has had its day; we may be said to be living in an era similar to when Cromwell laid the foundations of a New Britain. We are looking for something new, and that planned something may not be democratic. This is the tragic danger we have to confront. It is our job to see that it is not a few powerful organizations who will offer the masses a new kind of feudal industrialism. The time has come when we must make a planned democracy for all people.

HAROLD LASKI, 1944

SOCIALISM AND THE WELFARE STATE

The peculiar—and I think unique—quality of British Socialism is that it contains in it a greater faith in the power of the
individual and group to fashion its own destinies within the
Socialist structure. There is nothing written in history, for
instance, to show that if the State takes over the means of distribution, production and exchange then the administration
must be completely centralized. On the contrary: we need
small units of administration with local 'participation' to the
utmost within a general, central framework. The alternative,
as a Frenchman said, is 'apoplexy at the centre and anaemia
at the extremities'. The Welfare State, which involves far
more attention to the private lives of citizens than the
Englishman has been accustomed to relish, can nevertheless
be compatible with the rights of free speech, personal and
civil freedom. It is because British Labour has maintained
this conception—and to some extent put it into practice—
that one meets all over the world today anxious people who
will tell you that they fear both Soviet Communism and the
American way of life. Their hopes, they say, hang on the
survival and development of the British Welfare State. They
fear that it too may become too centralized, that the acqui-
sition of the new social and economic rights may be allowed
to endanger the personal and civil ones. The answer to these
questions is not to be found in Marx, who dealt only with the
structure of society, and who knew what modern Communists are apt to deny—that the superstructure is not
mechanically determined. Within the limits of the structure,
the superstructure depends on our wills. I remember years
ago asking Tawney how he conceived Socialism. He replied,
'A society in which everyone can say "Go to hell" to
everyone else, but no one wants to.'

KINGSLEY MARTIN, 1951
A lecture to the Fabian Society

SPEECH AT THE LABOUR PARTY CONFERENCE

This was Aneurin Bevan's last speech.

I have enough faith in my fellow creatures in Great Britain to believe that when they have got over the delirium of the television, when they realize that their new homes that they have been put into are mortgaged to the hilt, when they realize that the money-lender has been elevated to the highest position in the land, when they realize that the refinements to which they should look are not there, when the years go by and they see the challenge of modern society not being met by the Tories, who can consolidate their political powers only on the basis of national mediocrity, who are unable to exploit the resources of their scientists because they are prevented by the greed of their capitalism from doing so, when they realize that the flower of our youth goes abroad today because they are not being given opportunities of using their skill and their knowledge properly at home, when they realize that all the tides of history are flowing in our direction: then, when we say it and mean it, then we shall lead our people to where they deserve to be led.

ANEURIN BEVAN, 1959

SPEECH AT BIRMINGHAM TOWN HALL

We are living in the jet age but we are governed by an Edwardian establishment mentality. Over the British people lies the chill frost of Tory leadership. They freeze initiative and petrify imagination. They cling to privilege and power for the few, shutting the gates on the many. Tory society is a *closed* society, in which birth and wealth have priority, in

256

which the master-and-servant, landlord-and-tenant mentality is predominant. The Tories have proved that they are incapable of mobilizing Britain to take full advantage of the scientific breakthrough. Their approach and methods are fifty years out of date.

Labour wants to mobilize the entire nation in the nation's business. It wants to create government of the whole people by the whole people. Labour will replace the closed, exclusive society by an open society in which all have an opportunity to work and serve, in which brains will take precedence over blue blood, and craftsmanship will be more important than caste. Labour wants to streamline our institutions, modernize methods of government, bring the entire nation into a working partnership with the state....

This is the time for a breakthrough to an exciting and wonderful period in our history, in which all can and must take part. Our young men and women, especially, have in their hands the power to change the world. We want the youth of Britain to storm the new frontiers of knowledge, to bring back to Britain that surging adventurous self-confidence and sturdy self-respect which the Tories have almost submerged by their apathy and cynicism.

HAROLD WILSON, 19 JANUARY 1964
Published in The New Britain

NOTES FROM A STUDENT

In the six weeks of the Hornsey Revolution I had more education than I had ever previously experienced. A new sort of freedom emerged, a freedom to work, learn and develop. A new surge of life. The network system we developed was flexible and humane. We evolved a dynamic house of our own design. A direct democracy where people were informed and given time to make their decisions, good organization without the dysfunctions of bureaucracy, a new language, and primarily control over our own education, our own lives. We had freedom to express ourselves creatively and yet end our isolation from the world, the helplessness of the individual was at an end, we began to realize that art was revolutionary but our aims remained educational.

A HORNSEY ART COLLEGE STUDENT, 1968
From Revelations, *the students' paper published during the student unrest at Hornsey*

ADJUSTING THE BALANCE

Our first and prime objective is to bring about a fundamental and irreversible shift in the balance of power in favour of working people and their families.

TONY BENN, 1973

AN OPEN LETTER TO LESZEK KOLAKOWSKI

My own utopia, two hundred years ahead, would not be like Morris's 'epoch of rest'. It would be a world (as D. H. Lawrence would have it) where the 'money values' give way before the 'life values', or (as Blake would have it) 'corporeal' will give way to 'mental' war. With sources of power easily available, some men and women might choose to live in unified communities, sited, like Cistercian monasteries, in centres of great natural beauty, where agricultural, industrial and intellectual pursuits might be combined. Others

258

might prefer the variety and pace of an urban life which re-discovers some of the qualities of the city-state. Others will prefer a life of seclusion, and many will pass between all three. Scholars would follow the disputes of different schools, in Paris, Jakarta or Bogota. . . .

But one stirs uneasily within such dreams. The utopian imagination today has been diverted into the realm of space-fiction, whose authors examine, exactly, what societies might be created if social consciousness could impose itself upon social being. Their imaginings are not always comfort-ing. Nothing will 'happen' of its own accord, without conflict and without the assertion of choice. . . .

To be a Utopian in 1973 is to be written off, in most 'reput-able' quarters, as a romantic and a fool. But perhaps to fall into a 'realism' which is derivative from an obsession with men's evil propensities is only the symptom of an inverted or depressive romanticism. For to lose faith in man's reason and in his capacity to act as a moral agent is to disarm him in the face of 'circumstances'. And circumstances, mounted on man's evil will, have more than once in the past decades seemed likely to kill us all. It is the utopian nerve of failure, to which you were once a most eloquent witness, that we must still nourish.

E. P. THOMPSON, 1973

SPEECH AT THE LABOUR PARTY CONFERENCE

Socialism [is] the deliberate organization of all of the re-sources of humankind by all of the talents of humankind. That is the definition of Socialism—productive, systematic, liberating Socialism.

NEIL KINNOCK, 2 OCTOBER 1983
after his election as leader

PART SIX

PEACE AND INTERNATIONALISM

the natural bond / Of brotherhood . . .
WILLIAM COWPER, 1785

Of all the themes running through this book the insistent demand for peace must strike the deepest chord with us today. As we read some of the speeches made by conscientious objectors appearing before tribunals, or by others hauled before the courts accused of sedition, we can find early statements that reveal a yearning for an end to bloodshed, and a deep hatred for war and the militarism it encourages. As recently as 1982, we hear the moving words of a Greenham Common woman sentenced by the Magistrates.

There are denunciations of hypocrisy reserved for those who preach the gospel of Jesus and yet support the use of force, and of others who argue for a foreign policy based on the idea that we should always aim to maintain a balance of power. But this is not just a collection of pacifist declarations, and as we reach more modern times the idea of internationalism and the need for solidarity to express it surface most strongly and come together with anti-imperialism and opposition to the doctrines of fascism. Towards the very end of the book the warnings about re-armament acquire a note of even greater urgency with the development of nuclear weapons and the real possibility that they might be used in war.

The Peace Movement is now immensely strong in Britain, and this final section should help us to understand its roots. It is not the creation of a little band of defence experts who have a preference for conventional, rather than atomic, weapons nor is it a new movement born out of the Aldermaston marches. The Peace Movement is, in fact, a very old and very broad movement. It embraces the needs of all peoples everywhere, espousing their aspirations for an international order that would replace nationalism to meet the needs of the Third World, and lifting the threat of obliteration from the superpowers and their client states—of which Britain is now one.

These affirmations of internationalism bring this anthology to a close. They also provide a bridge that we must cross if we are to reach those, in other countries, whose own radical and revolutionary traditions we shall need to understand if the peace we desire is ever to be built.

TONY BENN

IN PRAISE OF PEACE

Peace is the chief of all the worldès wealth,
  And to the heaven it leadeth eke the way;
Peace is of man's soul and life the health,
  And doth with pestilence and war away.
  My liegè lord, take heed of what I say,
If war may be left off, take peace on hand,
Which may not be unless God doth it send.

With peace may every creature dwell at rest;
  Withoutè peace there may no life be glad;
Above all other good peace is the best;
  Peace hath himself when war is all bestead;
  Peace is secure, war ever is adread;
Peace is of all charity the key,
That hath the life and soulè for to weigh.

For honour vain, or for the worldès good,
  They that aforetimes the strong battles made,
Where be they now?—bethink well in thy mood!
  The day is gone, the night is dark and fade,
  Their cruelty which then did make them glad,
They sorrow now, and yet have nought the more;
The blood is shed, which no man may restore.

War is the mother of the wrongès all;
  It slayeth the priest in holy church at mass,
Forliths[1] the maid, and doth her flower to fall;
  The war maketh the great city less,
  And doth the law its rules to overpass,
There is no thing whereof mischief may grow,
Which is not caused by the war, I trow.

JOHN GOWER, 1399
To Henry IV

THE FURIES

War is the mistress of enormity,
Mother of mischief, monster of deformity;
Laws, manners, arts she breaks, she mars, she chases,
Blood, tears, bowers, towers, she spills, smites, burns, and
*   razes.*
Her brazen teeth shake all the earth asunder:
Her mouth a firebrand, and her voice a thunder,
Her looks are lightning, every glance a flash,
Her fingers guns that all to powder smash;
Fear and despair, flight and disorder, post
With hasty march before her murderous host.
As burning, waste, rape, wrong, impiety,
Rage, ruin, discord, horror, cruelty,
Sack, sacrilege, impunity and pride are still stern consorts by
*   her barbarous side;*
And poverty, sorrow, and desolation
Follow her armies' bloody transmigration.

JOSHUA SYLVESTER, 1598 [?]

THE TEMPEST

CALIBAN: *This island's mine, by Sycorax my mother,*
Which thou tak'st from me. When thou cam'st
*   first,*
Thou strok'st me, and made much of me; wouldst
*   give me*
Water with berries in 't; and teach me how
To name the bigger light, and how the less,
That burn by day and night: and then I lov'd thee,
And show'd thee all the qualities o'th' isle,
The fresh springs, brine-pits, barren place and
*   fertile:*
Curs'd be I that did so! All the charms
Of Sycorax, toads, beetles, bats, light on you!
For I am all the subjects that you have,
Which first was mine own King: and here you sty
*   me*
In this hard rock, whiles you do keep from me
The rest o'th' island.

WILLIAM SHAKESPEARE, 1613
Act I scene 2

THE BLOODY PROJECT

In all undertakings, which may occasion war or bloodshed, men have great need to be sure that their cause be right, both in respect of themselves and others: for if they kill men themselves, or cause others to kill, without a just cause, and upon the extremest necessity, they not only disturb the peace of men, and families, and bring misery and poverty upon a Nation, but are indeed absolute murderers.

WILLIAM WALWYN, AUGUST 1648

JOURNAL

The keeper of the house of correction was commanded to bring me before the commissioners and soldiers in the market-place; and there they offered me that preferment, as they called it, asking me, if I would not take up arms for the Commonwealth against Charles Stuart? I told them, I knew from whence all wars arose, even from lust, according to James's doctrine; and that I lived in the virtue of that life and power that took away the occasion of all wars. But they courted me to accept their offer, and thought I did but compliment them. But I told them, I was come into the covenant of peace, which was before wars and strife were. They said, they offered it in love and kindness to me, because of my virtue; and such like flattering words they used. But I told them, if that was their love and kindness, I trampled it under my feet. Then their rage got up, and they said, 'Take him away, gaoler, and put him into the dungeon amongst the rogues and felons.' So I was had away and put into a lousy, stinking place, without any bed, amongst thirty felons, where I was kept almost half a year. . . .

All that pretend to fight for Christ are deceived; for his kingdom is not of this world, therefore his servants do not fight. Fighters are not of Christ's kingdom, but are without Christ's kingdom; his kingdom starts in peace and righteousness, but fighters are in the lust; and all that would destroy men's lives, are not of Christ's mind, who came to save men's lives.

GEORGE FOX, 1654

PARADISE REGAINED

They err who count it glorious to subdue
By conquest far and wide, to overrun
Large countries, and in field great battles win,
Great cities by assault. What do these worthies
But rob and spoil, burn, slaughter, and enslave
Peaceable nations, neighbouring or remote,
Made captive, yet deserving freedom more
Than those their conquerors, who leave behind
Nothing but ruin wheresoe'er they rove,
And all the flourishing works of peace destroy;
Then swell with pride, and must be titled Gods,
Great Benefactors of mankind, Deliverers,
Worshipped with temple, priest, and sacrifice?
One is the son of Jove, of Mars the other;
Till conqueror Death discover them scarce men,
Rolling in brutish vices, and deformed,
Violent or shameful death their due reward.
But, if there be in glory aught of good,
It may by means far different be attained,
Without ambition, war, or violence—
By deeds of peace, by wisdom eminent,
By patience, temperance.

JOHN MILTON, 1667
Book III, lines 71–93

AN EPISTLE OF LOVE AND FRIENDLY ADVICE

'*To the ambassadors of the several princes of Europe met at Nimeguen, to consult the peace of Christendom....*'

The chief ground, cause and root then of all this misery among all these called Christians, is because they are only

such in *Name*, and not in *Nature*, having only a form and profession of Christianity in show and words, but are still
strangers, yea and enemies to the life and virtue of it. . . .
They sheath their swords in one another's bowels, ruin,
waste and destroy whole Countries, expose to the greatest
misery many thousand Families, make thousands of
Widows, and ten thousands of Orphans, cause the banks to
overflow with the blood of those for whom the Lord Jesus
Christ shed his precious blood, spend and destroy many of
the good creatures of God: And all this while they pretend to
be followers of the Lamblike Jesus, who came not to destroy
men's lives, but to save them. . . .

ROBERT BARCLAY, 1677

QUESTIONS TO A CONSCIENTIOUS
· OBJECTOR

'The account of PHILIP FORD's *being summoned to appear
before the Lieutenancy at Guildhall . . . where Sir Thomas
Davies was chairman, with queries proposed and answers
thereto'.*

QUESTIONER: Complaint is made that you appeared not with
your arms according to summons.
PHILIP FORD: Here's a summons dated the 7th of February last
which I received.
QUESTIONER: Received you not one before?
FORD: Yes.
QUESTIONER: Wherefore did you not then appear?
FORD: Before the first summons came I received a summons
from the Prince of Peace to march under his banner,
which is love, who came not to destroy men's lives but to
save them. And being listed under this banner I dare not
desert my colours to march under the banner—shop—of
the kings of the earth. . . .

QUESTIONER: Do not you believe a man may be killed with an halbert?

FORD: I make a distinction betwixt the military power and the civil. The military power's command is, Go, fire, kill and destroy. The civil power's command is, Go, keep the peace.

QUESTIONER: The military power is not so.

FORD: Be pleased to read your commission.

(It was read, the substance being to exercise the soldiers and be subject to superior officers, and they to the King, etc.)

Be pleased to take notice, you are first to exercise the soldiers and make them expert to kill one another. Then when the word of command is given, Go charge, horse, foot, cannon, fire, kill and destroy, you must be subject to superior officers, and so fall on and deface the workmanship of God.

QUESTIONER: You must be subject to the King's laws.

FORD: I am so. All laws being fulfilled by active or passive obedience. And that which for conscience' sake I cannot comply with I shall endeavour patiently to undergo the penalty.

QUESTIONER: Then fine him five pounds a time.

JANUARY 1679

DEATH

One *Murder made a Villain,*
Millions *a Hero. Princes were privileg'd*
To kill, and numbers sanctified the crime.
Ah! why will Kings forget that they are Men?
And Men that they are brethren? Why delight
In human sacrifice? Why burst the ties
Of Nature, that should knit their souls together
In one soft bond of amity and love?

271

Yet still they breathe destruction, still go on
Inhumanly ingenious to find out
New pains for life, new terrors for the grave,
Artificers of Death! Still Monarchs dream
Of universal Empire growing up
From universal ruin. Blast the design,
Great God of Hosts, nor let thy creatures fall
Unpitied victims at Ambition's shrine!
DR BEILBY PORTEUS (*Bishop of London*), 1772

JAMES HASTIE,
A CONSCIENTIOUS OBJECTOR

While James Hastie was serving as corporal in the army, he decided he could no longer participate in military life. This account is taken from the diary of Mary Shackleton, a young Quaker.

He now resolved upon his sacrifice and instead of going to parade, stayed in his barrack room. The sergeant came to see what was the reason, and said he must acquaint the colonel. James said he would have him do so. The colonel ordered him to the guard-house, and had him tried by a court-martial. They said he was mad ... they sent him away to the black hole, denied him pen and ink, and to see his friends, but had him again and sentenced him to receive two hundred lashes which was executed with a whip of small cords, laid on with the strength of a man, and a fresh man every twenty-five strokes. But he was enabled to rejoice in his sufferings. The soldiers brought him his clothes, washed his back with milk and water, applied dock leaves to it, and wept over him. He bid them not to weep for him, but for themselves. The soldiers' wives came to him with jugs of tea, and bread and butter, but though he accepted their kindness he refused their refreshment.

MARY SHACKLETON, 1782

THE TIMEPIECE

There is no flesh in man's obdurate heart—
It does not feel for man; the natural bond
Of brotherhood is severed as the flax
That falls asunder at the touch of fire.
He finds a fellow guilty of a skin
Not coloured like his own, and having power
To enforce the wrong, for such a worthy cause
Dooms and devotes him as his lawful prey.
Lands intersected by a narrow frith
Abhor each other. Mountains interposed
Make enemies of nations who had else
Like kindred drops been mingled into one.
Thus man devotes his brother, and destroys;
And worse than all, and most to be deplored,
As human nature's broadest, foulest blot,
Chains him, and tasks him, and exacts the sweat
With stripes that Mercy, with a bleeding heart,
Weeps when she sees inflicted on a beast.

WILLIAM COWPER, 1785
Thc Task, *Book II*

A PLAN FOR AN
UNIVERSAL AND PERPETUAL PEACE

Hitherto war has been the national rage; peace has always come too soon, war too late. To tie up the Ministers' hands and make them continually accountable would be depriving them of numberless occasions of seizing the happy advantages that lead to war; it would be lessening people's chance of their favourite amusement.

JEREMY BENTHAM, 1786–9

THE RIGHTS OF MAN

Whatever is the cause of taxes to a Nation becomes also the means of revenue to a Government. Every war terminates with an addition of taxes, and consequently with an addition of revenue; and in any event of war, in the manner they are now commenced and concluded, the power and interest of Governments are increased. War, therefore, from its productiveness, as it easily furnishes the pretence of necessity for taxes and appointments to places and offices, becomes a principal part of the system of old Governments; and to establish any mode to abolish war, however advantageous it might be to Nations, would be to take from such Government the most lucrative of its branches. The frivolous matters upon which war is made show the disposition and avidity of Governments to uphold the system of war, and betray the motives upon which they act.

TOM PAINE, 1791–2
Part II

POLITICAL JUSTICE

Society was instituted, not for the sake of glory, not to furnish splendid materials for the page of history, but for the benefit of its members. The love of our country, if we would speak accurately, is another of those specious illusions, which have been invented by impostors in order to render the multitude the blind instruments of their crooked designs. . . .

We can have no adequate idea of this evil [war], unless we visit, at least in imagination, a field of battle. Here men deliberately destroy each other by thousands without any resentment against or even knowledge of each other. The plain is strewed with death in all its various forms. Anguish and wounds display the diversified modes in which they can torment the human frame. Towns are burned, ships are blown up in the air while the mangled limbs descend on every side, the fields are laid desolate, the wives of the inhabitants exposed to brutal insult, and their children driven forth to hunger and nakedness. It would be despicable to mention, along with these scenes of horror, and the total subversion of all ideas of moral justice they must occasion in the auditors and spectators, the immense treasures which are wrung in the form of taxes from those inhabitants whose residence is at a distance from the scene.

WILLIAM GODWIN, 1793
Volume II, book V

FEARS IN SOLITUDE

Secure from actual warfare, we have loved
To swell the war-whoop, passionate for war!
Alas! for ages ignorant of all
Its ghastlier workings (famine or blue plague,
Battle, or siege, or flight through wintry snows),
We, this whole people, have been clamorous
For war and bloodshed; animating sports
The which we pay for as a thing to talk of,
Spectators and not combatants! No guess
Anticipative of a wrong unfelt,
No speculation on contingency,
However dim and vague, too vague and dim
To yield a justifying cause; and forth,
(Stuffed out with big preamble, holy names,
And adjurations to the God in Heaven),
We send out mandates for the certain death
Of thousands and ten thousands! Boys and girls,
And women, that would groan to see a child
Pull off an insect's leg, all roar for war,
The best amusement for our morning meal!

As if a soldier died without a wound;
As if the fibres of this godlike frame
Were gored without a pang; as if the wretch,
Who fell in battle, doing bloody deeds,
Passed off to Heaven, translated and not killed;
As though he had no wife to pine for him,
No God to judge him!

SAMUEL TAYLOR COLERIDGE, 1798

THE EFFECTS OF CIVILIZATION
ON THE PEOPLE IN EUROPEAN STATES

It is to be feared that these wars, of which the poor bear the burden, and in which millions of them lose their limbs, their health, and their lives, are often entered into for the express purpose of increasing their subjection and oppression, and making them the instruments of it. It is highly probable, for instance, that wars have been concerted privately, and undertaken by neighbouring kings, for the sole purpose of gaining a pretence for increasing their forces and keeping up a larger standing army; the chief view in augmenting which was to keep their own people in closer subjection, and lay and enforce farther restraints and impositions upon them.... Whereas, were the people themselves, who bear the burden of the war, and who would gain no object, but suffer great loss, whatever the success might be, to be the persons by whom it was to be determined whether there should be war or peace, we should have few wars.

CHARLES HALL, 1805

AN ENQUIRY INTO THE ACCORDANCY OF WAR WITH THE PRINCIPLES OF CHRISTANITY

If we had a right to kill a man in self-defence, very few wars would be shown to be lawful. Of the wars which are prosecuted, some are simply wars of aggression; some are for the maintenance of a balance of power; some are in assertion of technical rights; and some, undoubtedly, to repel invasion. The last are perhaps the fewest; and of these only it can be said that they bear any analogy whatever to the case which is supposed; and even in these, the analogy is seldom complete. It has rarely indeed happened that wars have been undertaken simply for the preservation of life, and that no other alternative has remained to a people, than to kill, or to be killed. And let it be remembered, that *unless this alternative alone remains*, the case of individual self-defence is irrelevant.

JONATHAN DYMOND, 1823

THE AGE OF BRONZE

Alas the country! how shall tongue or pen
Bewail her now un*country gentlemen?*
The last to bid the cry of warfare to cease,
The first to make a malady of peace.
For what were all these country patriots born?
To hunt, and vote, and raise the price of corn?
But corn, like every mortal thing, must fall,
Kings, conquerors, and markets most of all.

LORD BYRON, 1823

TO THE PEOPLE OF CANADA

An address from the London Working Men's Association

WE ASSERT

That your petitioners are deeply impressed with the conviction that the colonial policy of England has for many centuries past been fraught with tyranny and injustice towards the mass of the people.

That by far the greater number of our colonies have been originated by means no-ways justifiable on principles of morality; and to establish and secure which have millions of money been wasted, and millions of our brethren been doomed to an untimely end.

That when by their sacrifices they have been secured, instead of regarding them as auxiliaries to the progress of civilization, and teaching them the most efficient means of developing their natural resources so as to promote the general welfare of humanity, we seem to have considered them as legitimate objects of our prey, or as places where the shoots and underlings of despotism might practise their oppression, shameless and regardless of consequences.

Drafted by WILLIAM LOVETT, 1837

SPEECH AT HIS COURT MARTIAL

William Dyne was a drummer in the marines. He was court-martialled for refusing to wear a sword.

I am well aware that, in thus refusing any longer to perform the part of a soldier, I am guilty of a breach of discipline, and am liable to the punishment which may be imposed by law in such a case. But my conduct proceeds not from a spirit of

278

insubordination, or wilful disobedience; it is simply the result of a conscientious conviction that all war is inconsistent with the gospel of our Lord and Saviour Jesus Christ, and a direct violation of His precepts. . . . I am a servant of the Prince of Peace, and I can be a soldier no longer. . . . I was taken into the service when only twelve years of age, and when, consequently, I was too young to form a judgement on this subject, or properly to understand the nature of the engagement into which I was required to enter; and no opportunity has ever since been given me to determine for myself how I would act.

WILLIAM DYNE, c. 1840

PRINCIPLES AND RULES OF THE SOCIETY OF FRATERNAL DEMOCRATS

The society was 'composed of natives of Great Britain, France, Germany, Scandinavia, Poland, Italy, Switzerland, Hungary and other countries' and was the forerunner of the First International.

Objects

The mutual enlightenment of its members; and the propaganda of the great principle embodied in the society's motto, 'All men are brethren.'

We declare that the earth with all its natural productions is the common property of all. . . .

'We condemn the 'National' hatreds which have hitherto divided mankind, as both foolish and wicked; foolish, because no one can decide for himself the country he will be born in; and wicked, as proved by the feuds and bloody wars

279

which have desolated the earth, in consequence of these national vanities. Convinced, too, that national prejudices have been, in all ages, taken advantage of by the people's oppressors, to set them tearing the throats of each other, when they should have been working together for their common good, this society repudiates the term 'Foreigner', no matter by whom or to whom applied. Our moral creed is to receive our fellow men, without regard to country, as members of one family, the human race; and citizens of one great commonwealth—the world.

1845

ALTON LOCKE

We were going through the Horse Guards, and I could not help lingering to look with wistful admiration on the huge mustachioed war-machines who sauntered about the court-yard. . . .

'Come on,' he said, peevishly clutching me by the arm; 'what do you want dawdling? Are you a nursery-maid, that you must stare at those red-coated butchers?' And a deep curse followed.

'What harm have they done you?'

'I should think I owed them turn enough.'

'What?'

'They cut my father down at Sheffield—perhaps with the very swords he helped to make—because he would not sit still and starve, and see us starving around him, while those who fattened on the sweat of his brow, and on those lungs of his, which the sword-grinding dust was eating out day by day, were wantoning on venison and champagne. That's the harm they've done me, my chap!'

'Poor fellows! they only did as they were ordered, I suppose.'

'And what business have they to let themselves be ordered? What right, I say—what right has any free, reasonable soul on earth, to sell himself for a shilling a day to murder any man, right or wrong—even his own brother or his own father—just because such a whiskered, profligate jackanapes as that officer, without learning, without any god except his own looking-glass and his opera-dancer—a fellow who, just because he is born a gentleman, is set to command grey-headed men before he can command his own meanest passions. Good heavens! that the lives of free men should be entrusted to such a stuffed cockatoo; and that free men should be such traitors to their country, traitors to their own flesh and blood, as to sell themselves, for a shilling a day and the smirks of the nursery-maids, to do that fellow's bidding!'

CHARLES KINGSLEY, 1850

ON THE DECLARATION OF
THE CRIMEAN WAR

Speech in the House of Commons

If this phrase of the 'balance of power' is to be always an argument for war, the pretence for war will never be wanting, and peace can never be secure.... This whole notion of the 'balance of power' is a mischievous delusion which has come down to us from past times; we ought to drive it from our minds, and to consider the solemn question of peace or war on more clear, more definite, and on far higher principles than any that are involved in the phrase the 'balance of power'.

JOHN BRIGHT, 1854

PEACE PLEDGE OF
THE LEAGUE OF HUMAN BROTHERHOOD

The Brotherhood had strong Chartist support.

I do hereby pledge myself never to enlist or enter into any army or navy, or to yield any voluntary support or sanction to the preparation for or prosecution of any war, by whomsoever, for whatsoever proposed, declared, or waged. And I do hereby associate myself with all persons, of whatever country, condition, or colour, who have signed, or shall hereafter sign this pledge, in a 'League of Universal Brotherhood'; whose object shall be to employ all legitimate and moral means for the abolition of all war, and all spirit, and all the manifestation of war, throughout the world; for the abolition of all restrictions upon international correspondence and friendly intercourse, and of whatever else tends to make enemies of nations, or prevents their fusion into one peaceful brotherhood; for the abolition of all institutions and customs which do not recognize the image of God and a human brother in every man of whatever clime, colour or condition of humanity.

1857

THE FRANCO-PRUSSIAN WAR OF 1870

Robert Spence Watson, a Quaker serving with the Friends' War Victims Relief Fund, describes his experiences in France.

I wish I could tell you how I loathe this war. It is too horrible. The misery which it brings with it is altogether incredible. I begin now to dream of it all night, for it has become a terrible reality. Bad I always thought it, but I never dreamed it could be so bad. I am glad I have seen what I have; it is a great lesson, and I wish all the editors in England could just see Bazaine's army; we should hear less of the glory of war for some years to come.

ROBERT SPENCE WATSON, 1870

THE MAN HE KILLED

Had he and I but met
  By some old ancient inn,
We should have set us down to wet
  Right many a nipperkin!

But ranged as infantry,
  And staring face to face,
I shot at him as he at me,
  And killed him in his place.

I shot him dead because—
  Because he was my foe,
Just so, my foe of course he was;
  That's clear enough; although

He thought he'd 'list', perhaps,
  Off-hand like—just as I—
Was out of work—had sold his traps—
  No other reason why.

Yes; quaint and curious war is!
  You shoot a fellow down
You'd treat if met where any bar is,
  Or help to half-a-crown.

THOMAS HARDY, 1902

LETTER TO MR BANKOLE BRIGHT

I am obliged by your approval of anything I have been able to do to assist your race, and I regret that I cannot do more. . . .

I hope the day will speedily come when your race will be able to defend itself against the barbarities being perpetrated against it by hypocritical whites, who regard the black man as having been created in order that they might exploit him for their own advantage. The Press and politicians for the most part keep the people of this country in ignorance of the real treatment meted out to the natives, and not until they, the natives, are in a position to hold their own can they expect to be treated as human beings.

JAMES KEIR HARDIE, 1906

ESSAYS IN SOCIALISM
NEW AND OLD

What Imperial extension, what the blessings of our beneficent rule, what the opening up of new territories *are supposed* to mean we all know. What these high-sounding terms *really* mean, few of us distinctly realize. The working class at home see that they are not materially benefited by the expansion of Greater Britain, as it is called. But they are assured by their pastors and masters that it is a necessary and glorious thing, and as this thought affords them some amusement now and then at the music-halls, in the shape of refrains and cheers, they are content to let the matter slide.

ERNEST BELFORT BAX, 1906

OPEN LETTER TO BRITISH SOLDIERS

This open letter was reprinted in the Syndicalist *which was produced under the chairmanship of Tom Mann. Mann was found guilty of incitement to mutiny and sentenced to six months' imprisonment.*

DON'T SHOOT

Men! Comrades! Brothers!

YOU are in the Army.

So are WE. YOU in the Army of Destruction. We in the Industrial, or Army of Construction.

WE work at mine, mill, forge, factory, or dock, producing and transporting all the goods, clothing, stuffs, etc., which make it possible for people to live.

YOU ARE WORKING MEN'S SONS.

When WE go on Strike to better OUR lot, which is the lot also of YOUR FATHERS, MOTHERS, BROTHERS, and SISTERS, YOU are called upon by your officers to MURDER US.

DON'T DO IT!

You know how it happens always has happened.

We stand out as long as we can. Then one of our (and your) irresponsible Brothers, goaded by the sight and thought of his and his loved ones' misery and hunger, commits a crime on property. Immediately YOU are ordered to MURDER US as YOU did at Mitchelstown, at Featherstone, at Belfast.

Don't YOU know that when YOU are out of the colours, and become a 'Civy' again, that YOU, like US, may be on Strike, and YOU, like US, be liable to be MURDERED by other soldiers.

BOYS, DON'T DO IT!

'THOU SHALT NOT KILL,' says the Book.

DON'T FORGET THAT!

It does not say, 'unless you have a uniform on'.

No! MURDER IS MURDER, whether committed in the

heat of anger on one who has wronged a loved one, or by pipe-clayed Tommies with a rifle.

BOYS, DON'T DO IT!

Comrades, have WE called in vain? Think things out and refuse any longer to MURDER YOUR KINDRED. Help Us to win back BRITAIN for the BRITISH, and the WORLD for the WORKERS.

1911
From the Irish Worker

INDEPENDENT LABOUR PARTY MANIFESTO ON THE WAR

We are told that International Socialism is dead, that all our hopes and ideals are wrecked by the fire and pestilence and European war. It is not true.

Out of the darkness and the depth we hail our working-class comrades of every land. Across the roar of guns, we send sympathy and greeting to the German Socialists. They have laboured unceasingly to promote good relations with Britain, as we with Germany. They are no enemies of ours, but faithful friends.

In forcing this appalling crime upon the nations, it is the rulers, the diplomats, the militarists who have sealed their doom. In tears and blood and bitterness, the greater Democracy will be born. With steadfast faith we greet the future; our cause is holy and imperishable, and the labour of our hands has not been in vain.

Long live Freedom and Equality! Long live International Socialism!

1914
Drafted by W. C. ANDERSON

A CALL TO MANHOOD

Man was destined for a nobler end than the feeding of cannon.

GUY ALDRED, DECEMBER 1914

LAST WORDS

Nurse Edith Cavell was shot by the Germans for assisting soldiers escaping from Belgium and for espionage.

Patriotism is not enough. I must have no hatred or bitterness for anyone.

EDITH CAVELL, 1915

THE POSITION OF THE CONSCIENTIOUS OBJECTOR

Our decision is based on varied grounds:

1 On definite Christian belief. We cannot inflict death upon our fellows because we hold that war is inconsistent with the teaching of Christ, and because we believe in the Fatherhood of God over all men.
2 On the ground that we hold either that human life is absolutely sacred under all circumstances, or that human personality is of such worth that the only person to decide such an issue as life and death is the man himself. We argue that the State, whatever may be its power, cannot compel men in matters of moral belief or conscience.

Some feel that there is something of divinity in every man, and that therefore no member of the human race should destroy his fellow.

3 On Socialist opinions and international faith, which find their expression in the Brotherhood of Man. We believe in a common unity between the peoples, as distinct from the Governments, of all nations. The only way to prevent war being forced by Governments upon peoples who do not seek war is by an increasing number of citizens with such convictions refusing to engage in war, whatever the pretext for which it is waged.

1916

A pamphlet issued by the No-Conscription Fellowship

THE MARCH-PAST

In red and gold the Corps-Commander stood,
With ribboned breast puffed out for all to see:
He'd sworn to beat the Germans, if he could;
For God had taught him strength and strategy.
He was our leader, and a judge of Port—
Rode well to hounds, and was a damned good sort.

'Eyes right!' We passed him with a jaunty stare.
'Eyes front!' He'd watched his trusted legions go.
I wonder if he guessed how many there
Would get knocked out of time in next week's show.
'Eyes right!' The corpse-commander was a Mute;
And Death leered round him, taking our salute.

SIEGFRIED SASSOON, 25 DECEMBER 1916

PEACE AND THE PUBLIC MIND

In my own experience, the sincere conviction that peace can only be achieved by preparing for war does seem to be held by men rather than by women. In masculine minds there is often a confused identification of virility with the possession and use of weapons, although the weapons of tomorrow could be invented and manufactured by the most anaemic of emasculated chemists, and would meet with no more effective resistance from the body of a full-grown, hot-blooded male than from that of a fragile infant female.

VERA BRITTAIN, 1934
From Challenge to Death *(Baker* et al.*)*

APOLOGY FOR ARMOURERS

It is no use simply to blame the traders and manufacturers. They are almost as much victims of a system as those whom their products destroy. Probably most have trained themselves not to think of the final end of their activities, or, having decided that final end to be inevitable, use Lord Hutchinson's excuse, that 'if arms are to be produced, let us at least produce the best we can'. And they are not alone responsible. As the world exists today hardly one of us can wash our hands and say that we are innocent of the blood of just men killed by British bombs. The stream of tainted profit runs through industry, affecting not armaments firms alone, but mines, banks, railways, engineering and chemical works, optical instrument-makers—even the groceries and drapers which supply necessities of life for the armourers. We may sell our shares, if we possess any, in Vickers or Imperial Chemical Industries; but that gives us no cause for complacency. We are not out, as in cases of banditry, against certain public enemies; we are all of us accessories, before or after the act, in a common crime perpetrated by a vicious system.

WINIFRED HOLTBY, 1934

From Challenge to Death *(Baker* et al.*)*

PRACTICAL SOCIALISM FOR BRITAIN

Today we are all like sleep-walkers, who walk near the sheer edge of a cliff. That edge may not be quite so near as some think. But it is not far off. We must wake soon, or crash. If we let the next years slip, as we have let slip these last years, then, I fear, our feet may slip too, and we shall fall into horrors too complete and too hideous to imagine.

There is but one way back from the cliff's edge. It leads toward world government, and a worldwide plan, for justice and plenty and peace. We must step boldly away from national sovereignty and capitalism, both too weak to bear our weight much longer. Someone must lead. Let us lead. Let a Socialist Britain, by her influence and her example, help to save the world from war.

HUGH DALTON, 1935

O WHAT IS THAT SOUND

O what is that sound which so thrills the ear
  Down in the valley drumming, drumming?
Only the scarlet soldiers, dear,
  The soldiers coming.

O what is that light I see flashing so clear
  Over the distance brightly, brightly?
Only the sun on their weapons, dear,
  As they step lightly.

O what are they doing with all that gear,
  What are they doing this morning, this morning?
Only their usual manoeuvres, dear,
  Or perhaps a warning.

O why have they left the road down there,
  Why are they suddenly wheeling, wheeling?
Perhaps a change in their orders, dear.
  Why are you kneeling?

O haven't they stopped for the doctor's care,
  Haven't they reined their horses, their horses?
Why, they are none of them wounded, dear,
  None of these forces.

O is it the parson they want, with white hair,
  Is it the parson, is it, is it?
No, they are passing his gateway, dear,
  Without a visit.

O it must be the farmer who lives so near.
  It must be the farmer so cunning, so cunning?
They have passed the farmyard already, dear,
  And now they are running.

O where are you going? Stay with me here!
  Were the vows you swore deceiving, deceiving?
No, I promised to love you, dear,
  But I must be leaving.

O it's broken the lock and splintered the door,
  O it's the gate where they're turning, turning;
Their boots are heavy on the floor
  And their eyes are burning.

W. H. AUDEN, 1933–8

ENDS AND MEANS

All statesmen insist that the armaments of their own country are solely for purposes of defence. At the same time, all statesmen insist that the existence of armaments in a foreign country constitutes a reason for the creation of new armaments at home. Every nation is perpetually taking more and more elaborate defensive measures against the more and more elaborate defensive measures of all other nations. The armament race would go on *ad infinitum*, if it did not inevitably and invariably lead to war.

ALDOUS HUXLEY, 1937

INTRODUCTION TO THE DECLARATION OF THE RIGHTS OF MAN

Everywhere war and monstrous economic exploitation are intensified, so that those very same increments of power and opportunity which have brought mankind within sight of an age of limitless plenty seem likely to be lost again, and, it may be, lost for ever, in a chaotic and irremediable collapse.

It becomes clear that a unified political, economic and social order can alone put an end to these national and private appropriations that now waste the mighty possibilities of our time.

H. G. WELLS, 1940

NOBEL PEACE PRIZE LECTURE

Lord Boyd-Orr was the first Director of the United Nations Food and Agriculture Organization.

The increase of territory and power of empires by force of arms has been the policy of all great powers, and it has always been possible to get the approval of their state religion. The destruction of the false Gods of the enemy, which threaten the true religion, has always justified propaganda of fear and hatred to overcome the natural reluctance of soldiers to kill their fellowmen with whom indeed they had no quarrel. Some wars have been due to the lust of rulers for power and glory, or to revenge to wipe out the humiliation of a former defeat. Most however have had an economic basis; the conquest of foreign territory in the interest of trade, or of land with rich agricultural or other resources. At the present time the control of oil-bearing land is an important factor in the foreign policy of some governments.

But we have reached the end of the age of competing empires. Science has produced such powerful weapons that in a war between great powers there would be neither victor nor vanquished. Both would be overwhelmed in destruction. Our civilization is now in the transition stage between the age of warring empires and a new age of world unity and peace.... We must not however delude ourselves that this transition phase of our civilization will be easy. Some politicians are still haunted by atavistic dreams of Empires, and hate the thought of submerging any of their absolute sovereignty in a world government.

JOHN BOYD-ORR, 1949

BRITAIN AND THE NUCLEAR BOMBS

One 'ultimate weapon', the final deterrent, succeeds another. After the bombs, the inter-continental rockets; and after the rockets, according to the First Lord of the Admiralty, the guided-missile submarine, which will 'carry a guided missile with a nuclear warhead and appear off the coast of any country in the world with a capability of penetrating to the centre of any continent'. The prospect now is not of countries without navies but of navies without countries. And we have arrived at an insane regress of ultimate weapons that are not ultimate.

But all this is to the good; and we cannot have too much of it, we are told, because no men in their right minds would let loose such powers of destruction. Here is the realistic view. Any criticism of it is presumed to be based on wild idealism. But surely it is the wildest idealism, at the furthest remove from a sober realism, to assume that men will always behave reasonably and in line with their best interests? Yet this is precisely what we are asked to believe, and to stake our all on it.

For that matter, why should it be assumed that the men who create and control such monstrous devices *are* in their right minds? They live in an unhealthy mental climate, an atmosphere dangerous to sanity. They are responsible to no large body of ordinary sensible men and women, who pay for these weapons without ever having ordered them, who have never been asked anywhere yet if they wanted them.

J. B. PRIESTLEY, 1957
From the New Statesman *(2 November 1957)*

294

THE CHALLENGE OF POLITICS

Today we march from Aldermaston. And in a world which sits and watches cataclysms of mankind from comfortable chairs by the fireside, our march is some new kind of miracle. It is no weak or phoney ideal that brings men and women by coach and bus and train from towns and villages all over Britain.

This is not just London marching. It is the housewife from Glasgow. It is the doctor from Manchester, the students from Cardiff, the miner from Durham, the office worker from Edinburgh. And the force that brings them to Aldermaston is the strongest and most powerful moral purpose this generation knows.

It is a moral purpose that springs from individual conscience. I suppose that it is essentially a protest against insanity. Acceptance of Britain's nuclear weapons policy seems to us to display a pathological nostalgia for suicide: the death-wish on a mass-scale. Most of us in the Campaign came into it primarily because the H-bomb seems to us to raise new moral issues—because it threatens to destroy a whole civilization, and to warp and cripple the human race itself. Once in it for this compelling reason, we examine its implications in more detail.

JUDITH HART, 1960
From Tribune *(15 April 1960)*

HAS MAN A FUTURE?

As I go about the streets and see St Paul's, the British Museum, the Houses of Parliament and the other monuments of our civilization, in my mind's eye I see a nightmare vision of those buildings as heaps of rubble with corpses all round them. That is a thing we have got to face, not only in our own country and cities, but throughout the civilized world as a real probability unless the world will agree to find a way of abolishing war. It is not enough to make war rare; great and serious war has got to be abolished, because otherwise these things will happen.

There are those who say: 'War is part of human nature, and human nature cannot be changed. If war means the end of man, we must sigh and submit.' This is always said by those whose sigh is hypocritical. It is undeniable that there are men and nations to whom violence is attractive, but it is not the case that anything in human nature makes it impossible to restrain such men and nations. Individuals who have a taste for homicide are restrained by the criminal law, and most of us do not find life intolerable because we are not allowed to commit murders. The same is true of nations, however disinclined war-mongers may be to admit it.

BERTRAND RUSSELL, 1961

NEW YEAR'S MESSAGE

For Socialists whose faith is based on our common humanity, the deepest offence against everything we believe in is comprised in the arms race, the nuclear arms race and its infinity of horrors. To stop that race, to turn it back on its tracks, to dismantle the nuclear armouries, to lift the crushing burden of armaments which obliterates life for growing hundreds of millions of our fellow citizens of the world—this is the greatest summons of all for Socialists in the rest of our century.

MICHAEL FOOT, JANUARY 1980

ZERO OPTION: BEYOND THE COLD WAR

*The Dimbleby Television Lecture—until the BBC
'withdrew the invitation'.*

What a discrepancy there is between the procedures of war
and those of peace! The decisions to develop new weapons—
to deploy the SS-20, to put the neutron bomb into
production, to go ahead with cruise missiles—are taken by a
few score people—at the most by a few hundred—
secretively, behind closed doors, on both sides. But to check,
or to reverse, any one of those decisions, nothing will do
except the voluntary efforts of hundreds of thousands—late
into the night and through weekends, month after month—
addressing envelopes, collating information, raising money,
meeting in churches or in school halls, debating in con-
ferences, lobbying parliaments, marching through the
streets of Europe's capital cities.

E. P. THOMPSON, 1981

STATEMENT TO
NEWBURY MAGISTRATES' COURT

I do not feel I stand here today as a criminal.

I feel this court is dealing in trivia by making this charge
against us, while those who are the real criminals (those who
deal in our deaths) continue their conspiracy against humankind. We will continue to make a peaceful stand against
them and continue to uphold our moral values which celebrate life.

We are all individuals whose responsibility it is to maintain
and nurture life, something all of us can do together—with
mutual support.

While we stand here the silos, which are intended to house the cruise missiles from December 1983, are still being constructed at Greenham Common. We all feel the urgency of this threat to our lives—and are determined not to remain silent.

As women we have been actively encouraged to be complacent, by sitting at home and revering men as our protectors: we now reject this role.

The law is concerned with the preservation of property. We are concerned with the preservation of all life. How dare the government presume the right to kill others in our names?

A GREENHAM COMMON WOMAN, 14 APRIL 1982

DEFEND US AGAINST OUR DEFENDERS

We must take back the language of freedom and the practices of democracy from the people who are perverting them. Who but ourselves can defend us against these defenders? Their policies impoverish us materially and oppress us politically. We have to take our country back, and defend it in our own way. The survival of our civilization depends on the elimination of the worst forms of destruction, but also on the encouragement and extension of the values of mutuality, co-operation, toleration, so that the most basic problems of the world can be solved by the joint exploitation of the world's resources and not frittered away in mutual destruction. These values have to be taught and encouraged in the home as well as in the schoolroom, in our organizations as well as in our propaganda. Every one of us is involved, and we are the only people who can do it—and in the short time we have left, we are accepting the challenge.

DOROTHY THOMPSON, 1983
From Over Our Dead Bodies

A VOICE FROM THE PEACE CAMPS

In 1983 Maggie Lowry was a full-time member of the Upper Heyford Women's Peace Camp.

Looking through the perimeter fence of the air base, listening to the roar of the FIIIs stationed there, I feel as if I am looking across a demarcation line between war and peace. As yet, peace has few victories to celebrate, but our protest continues. Our daily presence here is a permanent witness to our determination to work for peace, and it will be reinforced by action of many kinds in support. To begin with, we aim to make the American personnel think. This may sound condescending, but the fact is that military training discourages independent thinking or any questioning of their individual responsibility. We are here because we are afraid—afraid of the mindless commitment to destruction that these bases represent. We intend by our presence to remind ordinary people of the need to protest, to gain strength through co-operation, and to achieve the ending of the threat of nuclear war.

MAGGIE LOWRY, 1983

THE INTERNATIONAL

Arise! ye starvlings from your slumbers;
Arise! ye criminals of want,
For reason in revolt now thunders.
And at last ends the age of cant.
Now away with all superstitions,
Servile masses arise! arise!
We'll change forthwith the old conditions
And spurn the dust to win the prize.

Then comrades, come rally.
And the last fight let us face
The International
Unites the human race,
Then comrades, come rally.
And the last fight let us face
The International
Unites the human race.

We peasants, artisans and others
Enroll'd among the sons of toil,
Let's claim the earth henceforth for brothers.
Drive the indolent from the soil.
On our flesh has fed the raven,
We've too long been the vulture's prey;
But now; farewell the spirit craven,
The dawn brings in a brighter day.

Then comrades, come rally.
And the last fight let us face
The International
Unites the human race,
Then comrades, come rally.
And the last fight let us face
The International
Unites the human race.

From the French of EUGÈNE EDME POTTIER, 1880

BIBLIOGRAPHY

Books referred to by title in the text are not listed here. Nor are newspapers and journals.

Baker, Philip Noel, and fourteen others, *Challenge to Death*, London 1934

Barker, Theo, *Long March of Everyman, 1750–1960*, London, BBC/André Deutsch, 1975

Bealey, Frank, *The Social and Political Thought of the British Labour Party*, London, Weidenfeld & Nicolson, 1970

Beer, M., *History of British Socialism*, 2 vols., London, 1919

Behn, Aphra, *The Collected Works of Aphra Behn*, Montague Summer (ed.), London, Heinemann, 1915

Bellamy, Edward, *Equality*, London, Heinemann, 1897

Birrell, Augustine (ed.), *Crowned Masterpieces of Eloquence*, 10 vols., London, International University Society, 1895

Bliss, W. D. P., *Handbook of Socialism*, London, Swan Sonnenschein, 1895

Boulton, David, *Voices from the Crowd: Against the H Bomb*, London, Peter Owen, 1964

Brittain, Vera, *Humiliation with Honour*, London, Dakars, 1942

Brock, Peter, *Pacifism in Europe to 1914*, Princeton, New Jersey, Princeton University Press, 1972

Brockway, Fenner, *Socialism over 60 Years: The Life of Jowett of Bradford, 1864–1944*, London, Allen & Unwin, 1946

Cartwright, J., *Life and Correspondence of Major Cartwright*, London, 1826

Coates, Ken, and Topham, Anthony (eds.), *Industrial*

Democracy in Great Britain, London, MacGibbon & Kee, 1968

Cole, G. D. H., and Filson, A. W., *British Working Class Movements: Select Documents, 1789–1875*, London, Macmillan, 1951

Connolly, James, *Selected Political Writings*, R. Miliband (ed.), London, Jonathan Cape, 1973

Cook, Alice, and Gwyn Kirk, *Greenham Women Everywhere*, London, Pluto Press, 1983

Cowan, Edward J., *The People's Past*, Edinburgh, Polygon Books, 1980

Dalton, Hugh, *Practical Socialism for Britain*, London, Routledge, 1935

Divine, David, *Mutiny at Invergordon*, London, MacDonald, 1970

Douglas, D. (general editor), *English Historical Documents*, London, Eyre & Spottiswoode, 1955

Fishman, William J., *East End Jewish Radicals*, London, Duckworth, 1975

A First Trade Union Annual 1983, Preston, Lancs, Association of Trades Councils, 1983

Foner, Philip S., *Karl Marx Remembered*, San Francisco, Synthesis Publications, 1983

Froissart, Jean, *The Chronicles*, translated by H. P. Dunster, London, Routledge, 1891

Frow, R., Frow, E., and Katanka, Michael, *Strikes: A Documentary History*, London, Charles Knight, 1971

Gallacher, Willie, *Revolt on the Clyde*, London, Lawrence and Wishart, 1936

Gangulee, N. (ed.), *There shall be Peace*, Bombay, 1953

Glasier, J. Bruce (ed.), *Minstrelsy of Peace*, London, National Labour Press, 1920

Gower, John, *Gower's Complete Works*, G. C. Macauley (ed.), London, 1861

Griffiths, W. D., *Fifty Standard Definitions of Socialism*, Glasgow, Reformers' Bookstall, 1912

Haller, William, *Liberty and Reformation in the Puritan Rev-*

olution, New York, Columbia University Press, 1955

Haller, William, and Davies, Godfrey, *The Leveller Tracts, 1647–1653*, New York, Columbia University Press, 1944

Harland, John (ed.), *Ballads and Songs of Lancashire*, London, 1865

History Workshop Journal, London, Routledge & Kegan Paul, 1977

Hobsbawn, E. J., and Rudé, George, *Captain Swing*, London, Penguin, 1973

Holton, Bob, *British Syndicalism, Myths and Realities*, London, B. Holton, 1976

Huxley, Aldous, *Ends and Means*, London, Chatto & Windus, 1937

James, Louis (ed.), *Print and the People*, London, Allen Lane, 1976

Johnson, Thomas, *History of the Working Classes in Scotland*, Glasgow, n.d.

Kingsford, Peter, *The Hunger Marchers in Britain, 1920–40*, London, Lawrence and Wishart, 1982

Knowles, G. W. (ed.), *Quakers and Peace*, London, Grotius Society Publications, 1927

Labour Party Song Book, The, London, Labour Party Publications, 1955

Leeson, R. A., *Strikes: A Live History, 1887–1971*, London, Allen & Unwin, 1973

Llewelyn-Davies, Margaret, *Life as We have Known it*, London, Hogarth Press, 1931

Lloyd, A. L. (ed.), *Come All Ye Bold Miners*, London, Lawrence and Wishart, 1952; rev. ed., 1978

Lovett, William, *The Life and Struggles of W. L.*, London, 1876

Lowery, Robert, *Autobiography*, B. Harrison and P. Hollis (eds.), London, Europa, 1979

MacKenzie, Norman (ed.), *Convictions*, London, MacGibbon & Kee, 1958

Mann, Tom, *Memoirs*, London, London Labour Publishing Co., 1923

Mayer, Peter (ed.), *The Pacifist Conscience*, London, Rupert Hart-Davis, 1966

Mitchell, Adrian, *Ride the Nightmare*, London, Jonathan Cape, 1971

Morrison, Herbert, *Socialisation and Transport*, London, Constable, 1933

Orwell, George, and Reynolds, R. A., *British Pamphleteers*, 2 vols., London, Allan Wingate, 1948, 1951

Owen, Robert, *A New View of Society and Other Writings*, London, Dent, 1927

Palmer, Mary (ed.), *Writing and Action*, London, Allen & Unwin, 1938

Pelling, Henry (ed.), *The Challenge of Socialism*, London, 1954

Pollitt, Harry, *Serving My Time*, London, Lawrence & Wishart, 1950

Postgate, Raymond W., *Revolution from 1789 to 1906*, London, 1920

Read, Herbert, *The English Vision*, London, 1933

Reid, Jimmy, *Reflections of a Clyde-Built Man*, London, Souvenir Press, 1976

Rickword, Edgell, and Lindsay, Jack, *Spokesman for Liberty*, London, Lawrence & Wishart, 1941; first published, 1939, as *Handbook of Freedom*

Robottom, John (ed.), *Keir Hardie and the Labour Party*, London, Longman, 1975

Rowe, Marsha (ed.), *The Spare Rib Reader*, London, Penguin, 1982

Russell, Dora, *The Dora Russell Reader*, London, Pandora, 1983

Sassoon, Siegfried, *The War Poems*, London, Faber and Faber, 1983

Seabrook, Jeremy, *Unemployment*, London, Paladin, 1982

Skelton, Robert (ed.), *Poetry of the Thirties*, London, Penguin, 1964

Taylor, Barbara, *Eve and the New Jerusalem*, London, Virago, 1982

Thompson, Dorothy (ed.), *Over Our Dead Bodies*, London, Virago, 1983

Thompson, E. P., *Zero Option*, London, Merlin Press, 1982

Thompson, E. P., *The Making of the English Working Class*, London, Gollancz, 1963

Thompson, Wilfred, *Victor Grayson: His Life and Works*, London, 1910

Wainwright, Hilary, Segal, Lynne, and Rowbotham, Sheila, *Beyond the Fragments*, London, Merlin Press, 1979

Walsingham, Thomas, *Historia Anglicana II*, T. H. Riley (ed.), London, Rolls Series, 1863–4

Webb, Beatrice, *My Apprenticeship*, London, Longman, 1926

Wedgwood, Josiah, *Forever Freedom*, London, Penguin, 1944

West, Rebecca, *The Young Rebecca: Selected Essays by Rebecca West, 1911–17*, Jane Marcus (ed.), London, Macmillan, 1982

Widgery, David (ed.), *The Left in Britain, 1956–68*, London, Penguin, 1976

Wolfe, Don M., *Leveller Manifestoes of the Puritan Revolution*, New York and London, Nelson, 1944

Wright, Thomas (ed.), *Songs and Ballads Chiefly of the Reign of Philip and Mary*, London, 1860

Wright, Thomas, *Political Songs of England from the Reign of John to Edward II*, London, 1839

Wyncoll, Peter, *Nottingham Chartism*, Nottingham, 1966

INDEX

311

312

315

316

ACKNOWLEDGEMENTS

For permission to reprint extracts from copyright material the editors and publishers gratefully acknowledge the following:

Blond & Briggs Ltd for *1968 and After* by Tariq Ali; Victor Gollancz Ltd for *The Labour Party in Perspective* by Clement Attlee; Faber & Faber Ltd for 'O what is that sound' from *Collected Poems* by W. H. Auden; David Higham Associates Ltd for *In Place of Fear* by Aneurin Bevan; the PA for *Merrie England* by Robert Blatchford; Constable Publishers Ltd for *Peace and the Public Mind* and *Humiliation with Honour* by Vera Brittain; Allen & Unwin for *Inside the Left* by Fenner Brockway; Virago Press Ltd for *Wigan Pier Revisited* by Beatrix Campbell; Bell & Hyman Publishers Ltd for *Self-Government in Industry* by G. D. H. Cole; Routledge & Kegan Paul for *Practical Socialism for Britain* by Hugh Dalton; Mr Jack Davitt for 'Leaders of Men' from *Shipyard Muddling*; the Estate of Walter Greenwood and Jonathan Cape Ltd for *Love on the Dole*; *Tribune* for 'The Challenge of Politics' by Judith Hart; Constable Publishers Ltd for 'Apology for Armourers' by Winifred Holtby from *Challenge to Death*, ed. P. N. Baker; Mrs Laura Huxley and Chatto & Windus Ltd for *Ends and Means* by Aldous Huxley; Independent Labour Publications, 49 Top Moor Side, Leeds 11, for three ILP pamphlets, 'Parables of the Water Tank', 'Socialism in Our Time' and 'Manifesto on the War' (the ILP was founded in 1893 and still publishes the monthly *Labour Leader*, founded by Keir Hardie; since 1975 it has been known as Independent Labour Publications, a registered and recognized group within the Labour Party which continues to publish and permeate socialist ideas and practices); International Brigade Association for 'Memorial Souvenir' on the International Brigade; Granada Publishing Ltd for 'A Sense of Outrage' by Paul Johnson from *Conviction*, ed. Norman MacKenzie; the PA for *My England* by George Lansbury; Allen & Unwin Ltd for *Communist Manifesto* by Harold Laski; Allen & Unwin Ltd for *Strikes: A Live History 1887–1971* by R. A. Leason; the Hogarth Press for *The Women's Co-Operative Guild 1883–1904* by Margaret Llewelyn-Davies; Virago Press Ltd for 'A Voice from the Peace Camps' by Maggie Lowry from *Over Our Dead Bodies*, ed. Dorothy Thompson; Macmillan Publishing Co. Inc. for *Socialism: Critical and Constructive* by Ramsay MacDonald, first published in 1921 by Cassell and Co. Ltd; the Labour Party for *Memoirs* by Tom Mann; Jonathan Cape Ltd for 'Old Age Report' from *Ride the Nightmare* by Adrian Mitchell; *New Left Review* for 'Women: the Longest Revolution' by Juliet Mitchell; Penguin Books Ltd for *Utopia* by Thomas More, trs. Paul Turner; Constable Publishers Ltd for *Socialization and Transport* by Herbert Morrison; the Estate of the late Sonia Brownell Orwell and Martin Secker & Warburg Ltd for *The Road to Wigan Pier* and *The Lion and the Unicorn* by George Orwell; the *New Statesman* for 'Britain and the Nuclear Bombs' by J. B. Priestley; the Hogarth Press for 'Changes in Public Life' by Eleanor Rathbone from *Our Freedom and Its Result*, ed. Ray Strachey; Souvenir Press Ltd for *Reflec-*

tions ·of a Clyde-Built Man by Jimmy Reid; Penguin Books Ltd for *Woman's Consciousness, Man's World* by Sheila Rowbotham; Merlin Press Ltd for *Beyond the Fragments* by Sheila Rowbotham, Lynne Segal and Hilary Wainwright; Penguin Books Ltd and the Estate of Bertrand Russell for *Has Man a Future?* by Bertrand Russell; Routledge & Kegan Paul for 'In a Man's World: the Eclipse of Woman' from *The Dora Russell Reader*; Faber & Faber Ltd for 'The March Past' from *The War Poems* by Siegfried Sassoon; Quartet Books Ltd for *Unemployment* by Jeremy Seabrook; Marian Boyars Publishers Ltd for *This New Season* by Chris Searle; the Society of Authors on behalf of the Bernard Shaw Estate for *The Intelligent Woman's Guide to Socialism, Capitalism, Sovietism and Fascism*, published by Penguin Books Ltd; Collins Publishers Ltd for *What We Want and Why* by Ethel Snowden; *Tribune* for 'The Road to Aldermaston' by Donald Soper; *Spare Rib* for the interview with Grunwick women by Bea Campbell and Val Charlton from *Spare Rib Reader*, published by Penguin Books Ltd; Victor Gollancz Ltd for *Contemporary Capitalism* by John Strachey; Bell & Hyman Publishers for *The Acquisitive Society* by R. H. Tawney; Virago Press Ltd for 'Defend Us Against Our Defenders' by Dorothy Thompson from *Over Our Dead Bodies*, ed. Dorothy Thompson; Merlin Press Ltd for *Zero Option: Beyond the Cold War* and *An Open Letter to Lezek Kolakowski* by E. P. Thompson; the Trouble and Strife Collective for the editorial from the first edition of *Trouble and Strife* (Winter 1983); the London School of Economics and Political Science for *A Constitution for the Socialist Commonwealth of Great Britain* by Sidney and Beatrice Webb; Virago Press Ltd for *The Diary of Beatrice Webb*, vol. 1, 1873–1892 (*Glitter Around and Darkness Within*), editorial matter and arrangement copyright © Norman and Jeanne MacKenzie 1982, the Diary of Beatrice Webb, the Passfield Papers © the London School of Economics and Political Science 1982, first published by Virago Press Ltd 1982 in association with the London School of Economics and Political Science; A. D. Peters and Co. for *The Young Rebecca: Selected Essays by Rebecca West 1911–17*, ed. Jane Marcus, published by Macmillan and Co.; A. P. Watt Ltd and the Literary Executors of the Estate of H. G. Wells for *New Worlds for Old* and *Introduction to the Declaration of the Rights of Man*; Granada Publishing Ltd for 'Culture is Ordinary' by Raymond Williams from *Conviction*, ed. Norman MacKenzie; May Day Manifesto Committee 1968 for *May Day Manifesto*, ed. Raymond Williams, published by Penguin Books Ltd; David Higham Associates Ltd for *The New Britain* by Harold Wilson, published by Penguin Books Ltd.

Faber and Faber Limited apologize for any errors or omissions in the above list of acknowledgements and would be grateful to be notified of any changes that should be incorporated in the next edition of this volume.